The Silver Knight

Cast From Camelot: Book 1

By: M. Francis Lamont

For Tanya, my real knight in shining armor.

The first thanks is, as always, to my own little princess; Morgan. Your support and encouragement mean the world to me. I hope you follow your dreams to write your own stories.

To my work families, at the store: Diane, Emily, Amber, Analyn and the rest of the Geoffrey crew and the Club: Amanda, you got the real-life fairy tale and Dillion you're a knight in a suit and tie instead of armor. Thank you for your and belief in me.

My red pen team, Steffany, Kerri, Sarah, and Colin, you make sure I'm on track.

To "The Team": Lila, Hedda, Erin and Jessa. Thanks for the things you do to keep me sane and for the hard work you put into the creation every time.

The last two people are the two that this story wouldn't exist without, Tanya, you know what you did and I'm eternally grateful.

Kevin, my very own Sir Liam. You advised, corrected, suggested, and helped weave the story into something beyond what I would have been brave enough to try on my own. Your creative contributions, on the cover and on the pages, were and will continue to be the heartbeat of Redbourne. Thank you, you truly are a hero.

COVER CREDIT:

Photography: Golden Czermak
Design: Southern Fried Creative
Model: Kevin R Davise

Chapter 1

"No. I refuse. I can not marry him. I will not marry him!" Caelia cried, throwing the logs in her arms into the fireplace. "Father, please?" She begged, dropping to her knees beside the enfeebled man's chair. "Do not force me to do this. I have no wish to be married to any man and certainly not Liam of Redbourne."

"You have refused every suitable man in Durham." Her father, Hebron of Durham, barked, before coughing into his sleeve.

"And more than a few of the unsuitable ones." Added her brother, Cador, frowning in the doorway.

"As well as offending the wives of each your brothers to the point that they will not have you in their homes without me there to keep you from driving them from sanity." Her father concluded, taking a careful sip from the cup beside him.

"Well, father, then I will not go to their houses without you, since my brothers all seemed fit to marry a trio of demure prigs." Caelia said, rolling her eyes.

Her opinion of the women her brothers chose to marry was no secret. When Alis, her oldest brother had chosen to marry Enid, a model of manners and decorum Caelia had thought the boring woman was a fluke. That the woman to marry her dashing, adventurous brother was as dull as the white-washed walls of the hen house had to be an accident, not the way that women were expected to be in order to get married. It was when Elsa and Ade joined the family, marrying Ban and Cador, and were both just as slow to laugh, mannerly and courtly as Enid was, that Caelia realized that her family had not been joking when they said she was unlike the other girls in Durham or the kings court.

"That may have been enough in the past, my darling headstrong daughter." Hebron said, his voice rasping from the cough. "But we all know that I am not likely to be among the living by the first snowfall. I want to make sure that you are taken care of and since your brothers cannot see it done then I must find you a husband. Liam is a good man. The last few years have not been kind to him, but he is no monster." He looked at his sons as they all moved closer, ready to support what he was going to say. "Caelia. You cannot remain unmarried unless you wish to go to a convent and commit your life to the celibate service of god. Do you not wish children?"

Her heart had worried that he would confirm her worst fears and now it was so, the words now unable to be denied.

"Oh father. I would honor you with a child while you live. If only a man that I could love was willing to see past what others deem to be my faults." Caelia tried to keep her emotions from her voice, but confronting the reality that her father was right, regarding his health and the need for her marriage to happen soon took more strength than she had.

Tears welling in her eyes, she knelt at her father's feet and took his hand in hers. "My mind wishes to please you in this as all other things in my life father, but my heart is what pauses. Would you, as a final command, send me to a life absent the chance of love? Of happiness?"

"What do you know of such things Caelia?" Scoffed Alis. "There is more to marriage than your childish dreams spawned by nights of reading poetry in bed, when you should have been practicing your needlework, or afternoons uselessly spent on horseback when you could have been baking bread or cleaning like a woman who desires to become the wife of a man of note."

"I do what I must to a woman of interest, instead of that dull…mushroom of a woman you married, the one yet to provide you with the promised heir to this house. Now instead of your wives it falls somehow to me!" Caelia yelled, rising to her feet, and rushing past them all and out into the yard.

Even with her eyes burning with tears she was able to find her favorite tree, the one she had been climbing since she was able to reach it's lowest branches, and scramble up to the cradled seat made by the splitting of the main trunk. Hidden by the summer leaves she was able to let loose the damn of her emotions. Tears streamed down her cheeks as she stared out across the yard and fields of her home. She had only spent time away from the house the winter that her mother died, and she had been sent to live with a married aunt in the city of Camelot. Even though she had been taken to court and presented to the King and Queen she was much more excited to go home than she had been to watch the knights of the round table dancing with the ladies of the court.

"Caelia? Are you up there again?" Cador called from the bottom of the tree. He was the most understanding of her brothers, being the one closest in age to her.

They had spent many afternoons riding through the fields and playing at the river. If anyone in the family understood how much she did not want to get married to a man that she did not know, it was him.

"I cannot do it Cador. You know this. I just...I cannot do it. He's a drunk and a womanizer. How can I marry a man that will not even remember that I am his wife? And if he does recall it, he will not care."

"You are fairly unforgettable little sister." Cador chuckled, climbing up to sit opposite her and look out over the land. "And if he does forget that he is a married man then you will remind him, loudly I have no doubt. Caelia of Durham is not the kind of woman who meekly accepts infidelity from any man."

She shrugged, resting her head on her arms. "Why should I care about him if he will not care for me, for the sanctity of a marriage?" He did not understand, she wanted to be the love of someone's life, not an afterthought to provide an heir.

Cador reached out to tap her on the top of her head so that she would look up at him.

"Since when do you accept insult from anyone? Do you remember what you did to Ban when he was caught kissing someone other than Elsa once they were engaged? He could not walk for the rest of the day. Your husband, no matter his age or ability, will never stray from your bed more than once. Of that I am certain."

She could not help the smile that the story brought to her lips. "Alright. I will concede that point, but he is so much older than I am. He is going to think me a child."

"He is not Merlin. For saint's sake he is only ten years older than Alis." Cador laughed. "I have met your intended myself. That is where I was a fortnight ago, negotiating for you."

Her head whipped up. "You were a party to this? You did not tell me?" She wanted to push him from the tree for the betrayal, but he was the only ally she had left in this matter.

"I was told not to. I wanted to. I wanted to take you with me to meet him for yourself but Alis and father said not to." Cador raised his hands in surrender. "I can tell you about him though, if that will save me from being removed from the tree."

"Alright. Tell me what I am supposed to marry into. Does he smell?"

"Only of leather and horses." Cador chuckled. "Sir Liam is a widower, lost his bride and babe to childbirth eight years ago. That is when he started to drink, before that he was the right hand of Sir Lancelot himself."

"Truly? Lancelot? Maybe he is not such a beast after all?"

"I would think not though he does have his temper and his moods. Not unlike someone else I know."

"Oh brother, you are in a humorous mood for a man about to be pushed from a tree are you not?" She retorted with a roll of her eyes. "What about now? The taverns and his reputation with women? He was banished from court was he not? For disgracing a woman and refusing to wed her? Why would he not marry her but is willing to marry me?"

"Well I was not old enough to be at court to know the truth of what happened but that is the rumor. His men vouched for him and all, but Sir Mark reside with him now at Redbourne as they are loyal to him still. Remember that, a half dozen knights left the glory of Camelot to stand at his side in this. As for why he is willing to remarry now, father has offered a significant dowry and the king has offered Sir Liam the chance to return to court if he comes as a married man."

"So, he took the first girl offered to him in order to return to court?" She frowned "Maybe he will leave me at Redbourne, and we will have a marriage at a distance. I have heard that it is a beautiful place. A prosperous farm and his tenants? They are well treated and loyal?"

"Ah little sister, already mistress of the manor." He shook his head and climbed down the tree. "Only you would wish for your husband to leave you behind when he goes to Camelot and worry about the tenants before you set foot upon the road. Give Liam a chance, you might wish to be at his side more often than you think now."

Scoffing under her breath Caelia joined her brother on the ground. "I do not have much of a choice, do I? I must wed him or join a nunnery."

"I do not see your future in a nunnery. Take the chance Caelia, it is the only one that offers a chance at joy." He held her hands and stared, pleading, into her eyes. "It will give our father some peace to know that you are well looked after when his time comes."

"That is a pain I am not yet ready to face. Do not remind me of it, not yet." She said with a sigh. "Let us return to the house and I will tell father that I will at least meet the man and see what he has to offer as husband. Let him have that hope at least?"

"As long as you are happy when the year is done, that will be enough for him and for me."

Caelia took his arm as they started back towards the open doors of the house. "I hope, then, that you are not wrong about the man, for I cannot seem to find the faith in his honor that you do, dear brother."

Chapter 2

Liam rubbed a rough hand over his face and snarled at Rion. "I do not need the lot of you to escort me to pick up this child-bride I am supposed to retrieve from Durham." The young man was aggravatingly protective, to the point of making the senior knight feel as though they were worried about him either being attacked and killed or have a seizing of his heart, leaving the girl alone on the side of the road. "I promise that I will bring her back with me."

"If we believed that then Saffir and Emrys would not be waiting with the horses." Rion joked, grabbing Liam's cloak and sword. "So, unless you are going uncloaked and unarmed, we are going with you."

"He is right, Sir Liam." Emrys said, holding tight to the reigns of his leader's chestnut brown charger. "We are ready, Sir, to accompany you to bring the young lady of the manor home. Emrys will drive the cart, are you certain that you do not wish a carriage for her?"

"Very sure." Liam said, mounting the horse after retrieving his cloak and sword from Rion. "Her brother assured me that she can ride and enjoys it. If I am to take her as wife, I will have exactly what I want in a woman and nothing less."

"Then I pity the girl if she does not live up to expectations." Saffir said with a laugh as they started out down the road. "Though if she is half as amusing as Cador said then I expect we shall all be in for an interesting time. Do you not agree Liam?"

"If I wanted interesting, I would not be getting married." He called over his shoulder, joining them in the laughter of a group of bachelors as they began the journey.

He knew that the house and grounds would be well looked after in his absence, it was not that which worried him. It was what was waiting for him in Durham.

Hebron was not a knight, but he was a good and honorable man. His sons were married men of good reputation, unlike the daughter he was contracted to. She should have been married years ago but, according to her brother Cador, she had done everything short of bedding a man to make sure that she was deemed unmarriable by the local men.

As they rode through the predawn light Liam wondered what would drive a girl so such extremes. In all his years at court and those beyond its walls he had never met a woman who did not seek a husband, someone to take care of them while they lord over his household and pretty themselves for the court. This girl, Caelia, was rumored to be so opposed to the idea that she had turned down three proposals, including one, in writing, from Gareth, the youngest of Arthur's knights. What could bring a girl to do such a thing after being raised by parents who were kind and loving to each other and their children?

"Emrys?" Liam called back to the young man on the cart. "Did you get a feeling from Cador what the girl looks like? My options, if I am to return to Arthur's court by summer's end, may not be many, but I would not enjoy the surprise of an ugly wife." Rion and Saffir chuckled, Emrys smirked, but Liam remained as stone-faced as ever. "I will marry her, despite her appearance, whatever it is, but I would not wish to insult her feelings by showing surprise if she is unattractive."

"I stand sure that it is her feelings you are worried about and not the face that you have to see across the table." Emrys chided.

"Or across the bed!" Rion called from the back of the group, bringing laughter from all of them, including Liam.

"Alright. I admit that is a concern and I would rather not feel the need to spend nights at the tavern to enjoy the company of a beautiful woman." Liam admitted, scanning the road ahead of them as it began to get lighter. "Though I suppose I cannot expect her to be intelligent, a capable horsewoman, able to manage a household and be beautiful on top of all that."

"Unless of course she is Queen Guinevere." Saffir said. "But as there is only one of her it is safe to assume that your bride to be is, if not uncomely, then plain. I would resign myself to such a thing if I were you Liam."

"I shall simply have to do my husbandly duty and hope that she is with child, often, and then I will not be formed to endure pitying glances from Mark and the rest of that lot. They will see her at the wedding and then that duty will be performed, and I will not have to bring her again unless Arthur commands it."

He did not need to look to know that the three younger men were exchanging looks of disbelief at his surrender to the bleak outlook his marriage was offering him. They did not know how the pain of losing a wife and child could linger for years. Nor could they know that even though he was doing this, marrying Caelia, to get a chance at returning to Camelot, he had no intention of falling in love with the girl. None. He would be a good husband to her, she would never feel ashamed of him or his actions, but he fully intended to keep his heart well guarded.

"I doubt you will need to take such drastic measures Liam." Emrys chuckled, bringing his horse alongside his leader. "Cador assured me that his sister is a lovely girl, though on the wild side."

Liam turned his head a skeptical smirk on his face. "What brother would say otherwise if he is hoping to marry her off? Why did he not offer the marriage contract to you or one of the other younger men? Why me?"

"You underestimate your appeal old man." Emrys said. "There are plenty of women who find an older man more attractive than us young pups. It is not as though you are of the...girth, of Sir Kay nor are you as verbally repulsive as Sir Palamedes." The young man shrugged. "If I were to hazard a guess it would be that the young lady will likely find you attractive enough, if you remember to smile."

"What are you jesting about? I smile, do I not?" Liam looked at the other two men, expecting support but finding them doing their best to hide laughter.

"My dear Liam, you are not known as both The Silver Knight and Stone Face of Redbourne because of your dazzling smile." Saffir answered, trying to be respectful but unable to stop the laughter. "Just try not to glare at the girl and I am sure that you will be fine. Why worry so much if you intend to leave her at Redbourne. I would be much more concerned about leaving her alone with our dear Gerard. The local girls are once again making quite the fuss about him apparently."

"If he values his manhood Gerard knows better than to tamper with that which is mine." Liam growled, then shot a glance at Emrys. "Do you trust his words about the girl? Perhaps I am not one to cast stones, but I need for there to be no scandal about her. I have enough enemies left at court that I cannot risk even a rumor of impropriety. Arthur will not forgive a second time."

"I trust him as much as I would trust one of our own Liam. If you are determined to do this, then I cannot see any better option than Caelia of Durham. She is more likely to suit you than a woman from the city."

"There are no women left that suit me, but she will have to do, since there is little other option." Liam nudged his horse to trot down the road.

He was hoping to arrive at the house before noon the next day. If the years had taught him anything it was that women always made everything take at least twice as long as a man would plan for and, with the weeping and farewells, he did not expect to leave Durham before dawn the day after they arrived. If she was half the woman her brother described then, he hoped, that they would be able to ride for the entirety of that day, spend the night at the inn within the town on Dunstable and then he would bring his bride home to Redbourne at dawn so that she might see it at one of it's most beautiful times. It might make it easier for her to become accustomed to his home.

Redbourne was affectionately known as 'Meadow Hall' in the surrounding area. With the soft green fields that rippled like water, leading up to the forests of oak, birch and ash trees that surrounded the hall and outbuildings, it was a name well earned. He was certain that the light of dawn would paint the property, the great red-stoned house with it's entry tower and big windows, the armory, as well as barns and several cottages would appeal to the poetic nature of his young bride-to-be. In his experience, from the young women that his companions brought to the property for festivals and feasts, it was the kind of place that girl dreamed of presiding over.

Though he would continue to jest with the members of his brotherhood about his dislike of relatively forced marriage Liam held a genuine concern that a girl so many years his junior would not be happy, with him, his estate or his work.

The next morning the feeling of dread in her disappointment and how she would reaction to him on the ride home had not fled with his dreams. As the men mounted up and he looked into the pouch that contained his engagement gift to Caelia, a pendant of deep blue sapphire to go around her neck and a ring, a simple silver band, that would be moved from her right hand to her left once they said their vows before the Bishop, he muttered to himself. "Will this be enough? All of this, to return me to my proper place?" He looked upwards to the heavens, hoping, praying, that his dearly departed wife would hear him and soften the disposition of the girl towards accepting him as he was; flawed and scarred, inside, and out.

The hours seemed to slip by as they rode towards Durham. He was relieved that Hebron did not live on the far side of the city so that he did not have to deal with the calls of every person that Caelia knew as they departed the city. His pride could not take the looks of pity that would come to the faces of her friend when they realized it was not one of his handsome companions that she was to marry but the solemn man more than fifteen years her senior.

As they reached the road that led to Hebron's manor even the laughter of Saffir and Emrys had died down to nothing as his friends sensed his apprehension. It was hours before they had intended to arrive, and Liam was not sure if he were pleased or not that he would have less excuse to delay their departure.

Cador met them at the gate, he had obviously been waiting for them, his smile was certainly encouraging.

"Sir Liam? It is good to see you so early. Caelia has had her things prepared since yesterday. She is…punctual and waiting for your arrival in the main hall with my father. She is bidding farewell to her sisters-in-law and my brothers. My father will, I am sure, walk her right to her horse."

"That is good. Very good. I suppose that we can stop in one of the inns for the noon day meal. We arrived a few hours before I had intended, but there is plenty of time to walk the properties."

"There will be no need for that, unless you are curious yourself." Cador chuckled. "I think my father is worried that she will change her mind. Even her horse is ready to go."

He gestured towards a black charger that was impressive even to the eyes of the knight.

"That is horse belongs to Caelia? She can manage one that size?" Rion asked, awe in his voice.

"She is the one that broke him to ride. No one else has ever sat on his back, for long." Cador said proudly.

"Well, then let us go and meet the girl herself. I feel like there may be more in common than I have hoped."

Leading them towards the house Liam felt a spring in his step that had not been there that morning. Perhaps this would not be so bad.

They were laughing and joking about how a girl was going to be able to manage the spirited charger in the yard and if Liam was going to be jealous of his wife's horse. He was about to silence them with a searing reminder of his days working in the stables of Camelot when a sole female voice, as like to an angel as Liam could imagine, caught his ear. The smile that had risen to his lips swiftly fell to the pit of his stomach as he registered the words of his future bride.

Chapter 3

It was two days after she had been told that she was going to marry a man she had never met, and Celia did not feel any better about the fact. Her trunks were packed and by the door outside and one of her brothers would be saddling her horse, she had insisted on that. She was not going to ride in a carriage like some delicate little flower.

She looked around the room that had been the home of so many memories; hopes and dreams as well as tears and disappointments. The only way that she would be back here again would be if the knight chosen for her to marry rejected her or if he died before they had children that would inherit his land and perhaps his title if the king felt it the right thing to do. Would she end up like so many of her friends? Would she be pregnant constantly to ensure that the bloodline of her husband continued? That was not the life that she had ever wanted for herself, but there did not seem to be any choice now.

Closing the door behind herself felt like an ominous metaphor that she refused to consider in the bright light of day. Her steps down to the great hall were slow, she wanted to savor the sounds and smells of home before she was gone from it for who knew how long. Her father must have been waiting, he was staring at the doorway as she entered. He was on his feet, so he must have been feeling better knowing that she was to be taken care of now. With a sigh Caelia draped her cloak over her arm and joined him, taking his hand in hers.

"Father? Are you certain that this is what I must do? I am afraid, of the distance, the court and Sir Liam himself."

Her father looked horrified at her words and she turned to see the man in question had entered the hall just behind her.

"You are Caelia?"

She nodded mutely, unable to believe that of all things he could have overheard it was that.

"Well then, we should go. Since you fear the distance so greatly. The road is not getting any shorter by standing here."

She stared at the broad handsome face glaring at her, his dark eyes sparking as he pulled leather riding gloves over calloused hands. The calloused hands that would be touching her body if she agreed to the marriage. The lips pressed in a firm line would be the ones that would kiss her.

Following behind, staring at him while her brothers took her last trunk out to strap onto an open cart, Caelia finally found her voice. "Where is it that I am to sit Sir Liam?" She asked, noting that there was no covered carriage, only the wagon holding her things. Did he think she was going to ride upon his lap? Even if she did not have her own horse, she would rather sit on her luggage than a man.

"I was told that you can ride? Was that untrue?" He asked casually, walking back to stand before her. He was looking down at her, disapproving of everything about her.

"I can. Well actually." She retorted, feeling childish in her need to impress the man who was marrying her to save his reputation.

"Good. Since your horse is saddled and ready" He waved a hand and her glistening black horse was brought right to her. "Say good-bye. We're leaving."

The wives of her brothers each gave her a brief, dutiful hug. Ade, Cador's wife who had helped her pack, gave her a kiss to the cheek and whispered. "Do not worry. He is a knight. You will be safe and maybe, someday, happy."

Cador joined them and gave her a quick hug. "Give him a chance Caelia. Liam is a good man, and his company are honorable. I would not have been a part of this if I thought you would be unhappy."

"I will try and give him a chance." Caelia said, looking at the group of men by the horses.

Moving to her father she did her best to hide her fear and the desire to cry as she hugged him tight. This was not easy for him and in case it was the last time she saw him alive she wanted him to think that she was brave and happy to be off on a new adventure.

"If all goes well, I will see you at the wedding, my daughter. I look forward to raising a cup as you dance with you husband. Be safe and happy, my dear." He kissed her cheek as Liam joined them.

"She is in good hands, Hebron. We will see you at Redbourne in a month's time for the celebration." Sir Liam said, taking her hand and leading her away from everything she ever knew.

"I am not a man for public displays of emotion so if you need to weep, please keep it to yourself if you cannot wait until we have stopped for the night." He said, quiet enough so as not to be overheard but the tone of his voice left no room for mistaking his meaning.

She barely had time to think before he had lifted her onto the horse. In moments he was next to her on his own horse.

"Oh, and Caelia? Remember this about me; you have nothing to worry about, and everything to fear."

"You need not worry, my lord. I am not a woman given to tears and emotions. I would not wish to bring you shame, especially on what is supposed to be a happy occasion for all." She felt like her brave words might turn to lies as she stole a final glance at her childhood home over her shoulder before they entered the forest. Tears threatening to roll down her cheeks burned behind her eyes when one of Liam's companion's spoke for the first time.

"Do not let his stony façade fool you, my lady of Redbourne." Said a cheerful voice. "He is more afraid of you than you are of him."

Looking into the eyes of a man no older than herself, Caelia found her voice enough to say. "Your words bestow the honor of a title not yet mine, sir, but I do not think that my intended is a man that would fear something as unthreatening as an unarmed woman surrounded by knights of the realm. I pose no risk to anyone without a sword, or a staff at the least."

"Oh, I like her already Liam." The young knight laughed. "My name is Sir Emrys, please just call me Emrys though, Lady Caelia." He nodded with an infectious smile. "That serious fellow with the hood up is Saffir and driving the cart is Rion. He is in a bit of a sour mood as he hates to drive, preferring to ride but my backside was stiff, so I get the saddle for the return trip."

Saffir and Rion both laughed loudly, and even Caelia had to giggle a little before Liam turned to bark from the head of the group. "My wife-to-be does not need or want to hear about your ass, Emrys. Unless you wish to walk instead of riding you will cease talk on the subject."

All four of them stopped, like children scolded by their teacher. With a blush still on her cheek Caelia looked up at Liam she found that he was staring at her as well. With his solid jaw locked, and his lips pressed into a frown he exuded an authority that was unmistakable. This was not a man that could ever be mistaken for anything less than a knight, a commander of soldiers, a natural born leader, and every instinct she had told her to follow his order, no matter what it might be.

"Lady would you join me for a time?" He asked, his face softening slightly when he waved her forward. "I promise to provide better converse than those young rogues."

Nudging her mount forward she could have sworn that she saw the tease of a smile, perhaps there was more to him than she first supposed. Caelia wondered, could she get him to laugh before they reached Redbourne?

"You summoned me, my lord?" She said, smiling sweetly as they came side by side.

"I offered words that did not involve the foolishness of... boys." He said, not taking his eyes from the road. "Please, call me Liam and I will call you Caelia. I would not have us be so formal, unless that is what you wish." He turned to look at her, watching to see her reaction. Perhaps she would have enjoyed the younger men's company more, but he wanted the chance to get to know his future bride.

"Thank you, Liam." She nodded. It felt as though he were testing her. Perhaps he wanted to know if he had agreed to marry a courtly woman, or one of a more practical mindset?

She would not change who she was to please him, whichever it was that he had hoped for she was herself. When required she could play the part of a courtier, she knew all the proper manners and phrases though she dreaded the need. "I do not mind the company of men, after all, I grew up with brothers. What would you speak of with me?"

Caelia watched Liam try to decide what to ask her, making her wonder if he had invited her to join him simply to stop the flirtation of Emrys. He looked so flustered, almost boyish in his discomfort that she wondered when the last time he had a conversation with a woman was? Was it her age that made him uncomfortable or the fact that they were supposed to get married and were complete strangers?

"You mentioned a sword? Or staff?" He looked across at her, skeptically. "Was that a boast to join in the jest of the boys or do you have skill with a weapon?"

Caelia wanted to laugh. He thought that she would be so foolish as to declare herself capable of handling a weapon among knights that could easily challenge her ability?

"I assure you, though I may not be up to the standard of your knights, I was trained by my brothers to ensure that I would always be able to defend myself." She smiled proudly. "I was hoping that my brothers were going to gift me with my own sword for my birthday."

"You would know how to use it? Take care of it?" He asked, skepticism heavy in his voice.

"You mean, cleaning, sharpening, and polishing it?" She asked, arching a brow. "It is a lot less complicated than you men make it seem. Not like training a horse for the saddle or running a household. Both of which I can do as well."

She expected to see a look of either surprise or satisfaction on his face. Knowing that his future wife was accomplished in tasks beyond the normal household work, that she was able to participate in things that he would be interested in as well. She was surprised to see that his expression barely changed.

"Do you not think that it is important, my lord, for a woman to know things beyond the confines of kitchen, nursery and bedroom?" She asked, praying that she was not bound to a man that would never understand her.

Chapter 4

Liam was not sure how to address the bold question from the young woman beside him. She was right in that he had never expected sword skills in his future wife or anything besides the ability to manage the house and their future children. She was a fascinating creature that kept surprising him each time she spoke. Though her conversations with the younger men seemed normal enough, perhaps it was their similar ages that had something to do with that. Which was her true personality he wondered? The laughing girl or the serious young woman?

"Lady Caelia, I think it is important for a woman to know as much as she can learn, just like a man. What she needs to learn, well, that depends on the life that she intends to lead." He finally replied with a smile. "What could I offer to teach you?" He asked, his voice dropping to a husky growl.

He watched a blush creep from her cheeks down her neck and across her chest. She was most certainly a virgin if such a question made her colors rise so quickly.

"I am sure that there are many things I will learn under you, I...I mean from you, under your instruction." She stammered, looking down at the back of her horse's head.

Liam wanted to laugh. Finally, a subject that she was not the queen of confidence regarding. He might have the upper hand on this with his little wife, but he would not push that subject, not until they were closer to the wedding itself.

"I will be a patient teacher, no matter the subject." He said reaching to touch her hand through the riding gloves. When she smiled slightly and looked at him out of the corner of her eyes, he gave her another smile, trying to reassure her. "There is no hurry on some lessons, girl."

She looked as though she was about to make a reply when Emrys rode up beside them "Liam? If you are wanting to arrive at an inn before night fall then we need to increase our speed. I suggest that you and the lady go yourselves to secure the rooms and we will join you as soon as we are able."

Liam looked at the skyline, clouds joining the horizon so that he wondered if a storm would hit before the sun could set. The thought of losing another wife to illness filled him with dread. With a nod he nudged his horse to speed up and slapped the rump of Caelia's horse.

"Join us when you are able. Do not delay." He called, riding off down the road after Caelia. He was going to be alone, on the road and in inn for a few hours at least until the others arrived. He could not leave her alone with the women who worked in such places. What was he going to do with her, alone in the inn?

They rode in silence, the thunder of the horses the only sound as they moved through the trees towards the inn that Liam knew was beyond the edge of the forest. He wanted to get them there before the storm broke, but it was not long before the clouds had blanketed the sky and he could feel raindrops start to land upon his cheek.

"Liam, my lord." Caelia called over the rain, her face pale and teeth starting to chatter. "Are we near? And are you certain that the others will be alright? This is not the easiest road to follow."

"You look as though you are frozen through." Liam said with a frown. He knew how to warm her up, but it would take some trust from her that he did not think she had…yet. Drawing his horse to a stop and hers as well. He looked at her and cursed the weather under his breath. "Damnation. Come here." He reached towards her.

"What do you want? No. I will ride. I did not mean to complain." She pulled away from his reach, forcing him to move his steed closer to hers.

"You are not going to freeze in this rain, and I am not going to hurt you." Liam growled, reaching for her again and managing to grip both arms. "You will ride with me to the inn and I will hear no protest."

He could see that she was trying to think of a protest that he might listen to so while she tried to find words, he lifted her from the saddle and set her before him on his own.

"There. It is done." He lashed one of her charger's reins to his own and resumed the fast ride through the rain. It was only a few moments before he realized what he had forgotten to consider when he put Caelia before him. The last time he had ridden with a woman like this he had been in armor and she had been old enough to be his mother, not his bride to be.

She was pressed firmly against him and he could feel her shivering and, may the lord help him, he was affected in ways he had never expected to be. She let her hood fall back slightly, his own cloak more than surrounded her, and he could smell the honeysuckled sweetness of her hair. He hoped that the rain hid the sound of his groan of arousal. The roundness of her buttocks was nestled intimately against his manhood, which was becoming increasingly aware of her proximity. He had not considered the length of her legs until her thighs were aligned with his own and now, when she was nestled so close Liam could not help but wonder what it would be like when it was his time to be between hers.

"Hold on to me." He said when she started to slip. Instinctively he wrapped an arm around her slender waist and held her closer.

"I am sorry. I was reaching for the rein so you could concentrate." She said, leaning her head back against him.

"That would be helpful, thank you." He said carefully. He hoped that she did not realize how physically aware of her he was. He had to do something to distract her and himself from the sudden intimacy of the moment.

"We should be there soon, and I will ensure that there is a bath in your room so that you can get warm while the food is cooked." He said, urging the horses to go faster.

"I would welcome that after this cold." She replied cuddling against him further to avoid the whipping rain.

It seemed like hours later when they arrived in front of the lighted windows of the inn and Liam wondered if there was going to be enough rooms. The door opened and a few men stumbled out along with the roar of a crowd and the sound of songs sung around the fire.

"It looks like you may want to eat before the bath. It sounds like they are serving food already." He tossed the reins to the young attendant who came out from the barn door to take the horses and swung off the horse before reaching up for her.

"It is just as well. I feel as though I could eat a boar." Caelia said with a smile that warmed Liam through, despite the wind whipping down from the north. Holding her in his arms as they crossed the muddy, puddle filled yard he counted the darkened lights facing the yard and hoped that it meant that there were at least two rooms available, possibly three.

"Then let us see if they are serving it and see us both satisfied." He replied, setting her back on her feet at the threshold before pulling open the door and stepping into the warmth and noise of the inn. "Good sir, I will need at least two rooms, three if you have them. There are three more in our party that are following behind with the cart."

"I am not certain that I can accommodate your need, Sir." He added when he saw the sword at Liam's side and took in the quality of their attire. "There are only two rooms left, with four beds between them."

"I saw three unlit windows above. Did I see wrong or are you lying to me?" He bristled. "My lady is soaked through from the rain and I will not have her catch her death with the draft down here. I will take what rooms you have, and we will sort out the beds ourselves."

"As you say, m'lord." He handed him a pair of keys and gestured for a girl of Caelia's age to take them to their rooms.

"I would ask for hot water to be brought so that the lady may have a warm bath near the fire and supper for five, with wine, to be brought as well. My men will be here shortly, and I would ask that they be shown to these rooms immediately."

"Yes sir." The girl said, staring adoringly at him in the torchlight.

"Make the service as quick as can be managed and I promise a few copper coins for yourself and any that aid you."

"Yours are the last two rooms on this side of the house, Sir." She said with an eager smile. "The fires and candles will be lit now by my youngest sister. We will bring the food and hot water for your lady wife right away. Thank you, sir." She turned and raced back down the stairs and headed to the kitchen while Liam led Caelia towards the rooms.

"I am sure that we can hang some kind of partition to allow you your privacy to sleep. If it were not so rowdy a night then I would have seen if there was another lady you might share quarters with but I do not see any that would be suitable company for you and I would not trust that the innkeeper or his brood of daughters could keep you safe. I apologize if this is stressful for you Caelia but tomorrow night you will be in Redbourne and in a room all your own."

He was babbling, like a nervous boy instead of a knight of the realm that was widowed and of more experience with women than any man his young bride had yet met.

"I am sure that these rooms will be more than adequate Liam." She said, reassurance in her voice that he was almost certain was meant to calm them both. "It is only one night and with you and your men nearby I am certain that my virtue shall remain safe."

"Of that you can be certain. Now, let us worry about empty stomachs and chilled bodies." He opened the first door and saw two small beds crammed into the room. "Emrys and Rion can share it, Saffir will spend the night in the barn with the horses and cart."

"That is a good plan. I would not want to risk a theft in the night." Caelia replied, her body shaking with cold and making Liam wonder why her father had not sent the girl with a warmer robe.

He was just behind her when she turned the key and opened the door to the second room, which had two windows he noticed quickly as the reason for his miscount. The fire was lit and there were several candles around the room, at the table and on a stool next to a wooden tub, and on the nightstand of the large, solitary bed.

"Well, that is…what are we to do?" Caelia asked, turning to look at him with a face that had become very pale. It worried him almost as much as the sleeping situation that she was obviously now quite nervous about.

"Now we eat and get warm. The rest we can sort out when we are both feeling better." He said, leading her towards the fire and removing first her soaked cloak and then his own to hang up to dry. "Sit and warm yourself. I will see to the food."

He stepped into the hall with the door closed behind him. "Merciful god you find new ways to tempt me at every turn with this girl. How does a man keep his honor intact when every turn reveals a new temptation or obstacle?"

Chapter 5

Inside the room Caelia was shivering until the heat from the fire started to soak into her. She reached out towards the flames and tried to ignore the giant bed staring at her from the corner. Would she share it with Liam that night or would he bring her a cot to sleep near the fire? She was not certain that there would not be much choice since the inn was as full as could be and the rain was not showing signs of easing before morning.

The ride from her father's home had been more fun than she had thought it could be. Liam's companions were very much like her brothers, except that they were not trying to marry her off to every decent man that they saw. She had been enjoying the ease of their company when Liam had called her to ride with him. At first, she had seen it as an attempt to simply stop the four of them from being loud and laughing, but after a few minutes she realized that he wanted to know her and was nervous. She had been surprised to find that he was as nervous as she was. Soon they had begun to laugh and tease each other, and she was starting to think that they would be able to get along when the storm had begun to roll in.

The way that he had immediately reacted to keep her safe had amazed her, giving her a thrill, she had only dreamed of from her poetry books. The thrill had turned to unease and then fear when he had put her on the horse before him. She had never been so close to a man, tightly pressed against Liam she had felt his desire for her as a woman. He had been unable to hide it though she was sure he had wanted to.

As a knight his honor dictated that he do all that he could to help a woman feel safe and he had known that she was not used to such intimacy with a man. A glance over her shoulder at the bed made her wonder how intimate she might become with her handsome fiancé before she saw his home. Would honor be on his mind in the middle of the night while he was half asleep if they were in the same bed? Would she refuse him if he reached for her in the cold dark? The warmth in his eyes lingered in her mind as did his smile, as brief as it had been. He was handsome in all the ways that a romantic figure should be, and they would be legally married soon enough. All these things made her want to see what he was like beneath the layers that had been between them.

It was wrong of her, so very wrong from all her childhood lessons, but Caelia wanted to know if his kiss would be the same as the clumsy attempts of the stable boys and her brothers friends had been in the last year before the plan for the betrothal was begun? He had been married before so, perhaps, he knew how to kiss a girl and guide her to womanhood with skill. Instead of the painful, laughable wedding nights that her friends had gone through, would her first time with a man, with Liam, be something she would be able to smile about the next day?

When she thought of the handsome face of the man that she was going to marry she felt her entire body blush and tingle in ways that she did not understand. Was this the beginning of what her brothers' wives had told her falling in love could be like? Was it possible that she would get her romantic happily ever after?

The storm thundered above the inn and the shutters slammed against the walls with an enthusiasm that made

Caelia hope that it was the heavens signalling the answer to her prayers. Going to the window she opened it to pull the shutters closed and was relieved to see the trio of younger knights arrive in the courtyard.

"Lady Caelia." Called Saffir as Rion and Emrys rode to the barn. "Tell Liam we will join you in minutes for food and warmth."

She waved before closing the shutters against the wind. The camaraderie of the knights was heartwarming, like a brotherhood of misfits.

"Caelia! Get out of that window before you catch your death." Came the startling bellow from the doorway.

"Liam?" She said in surprise, sliding from the windowsill to stand with the bed between them. "I was simply closing the shutters. There is no danger from a bit of water and wind while I am inside."

"I would not have you catch your death of fever. Please, come to fire. The girl will bring water soon for your bath."

His steps paused at the side of the bed and Caelia wondered if he just realized that it was there and if he felt the intrusion of it as heavily as she did.

"I love to walk in the rain. This is not the kind of storm that I would choose to walk in, but I assure you that I am a picture of health." She sat on the bed and looked up at him. "What worries you so much?"

Her question hung on the air between them. She was not sure why a man who rode like a devil through the thunder and gusting wind was so fearful of her enjoying a moment of rain filled air before closing the shutters.

"Liam?" She tried to draw his attention back to her from wherever his mind had wandered to as he stared down at her. "What is it?"

"Caelia, your dress." He managed to choke out.

Her eyes dropped and she gasped. Her neckline had slipped, the fabric was heavy from the rain, and now the top edge was touching the pink edges of her nipples and revealing the white flesh of her bosom to his eyes.

Pulling the bedcover up in an attempt at modesty her cheeks were flaming. "I am sorry. That was...I am embarrassed."

***

Liam could not believe what he had just seen, and his body's reaction had been so instantaneous that he was glad that the bed was high enough not to show it. He had considered the possibility that he might have seen Caelia's ankle or her leg that night or the next morning but not her bosom. His body wanted to scream for her to not to hide herself. She was incredible and there was no doubt about that, but the flush of shame on her cheeks reminded him of her innocence.

Reigning in the thoughts of passion that came flooding to his mind the knight turned his back to the girl while she adjusted her dress.

"There is no need for any apology. If the dress is so heavy, then might I suggest that you remove it so that it can dry by the fire. I would not risk sending it downstairs with the crowd of people down there now. You can hang it by the fire and wear the blanket about yourself so that you feel...

comfortable." He hated that he sounded as unsure as Emrys or Rion would have been in the same situation, but he had to be sure not to scare her. If the night was about to go as he suspected, then she would have to trust him.

"Liam? You wish me to undress?" She asked in a tone he had not heard from her yet, fear.

"No man could deny that thought, my dear, but I want you to get warm and that dress is anything but."

He gestured towards the privacy screen in the corner of the room. "Just undress there and hand it to me. I will hang it up for you. The lads are bringing up food, stew and bread, simple fare for the future wife of a knight but I trust that the cook is good enough by the way it is being put away by those downstairs."

He watched her consider his words, her bottom lip pouted to the side, he knew that look would be imprinted on his mind for nights to come because she was unbelievably beautiful in her uncertainty. Her lips were a deep blush pink and a few strands of her chestnut brown hair were loose about her face. Some women at court were known to use the tint of flowers and berries to decorate their faces but his Caelia would never be one of those. She would never need it. Every new secret he learned about the girl made him more and more pleased that he had agreed to marry her when Hebron had sent his son with the proposal. Never had he gotten the better end of a bargain in all his life.

"That sounds reasonable." She nodded and he released the breath he had been holding as he waited. "I suppose I have nothing to fear in the company of knights of Arthur's court, do I?"

Her faith in the reputation of the men of Camelot was astounding and he hoped that it was never broken by the likes of Bedver and those he kept the company of. It was amazing that, even though he had been banished from the white city, he and his men were still regarded and trusted to be men of the same standing.

"I promise that you are as safe with me as you would be if you were at your home, at your father's home I mean."

He corrected himself but the slip of the tongue seemed to convince her to do as he suggested. She got off the bed and walked, as gracefully as the soaked gown would allow her, to go behind the screen so she could remove the dress. He stoked the fire, trying not to listen to her struggle with the fastenings. In a few weeks, maybe months, he would be able to offer her help with such things, but it was not proper or decent now. Her father was fool for dressing her in something so heavy just to impress him. Wealth and finery meant nothing to him and now the pride of the older man and his desire that his daughter should leave his house in her best gown, as though they were already wed, was causing her to whisper curses under her breath as though he could not hear her.

"Liam?" She called, and he straightened at the fireplace. The dress was being held out by a thin, pale arm for him. "Could you bring the blanket? Please?"

He swapped the dripping material for the thick plush quilt from the bed.

"Come and sit. I have built the fire higher so you will be warm."

She joined him and sat at his feet, wrapped in the faded blanket, one hand clutching it closed around her while the other reached out to catch the heat.

"They will come soon with the food? The others?" She asked, but before he could answer there was a sharp rap on the door and Emrys and Rion joined them, their hands filled with bowls and loaves.

"There is no room in the dining hall Liam." Rion said cheerfully, though he was dripping water. "To apologize, since we are a company of knights, with our damsel in distress, the cook has sent her freshest bread with a generous plate of cheese and butter."

"The damsel is not in distress, nor is she a shared care among us." Liam said sternly, handing the first dish to Caelia. "We will thank the lady when we depart tomorrow. Tonight, we eat, get warm and sleep."

"Speaking of warm." Emrys said, opening the door. "Here is the lady's bath."

A pair of boys brought in a giant copper vat and a trail of young girls followed behind with hot water.

"Well now that IS a luxury upon the road." Rion teased. "For us in the next room it will be a bowl of hot water and Saffir, in the barn, will have to make-due with what he can find for himself."

Liam smiled when Caelia's face lit up as the hot water continued to be brought in a revolving line of the children of the inn, but it fell when Emrys spoke, forgetting that there was a young innocent girl in the room before he spoke.

"I envy you two, giving each other a good washing in all that heat and then the feather bed. It looks to me like you were given the honeymoon suite just a bit before the wedding, but a good way to make sure there is no second thoughts. Clever man, Liam."

Chapter 6

Liam watched Caelia pale at Emrys' words and cuffed the boy on the back of the head. They were both lucky he wasn't wearing armor, or it would have been more than a reminder to watch his words.

"Emrys. You forget the presence of a lady, the future lady of Redbourne. You would do well to remember manners more fitting to her presence or when we return to Camelot you will offend every lady in attendance, especially the Queen."

He was relieved the boy had the good sense to be ashamed of the crude implication of his words.

"Maybe you two should take your plates to the other room and leave us to settle for the night since you have no useful words to share."

Rion and Emrys nodded and got to their feet, both bowing slightly to Caelia and stepping around the children who were still filling the tub with steaming hot water.

"Please make sure that Saffir has sufficient comfort and food for the night." Caelia asked as the younger men left.

"Yes m'lady." Rion said with a smile, closing the door behind him.

"It was good of you to remember Saffir. I did not expect you to, though the boys would have taken care of him. We outcasts tend to look out for our own."

"Is that what you see yourself as Liam? An outcast?" She asked him, looking up from her bowl and the hearth. The firelight shining in her eyes made him smile. It felt strangely intimate for the first night that they knew each other and yet it was also as if they had known each other for years. He felt strangely comfortable in that moment and sat down beside her.

"That is what we are, my dear. Outcasts of Camelot. At least for now. We all work towards earning re-admission to the round table. The younger men barely had a chance to prove themselves before we were sent away. I am grateful to them for sticking with me through it, it cannot have been an easy choice to make for them to make."

"You inspire them, I think." Caelia said, finishing the stew and delicately picking bites from the bread. "Good men respond well to a natural leader and the way they did as you said today, without pause, spoke of that."

He chuckled over his bowl. "Caelia. I told them to ride hard in the rain. It is not as though it was a battle situation."

"They would have obeyed either way, would they not?" She asked, getting to her feet to take his bowl and add it to hers on the tray to go downstairs.

"I suppose they would have. That is the way knights do things. We respect those that have earned it and obey the orders given by our commanders." He shrugged, watching her in the false scene of intimate domestic life. "If they see me as their commander it is a deference to my age, nothing more. I have never led them into real battle. Rion and Emrys have only done the quests needed to earn their knighthood. They did not have a chance to do more before following me to Redbourne."

"But they did follow you. If they were not forced to by command, then you have their loyalty because of who you are, and I am beginning to see what they admire." She said, returning to the seat by the hearth. The blanket fell a little from her shoulders as she tried to detangle her hair.

"Well I am glad that you see something of worth in the man you are supposed to marry." Liam said with a sigh. "That is more than some see."

"We will be married in a few weeks Liam. If I did not see someone to be admired, it would be a sad situation." She said, looking up at him. "Would you help me move the screen so that I can bathe while the water is hot?"

"Of course, I can help you with that." He carefully moved the dressing screen to hide her from sight while he sat on the bed. The tub was close to the fire and he wanted her to be as warm as possible. "I'll just rest here while you wash. Take you time and get warm. I do not wish for you to get sick. It would be ill luck for the wedding."

"I can sleep beside the fire so you may have the bed. I do not mind as long as it is warm." Caelia said as she stepped behind the screen. She must have been undressing while she spoke for soon the light linen of her underdress was draped over the top of the screen. "Nonsense." He said, taking the garment to hang by the fire to dry. "It is more than big enough to hold us both with a respectable distance between. There is no sense in getting a bad night sleep when there is no need." He crossed the room to sit on the bed and remove his boots. He just about dropped them on the floor when he turned to look towards the screen.

He could see a perfect outline of Caelia's body as she tested the water. The fire was behind her and while he had thought of the warmth it would provide, he hadn't considered that it would silhouette her so perfectly. He was glad that

Emrys and Rion were not there to see him staring. By heaven, he could see the bead of her nipples that must have tightened in the cool air, he could almost have sworn that he could see the fluff of curls that would hide the treasure of her femininity. Suddenly he realized that she was speaking. "My apologies Caelia. What did you say? My mind was elsewhere."

"It has been a long day, I understand." She replied, saving his resolve and sanity by climbing into the tub. "What I had said was that to sleep in the bed together would be to invite gossip that there was…that we…"

"That we had relations before the wedding vows were said?" He replied, removing his shirt and outer breeches, hanging them to dry overnight near the bed instead of the fire itself. "Since we share the room it will be whispered no matter where we sleep. There is no reason to be uncomfortable and sour the sleep we both need. You are safer here than if you had your own room. I will not touch you as a husband until you are my wife, on my honor as a knight of Arthur."

"That is reassuring, my lord, I mean Liam." She said from the tub. "I am still unconvinced that to share the bed is a good idea."

"It is the way it will be. I'll not have you on the floor while I take the bed and I intend to get a good rest tonight." Liam sighed. The outline of her washing was becoming more than he could bear to watch while speaking of the length of time before he could truly romance her the way a man romanced his woman. He had already decided that she would be his, not just his wife, but the woman who loved him as much as he could love her in return.

He moved to the other side of the bed in the hope of relief from the torment of her beauty. He got beneath the sheet, making sure that she would have not to worry about their bodies coming into contact, though he looked forward to the time when it would be him that warmed her instead of a blanket and when he could join her in the huge copper tub that he had in his chambers at Redbourne. With a smile on his lips at the thought of her on his lap in the warm water he turned towards the window, trying not to watch her silhouette, but the reflection that greeted him was impossible to turn away from.

He had not considered the angles of the screen when he chose this side of the bed and he cursed himself at the same time that he thanked the angels for the site of his bathing fiancé reflected in the dark glass before him. He would never tell a soul about this and could not bear to look away again. Her face was turned towards the fire, the light of which was giving her alabaster skin a glow of gold that made him think of chapel angels. She could easily have been a vision of divinity, but when she moved her arm in a graceful gesture that exposed the chest that he had been admiring through the screen all thoughts of the divine disappeared and sinning was all that he could think of. Closing his eyes, he pretended to be asleep while he committed the vision that was his soapy, glisteningly wet fiancé, to memory.

"Liam?" She called, the sound of water sloshing in the tub telling him that she was getting out. "Liam? Have you fallen asleep?"

He could not have said for certain that he would sleep at all that night, knowing what lay beside him and that he should not, could not, touch her. She did not need to know that though and so he coughed and sat up, slowly, as though he had dozed off.

"Hmm? No not asleep. Was close though. The bed is much more comfortable than the ground I slept on last night. Are you finished with the water?" He asked, smiling from the bedside when she came from behind the screen in her underdress. It made her slightly less tempting but with her hair down around her shoulders she now appeared less of a temptress and more of a lost waif. There was an unease in her eyes that changed to something else when her eyes raised from the floor and saw him.

He was bare-chested, in his breeches, showing nothing that she would not have seen when she grew up in a household full of men, but she still stared.

"Caelia? Is something wrong? Some scar or blemish that keeps you staring?" He asked, a nervous smile on his lips as she walked to the opposite side of the bed and kept staring silently. He was not as lean as a young man like Rion or Emrys. Even Saffir was considered slender and well muscled, but he knew the bulk of his arms was appealing and though he had more hair on his chest than the younger knights he was not a lazy man. There was also no man in his group of friends that could best him with the sword. He knew that if for some reason she thought him incomparable to a younger man then he would change her mind once she saw him training at Redbourne.

"Nothing wrong. Nothing wrong at all." She said softly. Her eyes were still on him while she covered the bed with the blanket that she had been wrapped in. "I was simply unprepared to see you...like that."

"Does it offend you, my lady." He teased, sensing that it might be appreciation and not shock that kept her face locked to him. "I can put on my shirt though it is still damp I think."

"No. There is no need for that and no offence, of course not. I would not wish for you to sleep in wet things, Liam." She said with a pretty, pink blush rising on her cheeks.

"Then, my dear, let us both get some sleep so that tomorrow you can appreciate Redbourne, your new home, in the way that I hope you will." He gestured towards the bed with a warm smile. "Why not get yourself comfortable and I will take care of the candles."

He doused the lights slowly, giving Caelia the chance to settle and get comfortable in the bed. When he got beneath the covers himself he was please to notice that she was not on the farthest edge, in danger of falling off, but was nearly asleep with her head turned inwards towards where he was now laying.

"Good night, Caelia. Dream sweet, my lady." He said, closing his eyes and praying for a solid night sleep to come easily.

Chapter 7

The bed was not nearly soft enough and something was burning in the kitchen, but Marianne was there, curled into him with her head on his arm, so nothing else really mattered.

"Good morning sweetheart." He said, kissing her neck and tightening his arms around her. He grunted in surprise when a sharp elbow jabbed him in the stomach. "Someone is cranky this morning."

"What in heavens name do you think you are doing?" Cried an unfamiliar voice as his eyes flashed open.

"What the…Caelia?" He groaned and let go of her, flipping to his back. "I am sorry. That was not supposed to happen. I thought you were my wife."

"Well I am not. Not yet." She said indignantly while she got out of the opposite side of the bed.

"No. Not yet." He said, sitting up and pulling on his boots.

The romance of the night had faded with the rising of the sun and he wished he knew how Caelia had ended up in his arms. It had felt so right to him, until the moment that she had cried out in protest. He looked around the room and sighed, this was not going the way he had hoped. She was looking at him like he was a monster, the kind of man that would do what had gotten him removed from Camelot. She would never believe him now if he told her that story and proclaimed his innocence. It might be best if he did not speak of it until he had no other choice, or she would run back to her father and he would never lay eyes upon her again.

"I am sorry, for the misunderstanding. I...um...you were not, I mean, are you alright?" He asked, looking over his shoulder at her.

"I am." She said sharply. "Do not look!" She cried, throwing a pillow at him. "I need to get dressed. May I do so in privacy?"

"Yes. Of course. My apologies."

Liam pulled on his shirt and gathered his things before stepping out into the hallway and right into both Rion and Emrys.

"Caelia is dressing. We will all eat and then we leave for Redbourne. Make sure that Saffir has the animals ready. Rion you drive the wagon today. I want to get my betrothed home as soon as possible so that she can begin to settle into her new life." The pair nodded and followed him down the stairs. Glancing up towards the door Liam added to the younger men "Make sure that the others know to not tell Caelia the details behind our expulsion from the court of Arthur."

"You want us to lie to her Liam?" Emrys asked, disapproval all over his face.

"No lad. I just wish to find the right time to tell her, to explain the truth. I would prefer if no one told her the more sordid version and scare her from the wedding."

"Well she won't hear that pack of lies from any of us. I would hope you would trust us by now Liam." Emrys said with the shake of his head.

"Rion, go find the innkeeper or cook, someone who can get us food. I will wait for my lady at the table. Remember I would like to be far from here before an hour has passed."

The men split to see their tasks completed while Liam finished tucking his shirt into his belt and sat down to wait for the arrival of the young woman he had left upstairs. He did not wait for long before she came skipping down the stairs. Her energy and smile bringing the smile back to his face.

"You look lovely, Caelia." He said, pulling out her seat and waving to Rion who looked to be in the process of trying to get their food ahead of the other orders in the kitchen. "Did you sleep well after the bath?"

"Thank you, Liam. I did."

He was grateful, as Emrys returned with their plates, that she did not broach the subject of their awkward awakening. He did not want the other knights to know that he had mistaken Caelia for the wife that had been gone for years.

He had not felt this comfortable with a woman since her passing and while it still hurt to say her name or even think about her, Liam believed he was on the way to healing at last. Bringing his focus back to the table he smiled to hear Caelia asking about Redbourne and the surrounding lands.

"I do my best to manage things, with the help of the other Knights. It's our duty to ensure all those under our care are safe, well treated and, of course, fed. As well in winter as summer, whenever possible." Liam said with some pride.

Not all Lords or Knights took the care and well being of surfs and vassals as seriously as he did, but he and his friends knew first hand what it was like to grow up in that kind of place and he was determined to never allow it to happen under his watch.

"That is reassuring. What about the years of failed harvest? I have heard tell of some who feed their warriors more than common folk during hard times. To ensure that they are strong enough to defend the lands if needed."

"Liam is not that sort Caelia." Emrys said, pointing towards him with the mug in his hands. "The last time that happened at Redbourne Liam was the last to eat at every meal and the first to go without on days where there was not enough."

Caelia turned eyes filled with admiration that made Liam blush slightly.

"Though to be fair those days were few because the men of Arthur's court stay together, helping one another in times of need. We share stores, seeds and armed men in times of need." Liam explained. Not wanting to seem arrogant and he also wanted to set the groundwork for her to feel comfortable around the knights that he would introduce her to, at Redbourne and Camelot.

"That shows a lot of wisdom. Is that the king's idea or did that come from one of you knights? I imagine he, the king, relies more on you and the other knights than most of us know. Is that so?"

"Well, we have not been to Camelot in some time." Emrys said, his eyes flicking to meet Liam's. "Due to…"

"Due to the fact that there has been so much going at Redbourne that has needed our care and attention. Then winter came and it was not safe upon the roads for man or beast. We have only just barely finished the birthing of livestock and nearly finished with the planting for the season."

"Then you will, we will, go there? To court? To Camelot?"

There was an eagerness in her voice that spoke of her innocent enthusiasm and the fact that her father had never taken her there himself. It would be up to him to introduce her to all of that when the time came, and he was invited back.

"We will go when Arthur, I mean the King, sends for us. Until then we will do our sworn duty by taking care of the land and people entrusted to me by his word."

"Oh, of course. I am sure that will come soon enough once he hears that you are to marry. Does he not have to give his blessing?"

Liam was not about to tell her that they may have a long wait before Arthur and those at the round table sent an invitation for his return. She was so excited at the prospect that it seemed cruel to crush her dreams.

"He does indeed. Once you have seen Redbourne and have settled in, then I will send word of our intent to marry. I am sure that the Queen will be eager to meet you. It has been years since there was a wedding of note among those of the round table."

"To that end, Lady Caelia." Emrys interrupted. "Let us be on the rode and get you where you belong before the noonday meal?"

Caelia rose and put her hand to Liam's arm. "Are we truly that close? Just a few hours ride?"

"It will be a hard ride, like last night, but yes." Liam smiled at her. "We can be there in a few hours."

Her enthusiasm was infectious, as was her smile heading out into the bright, early morning sunshine.

"Then let us ride Liam. I find myself anxious to explore this new home and sleep comfortable in my own bed." She said, her eyes lingering on Liam's face as Saffir brought the pair their horses.

"I thought that the two of you might prefer to get a head start on the rest of us. You will be faster just the two of you."

"Agreed." Liam said, picking Caelia up by the waist as he had the day before and settled her on the big horse. "We will have a nice ride together, I hope."

"I am sure we will arrive in no time at all." Caelia replied, flashing a smile and the trio of younger men that disappeared when her gaze returned to Liam's face.

They rode out of the courtyard of the inn and North up the road, heading towards his home. It was at least half an hour of riding steadily away from the inn before Caelia spoke to him.

"You spoke of your duty to the king and those he has put in your care. What part do you wish for me to play in that?" She aske him, unease in her sweet voice. "I know how to run my father's household, but I suspect there is much more required of the wife of a knight of Camelot that what I am used to."

He slowed his horse to a walk, easing hers to the same pace. He was silent for a few moments while he carefully considered his answer to her question. He did not want to put too much pressure on his young wife, but she was correct about the responsibility being greater than a farmer's household, even one as wealthy as her father.

"You are right, of course. There are more things that will need your attention, more people. I am sure that you will find the household things similar or perhaps easier with the staff that I have. The most complicated thing will be the things you will need to know for court. I am not going to worry you about those until we receive a summons to Camelot."

His guts twisted at how her face lit up at the mention of the city. How would she feel waiting for something that would not come?

"At Redbourne you will be the lady of the house, setting an example for all the women of the estate. I cannot tell you how pleased I am that you know how to run a household so well. I am sure that you and the servants will adapt well to each other with a little bit of time and compromise on both sides.

"I hope that I do not disappoint you. Am I required to consult with you on any changes I may with to make or is there a head of staff that I should speak with about them?"

"The cook, Hilda, would be the best person to speak to about most things." He said with a smile.

"Hilda? I shall make it my mission to get in her good graces so that we can make sure that nothing except improvements are brought to the house." He could hear the determination in her voice and hoped that Hilda knew what she was in for.

They continued to ride, increasing the pace and the conversation about the household and how she had managed things at her father's home. Time flew by and there was even some laughter between them. Before he knew it they were cresting the hill over Redbourne and he hung back just a little so that she could see the estate spread out at her feet and take it all in that this was now her home, if she chose it, if she chose him.

"Oh, Liam. I have never seen anything like it. Camelot itself could not be more beautiful. This is Redbourne?" She turned back to ask him.

"Yes, Lady Caelia of Redbourne. Welcome home." He said with a grin, nudging his horse past hers to move down the hill towards the house where a crowd would be gathered by the time they arrived. "Welcome home."

Chapter 8

Caelia stared at the property laid out at the bottom of the hill in amazement. It was bigger, grander, than anything she had ever seen. The red stone the manor house was built from was obviously where the name Redbourne came from. The main house was a massive building with windows on all three levels and a roof of clay tiles instead of timber or peat. She was delighted to see the tower on the far north corner. Though it was likely a tactical building it made her think of castles and princesses, damsels in distress and their knights on a white charger. She looked at Liam on his smoky grey charger, perhaps he was not the knight of her dreams, but she was beginning to suspect that he was a deeper man than she knew yet.

The cottages and outbuildings were made of the same stone, the cottages had telltale fences and gardens around them. She could not help but smile at the quaintness of the scene. It was good that the people not only had their own gardens to grow food but had the time to tend beautiful flower gardens that decorated the landscape. Such a simple thing told her that Liam and the other had not been lying about how he treated the people on his land. People were happy here.

They were getting closer to the buildings and Caelia saw the forge and she felt a surge of excitement that, perhaps, she might have a chance to watch swords being made and even have one of her own, made for her instead of borrowed.

"Liam? How do you manage all of this?" She asked him, bringing her charger beside him.

"Do not tell me that you are starting to doubt yourself Caelia?" He said, his voice teasing though his face was serious. "I am sure you will be running everything in no time at all."

Caelia did not share his confidence and, as they approached the gathering group of people at the house, she said with her most charming smile. "I will not believe you if you say that this is easy, Liam. No matter how much faith I have in you"

A man that was obviously a knight stepped forward to greet them as Liam replied to her in a rough voice.

"I never said that it was easy. I said that you could do it and you will."

She was surprised to hear the same hardness in his voice now as there had been at her father's house when they met. There was no more laughter and teasing in his eyes now that they were among his people. Caelia could not help but wonder which temperament was really him.

"Liam, it is good to see you back. This is the lady Caelia I presume?" The knight said.

"It is good to bring her home, Lionel." Liam said, dismounting his horse and reaching up for her.

Those big, strong, hands around her waist, lifting her down to the ground to face the people who would be her new family, her new community.

"Everyone, this is lady Caelia. My future bride and lady of the house. I hope that you will all make her welcome and aid her in learning the property. Work together to keep Redbourne running smoothly for all of us."

"Hello." Caelia said with a sudden feeling of shyness. Standing beside the proud knight, in front of his people, ones that had known him for years longer than she ever could, she felt incredibly young and even more inexperienced.

"This is Lionel and the surly looking man in the blacksmith's bib is Gerard and the one with the sword and without hair, is Lucas. They are the other knights that live here." Liam said to her, pointing out each man then continuing to introduce her to the rest of the household.

She was hardly able to keep track of all the names and faces as she greeted each one with a kind smile. Her eyes kept going back to the knights who were following her with their eyes and the blacksmith, Gerard, who did not look happy to see her. It might have been her imagination, but he seemed angry that she was there. Was it concern for Liam as a friend? Or was she not actually welcome at Redbourne? She shivered at the intensity of his stare and did her best to focus on the young woman in front of her.

"I am sorry, what was your name?" She asked, taking the hand of the fawn haired girl about her age.

"Lynn, my lady." She said with a curtsey. "I will be your handmaid, happy to help you with anything that I am able."

"Lynn." Caelia smiled, putting the angry blacksmith from her mind. "I am so glad to meet you. I hope you will help me from getting lost in the house? It is much larger than anything I have ever been in."

Lynn nodded with a smile. "I would be happy to show you anything and do not worry about the house. It is not that daunting once you are inside."

"Speaking of inside." Liam interrupted them. "Why don't you take Caelia inside and introduce her to Hilda. I have a few things to see to before Emrys and the others arrive with the lady's things."

"I could come with you?" Caelia said, not wanting to leave him and wanting to see more of the outside of the property before going into the intimidating house.

"No. Not this time. Gerard and I must talk in the forge and that is no place to take you on your first day at Redbourne."

She could have sworn that she saw a secretive smirk on Gerard's face as the pair of men walked off together.

"Do not mind Ger." Lynn said in her ear. "He is Sir Liam's oldest friend. They fought in the wars together and when given the choice to stay in Camelot or come to Redbourne he was the first to say that he would come here with him. They are seldom apart and regard each other very highly."

"I see. It is good to have such close friends. I wonder what is Sir Gerard's lady like? Perhaps she and I could become friends just as close?"

"I do not recall having ever seen him with a woman though I think most of the girls here have flirted a little with him. Those dark brown eyes of his are quite lovely up close."

"It sounds to me as though you favor him Lynn?" Caelia teased.

"I would never aim so high myself, but he is a handsome man, my lady."

"Please, call me Caelia. If we are to be good friends it will not do for you to call me by a title that is not even mine by right, yet. When we are alone together, I would like, if you are of the same mind, for us to call each other by our given names."

Lynn smiled and gestured towards the house.

"That does sound nice, Caelia. If we go now, we might be able to get something to eat from Hilda. You must be famished from the ride."

Caelia nodded, letting the groom take the rein of her horse. "Are you sure you do not want me to do that?" She asked him.

"Lady Caelia." The older man said, holding up a hand to stop her words. "It is not only my job but an honor to handle such a magnificent creature."

He bowed and led the charger off towards the barn, leaving Caelia wishing that she were going with them.

"Come on Caelia. I think I can get most of the tour of the house done before your things arrive with Emrys and the others. Do you like books?"

She followed her new friend with a last glance towards her departing knight and both horses, her eyes meeting Liam's for just a moment when he looked back at her. She flashed him a smile, but he did not return it before he put his arm around the shoulders of the blacksmith and headed into the shadows of the forge.

"Books? Oh yes. I love them. Is there a collection here?" Caelia said, rushing to catch up. "I have some that I have brought, they are in the wagon. I hope they are not…ruined." She almost forgot what she was talking about as they entered the house and moved into the largest hall she had ever imagined. It was the full height of the building and the light was pouring in from the windows across the long rectangular table.

"I have never…is that where we eat?" She asked in shock.

"Oh yes. All the knights, morning, and evening meal. Liam is a man that likes his friends around him. They have been through a lot, wars, quests and adventures that they love to share around the fire some nights."

"I will look forward to those. I have heard all the stories of my brothers and father so many times that I could tell them myself."

"Oh, they might like that, if you join them." Lynn said with a bright smile. "If not, you could tell all of us girls. We enjoy tales too and rarely get the good ones."

"I can promise you that there will be many nights, just us ladies, and they will be filled with stories so adventurous that even Sir Lancelot would find himself envious."

The pair giggled and wandered the main floor of the house, following the smell of bread with a hint of fruit.

"It smells like Hilda is making a pie. It must be to celebrate your arrival." Lynn said with an excited expression. "They are known for being the best and all the knights will be at dinner. It will be a wonderful affair."

"Should I wear something formal then? Would that be expected?" Caelia asked, stepping through the door that Lynn was holding open and into the bouquet of smells unlike anything she was used to. This place, this life, was going to take more getting used to than she had thought.

"If you wear something formal, in that room, you will make every single man at the table feel underdressed." Said a voice from the far side of the kitchen. "That is not a thing that most men like. Men of honor, like these boys that have been knighted alongside Liam and Gerard, like it less than most. Wear something clean, respectable but not too fancy or formal. Smile and make good conversation, but listen even more than you talk, for now."

Caelia followed the sound of the voice, Lynn behind her, trying to find the person behind the advice. She expected, with the name 'Hilda' to find a large, matronly woman instead of the tiny, white-haired being that could only be called a sprite that turned from the oven door to smile.

"You are the Lady Caelia that Liam has been so excited to bring home? Welcome to Redbourne. I am Hilda, the cook for the last twenty years. Sit down a spell and I will grab you a plate."

Both young women did as they were instructed, Lynn had a knowing and eager smile on her face while the tiny woman gathered food and sweet, cold, water for them to drink.

"Lord knows I love that boy, your Liam, but he is as thoughtless towards the needs of a woman now as he was when he first ran off to fight with young King Arthur."

Sharing a silent giggle with Lynn, the king was well into his forties and near the same age as her intended, Caelia took a deep drink of the water before digging into the plate of food. It was rich and flavorful, wholesome, and homely. She was going to enjoy getting to know and working with this woman, she could feel it.

"Well, Hilda, with a woman like you making sure that everyone is as well fed as we are right now, I am sure that his mind is freed to focus on other important things." Caelia said.

She smiled to herself when Hilda gave her an approving nod and slipped another sweet biscuit onto her plate.

"You girls finish that up and go look around some more. I have a dinner to prepare. Do you like pies Caelia?" She asked while they headed back the way they had come.

"They are my favorite." She replied, just before the door closed and Lynn led her off into the depths of Redbourne again.

Chapter 9

Liam looked at Gerard as soon as they were within the confines of the smithy. His friend's dark eyes were sparking with unspoken opinions and, though he was not certain they would be in Caelia's favor, he had to hear them.

"Alright Ger, what do you think of her? Of Caelia." He asked, leaning against a workbench covered with steel and tools.

"She is young, a little needy, but pretty." He said with a shrug. "If you can deal with the first two the last part should be pleasing enough, at least for making children and visiting Camelot. Arthur will approve because of her father and her youth. They all think we 'wild men' need to settle down finally."

"Never you though, my old friend?" Liam said with a smile. He had known that, after mourning had passed, his best friend had hoped that there would never be another lady of the house that they would have to censor themselves for. He never seemed comfortable around any of the women at court and only Hilda and young Lynn here at Redbourne.

"Never me. I have no time for such things and women are not interested in me after meeting the rest of the motely crew we keep here." Gerard laughed, though it sounded forced.

"Not even young Lynn? Marry the girl and then your wife and mine can be best of friends and our sons and daughters could grow together. One day they might even marry and join our families once and for all." Liam said, clapping his hand to the blacksmith's shoulder. "It would be the perfect life, would it not?"

"Liam, you have no idea how much I would like to join my last name to your house, but Lynn is too young, too innocent for me. It would never work."

"Oh, come now. Things can be overcome. The girl is lovely and would give you no grief. Unlike the one that I am to wed who has a voice she demands be heard, a mind of her own and, gods help us, a mind towards sword fighting. Can you imagine? The wife of a knight wielding a sword in the training yards?"

The two of them laughed together at the absurdity of it.

"If that is to be then you may as well have married a knight for all the tender qualities she will bring to your marriage." Gerard said once the laughter had stopped. "Are you certain that you wish to go through all this again Liam?

Liam shook his head and looked at the fire until Gerard put a hand on his shoulder and used the other to turn him back to face him.

"Do you want to marry the girl, Liam?" He asked with the same deep voice he would have used to ask if he wanted to make a risky maneuver on the battlefield. "There is time to get out of it if you want to. Let her stay a few weeks then send her back to her father. Tell him she is too young. You will not be lying. After that you can live your life as you wish, with whom you wish."

Liam stared into the eyes of his dearest friend, the man that had fought beside him in every battle he had ever faced and wondered, for the first time, at his motives.

"I intend to marry her Gerard. I gave my word and that girl needs a man to guide her, husband her. I pity the world if the wrong man married her. She would burn it to the ground with the strength of her will alone."

"You think that little scrap is that strong? She seemed scared of her own shadow just now." Gerard scoffed.

"I think it was the unexpected crowd and the fact that the three of you were not as warm as the younger fellows were. She is quite…unique." Liam said, unable to stop the smile from crossing his face. "The thing she desires most, the gift she said she wanted more than anything, is a sword. Can you believe it?"

Gerard laughed and stepped back to his fire to resume the work there.

"Do not ask that of me Liam. A sword for a woman. The balance has to be something so different than what we use, it will take so much time."

Was it that Gerard did not want to make a sword for a woman or was it Caelia herself that brought this animosity from him? Liam could not tell but from the way that he was focused on the blade in the fire he knew that this was not the time to press further.

"I will leave you to your work and go talk with Lionel and Lucas. Emrys and the others should be here soon. I want everyone in the dining room tonight to make my bride feel welcome. I do mean everyone Gerard." He said with a weight that was almost a command in his voice.

"I will be there and play my part Liam. If this is your choice, then I will do my best to support you." He growled, slamming the hammer in his hand against the hot steel, effectively ending the conversation without saying another word.

"Thank you." Liam said, knowing it was unheard, before heading to find the other two knights.

He hoped they had a better view of Caelia than Gerard did, or this was going to be a difficult marriage to pull off. He needed this to work or he would never get back to where he belonged: Arthur's side, with Lancelot and Gawain and the rest of the men at the round table. He had to bring the rest of the men back with him too, of course. After they had argued for his side, Gerard had even drawn his sword in the presence of the Queen, they had all been sent away with him, in shame and without their honor. He would find a way to see it and them all restored to where they belonged and the marriage to Caelia was the first step in that plan.

"Liam, does this horse really belong to that little girl you brought home with you?" Lucas called from within the barn.

Chuckling at the young man's question Liam strolled between the stalls to find both Lucas and Lionel with Caelia's horse. Lucas looked like a child presented with a puppy as he stroked the neck of the big stallion.

"Yes, that is hers. A gift from her family." He said, touching the cheek of the big animal carefully.

"Do you think she would let me ride him?" Lucas asked eagerly.

"You will have to ask her yourself. What I understand from her brothers is that no one else has ever been able to stay astride the horse. He chose Caelia and she chose him." Liam fought a smile when the horse turned to brush his lips over his hair. "He may not be that way now though."

Lionel rolled his eyes. "You two are dreamers to think that an animal like that chose a person. It is simply about the skill of the rider and the girl, I mean, Lady Caelia, is obviously a skilled one. It is well known that stallions often prefer a lighter rider so that their speed is not impeded. You two talk as though the creature understands our words, horse and female alike."

The big black nudged Lionel hard with his nose, throwing the younger man off balance.

"Careful Lionel. I think the horse and the lady who owns him might just surprise you." Liam said with a laugh. "If neither of you has any serious objection to my choice in wife, other than that she may or may not let you ride her horse, Lucas, then I suppose I can see you both at supper. I would like her to feel welcome."

Lionel simply nodded and headed in the opposite direction, to the office that Liam knew he kept there, in the peace and quiet of the animals that he loved. Lucas grinned and ran a hand over the horse's back.

"You have to do what you think is right Liam. She's a lovely girl and I will say whatever you want if it might get me the chance on this charger."

"Be yourself, you fool. She is kind enough to let you try if you are yourself with her and treat her with kindness. She will be missing her brothers and I cannot fill that void for her. I hope, perhaps, that you lads might treat her like a sister, for my sake if not for her own."

The young man grew serious, a rare thing for him.

"Of course, we will be as brothers to her Liam. She is one of us now, family. She may not know it yet or feel it, but there is no denying it. Once the two of you are joined in marriage she will be as dear to us as blood."

The relief he felt must have shown on his face because Lucas laughed.

"You did not think we were all going to react like Gerard, did you? The man has done little but complain about how things will have to change."

"I was not sure. He does not think that I need to get remarried, but I must. I have to prove to Arthur and the others that doubted me that night that I am better, that I am who they always thought I was before that night."

"Prove to Arthur, or prove to yourself?" Lucas asked, stepping out of the stall, and joining him on the walk to the house. "None of us believe Bedver or that girl. Not for moment."

"You have my gratitude for that." Liam shook his hand. "I am still trying to figure out how to tell Caelia why it is that we are not, exactly, welcome at court."

They walked in silence for a few moment, the older knight, the former hero of the king's court, and the wild young man who had risked a reputation he had not yet begun to earn to stand up for the honor of a friend.

"I do not know how you are going to approach it, but you had better do it before the wedding. No matter what, she deserves to know what she is getting herself into and you need to know what she has heard about you as well. Perhaps she already has heard the rumors and agreed to marry you regardless?

Liam shook his head. "No. No I do not think she knows, and I promise that I will tell her before the wedding. I want her to find out if she likes this life before I do that. You understand?"

Lucas shook his head. "Not even a little but it is not my business to try and figure that out."

"That's not so helpful. Get out of here and clean yourself up before supper, Lucas. You stink of horse and I'll not have you offending the nose of everyone around the table."

"I will smell as fresh as daisies." Lucas laughed and headed off towards his cottage, leaving Liam alone on the doorstep of his home.

The house already felt different when he stepped inside. It was as if Caelia was already making her presence known just by breathing. He could hear the echo of her voice and the sound of Lynn laughing at something that she had said. Liam had not realized that he was smiling until Hilda stepped out of the kitchen.

"Well now, I have not seen that smile in too many years." She said, touching his hand. "Your young bride is a force of nature."

"You have met her then?" Liam asked, turning to look at the woman he had grown up following around her kitchen while she learned her craft. Her opinion meant as much as Gerard's. If she did not like Caelia then it would not work, it would be impossible for her to feel welcome in a house where the most important people to him did not want her there.

"I have met her. Lynn brought her to get something to eat, since you forgot that most people eat more often than you." Hilda said with an arched brow.

"I suppose that I did forget. What do you think of her?" Liam said with a scoff, amused that she still made him feel like a little boy at times.

"I think that she is exactly what you need. Marry the girl and accept the happiness that she can bring to your life."

"Alright. You have yet to direct me wrong Hilda. I will try to convince her to accept the marriage."

"Do not convince her Liam. She is a young woman. Court her, win her over to this life, and let yourself fall in love, if that is what is meant to be. Let her fall in love with you."

"Let her fall in love with me." He said to himself as the sound of feminine feet came down the stairs.

Chapter 10

Caelia was delighted with the company of Lynn. She was amusing and eager to show her every little nook and cranny of Redbourne that she could. From the kitchen, dining hall and receiving hall on the main floor to each and every bedroom upstairs, including a secretive peek inside the room of her future husband.

It was a big room, bright and airy with a southern view, with simple and solid furniture that included an embarrassingly large bed with four tree sized columns at each corner and crisp white sheets. Across the foot of the bed was a deep blue blanket, gold thread embroidered stars, moons and trees across the surface and when Caelia dared to reach out and touch it she was surprised to find that it was the kind of soft, luxurious plush that made her want to wrap it around her shoulders and watch a rain storm roll through the valley.

"We should not linger in here." Lynn said. "Sir Liam will not like it. I just thought that you would want to know where he sleeps."

Caelia blushed and dropped the blanket back in place. She was not ready to admit that she had enjoyed waking in his arms that morning and, though she was sure they would be good friends, she was certainly not going to tell Lynn about it. She would not understand and might even think that it meant something more had happened.

"I am sure that I will not need to know that for some time yet." She replied, darting back into the hall as if she feared being caught in a bedroom with her intended. There was no doubt that he would never force anything from her, but the confusing feelings she had been flooded with all morning seemed even more real in his presence. If they were real then she would have to deal with them and Caelia was not prepared for that, not yet.

"Oh, now, do not worry about that. The wedding will be here before you know it. There is bound to be a letter from Camelot any day. That will be the official invitation for Sir Liam to bring you to meet the King and get the approval of the crown to marry you." Lynn smiled. "After that it is just as simple as preparing the dress and inviting your family. Less than a month from now it will be your room as well."

"Can you show me the room that is to be mine in the meantime. This talk of the wedding makes me nervous." It was not a lie. The feeling was not for the reason that she might have supposed but it was still the truth. "I would like to get an idea of where I will put my things before they arrive. After that, perhaps, we can see the library that you mentioned before?"

"I think that he wants to show you both of those himself." Lynn said, heading towards the stairs. "We should go downstairs to wait for him and the others. I would not want to spoil his plans. He went through a lot of work to make sure that things were nice for you."

"He did? Really?" Caelia asked, her curiosity about Liam returning while they descended to the hall.

"I did indeed see to your room myself."

His deep voice catching her off guard at the bottom of the stairs. She lost her footing and landed, hard on the bottom stair.

"Oof."

"Caelia?" He called and rushed to her side, pulling her to her feet.

"I am alright, Liam. Nothing injured but my pride that is all." She said, blushing horribly. When he cradled her face in his warm hands and made her look him in the eyes Caelia could feel her face burning.

"You are sure? There is no shame in admitting to pain." He said, the concern in his eyes making her believe that he meant what he said. He was not a man to lie and tease her about things later.

"He ought to know. He hides his every time I beat him in the training ring." The voice of the surly blacksmith, Gerard, called from the doorway. "Emrys and the others are here with the wagon and the lady's things."

Caelia was not sure but she thought that Liam had just cursed under his breath when his friend interrupted the prolonged look between them. Was he having the same confusing feelings that she was? Not love, that was a feeling she would have known right away from her books, but it was something she had never felt before. Whenever he was looking at her, she felt jittery and nervous. She blushed so much easier around him and she wanted him to see her, to smile at her and be proud to have her at his side. It seemed too much to hope that he, a celebrated and decorated knight, would ever see her as his equal, but she hoped that he might, one day, see her as a partner.

"They are? That's wonderful. I should be able to have things put away in time to help with dinner." Caelia said, taking a step away from the confusion that was Liam's touch.

"You are not expected to do anything like that, Caelia." Liam said with another heart fluttering smile. "Hilda is very territorial about her kitchen."

"I have always enjoyed cooking. Perhaps, in time, I will be able to convince her to let me join her at times." She replied hopefully before stepping outside to see the younger knights arrive with the wagon holding everything she owned. It was only a few seconds before she felt him behind her and when he touched a hand to the small of her back, she smiled. It was possible, perhaps, that they could build a relationship of affection after all. If she felt like this already it was bound to grow if they kept on this path. That was, of course, why her father had sent her here early, to get to know the man she was to marry, to fall in love with him.

"Come, my dear, let us see you settled before dinner." Liam said to her, squeezing her shoulder and heading towards the wagon.

She watched him join the other men, no airs or lordly attitude about him while they unloaded the trunks and few pieces of furniture that had been given to her. Each one was a treasure to her. From the chair her mother used to read her stories in, to the shelves her grandfather had made for her to put her treasured tales on. Each item, each box and small chest, were filled with the treasures of her young life. She was grateful to see that the men treated her things with a reverence and care that she had only imagined would be reserved for the Queen herself.

"Be gentle with my lady's things, lads." Liam called. Setting a chest on his shoulder that Caelia knew was not light and yet he handled it as though it was nearly empty. "Follow me if you will, Caelia. I would show you to your rooms."

"Rooms?" She asked, trying to keep up. "I do not need more than one."

Liam grinned at her and nodded towards the stairs. "Come along. Let me show you what I have had prepared for you."

She followed him past several doors, curious that they were going in the same direction as his own room, had she seen the room already and not known that it was for her?

"Here we are." He said, stopping near his door in the deeper part of the upper lever where there were rooms on both sides of a broad hallway.

She was about to protest that she was not going to share a room or bed with him again until after the wedding ceremony made them man and wife, when he opened the next door down from his.

"A suite of rooms for you to use." He said proudly, letting her in behind him. She was staring around a drawing room, plainly decorated but with well made, simple furniture and barely noticed when Liam opened two more doors.

"This is a shared drawing room. I thought that you might like to redecorate for both of us. Through here is a private room for you and your friends and, of course, your sleeping chambers."

When she turned to look at him Caelia could see a blush on his cheeks under the edges of his beard when he gestured towards the smaller version of his own bed.

"Thank you, Liam. I have never decorated any room besides my own at home, I mean, at my father's home. This will be a delightful challenge and of course for the drawing room I will consult for your tastes as well."

"Then you had best be prepared for it to look more like an armory than a drawing room, Lady Caelia." Gerard said, putting down the chest that he had carried in behind them.

"He is right. Liam would not know silk from cotton without someone to tell him." Emrys added with a laugh. "Where do you want this shelf?"

"I would enjoy a few swords around, as long as there was at least one made to measure for my own use." Caelia countered the blacksmith but smiled at Emrys. "Just in the bedroom. I will find a perfect place for it once everything is in here."

"What is left to be brought up?" She asked, heading towards the door.

"Nothing at all, now." Saffir said, as he and the rest of the knights arrived with their arms full of her things.

"You will find that we are an efficient group when we put our minds to it." Lionel said, looking around the room. "This does need a woman's touch, but that could be said of the whole house really. Good luck with that." He said with a nod before heading back out of the room.

Most of the other men left shortly after him, leaving Gerard and Liam in the drawing room.

"You think you will have time to play with swords while running this place and looking after the...children that you and Liam are bound to have?" Gerard scoffed at her, looking around the room.

She could have sworn that he sounded angry that she and Liam would, god-willing, have children. It did not make sense. She had never done anything to him that would cause him to hate her or even to dislike her.

"Sir Gerard? That is your name? I assure you, no matter the housework or children, I will always find time for sword practice. I will never be found helpless." Her voice carried more anger than she intended, but she could not let either of these men think that she was helpless or that she intended to rely on them for everything.

"I would not let you be in danger Caelia. You can trust that I am more than capable of keeping my wife and family safe." Liam said. He was meaning to be kind, but his words only confirmed her need to show them that she was not like the weak, ladylike girls of court. She was useful, she was a fighter and they would see it.

"Then I ask that you commission me a sword so that I may show you that I am unlike any other woman you have met. If you will not, then I shall borrow the smallest weapon at hand and demonstrate my skills." She said with a proud toss of her head and a glare at both men.

"Skills? I am a knight Caelia, all of us are. There is no need for you to learn such things." Liam said, his voice growing tense. "I need a wife that can stand beside me in the court of Arthur and help me with home and family."

"I can do all those things Liam. I am not a child playing with wooden sticks. I will make you proud the day we stand before the King and I can make you prouder still with a sword in my hand, fighting by your side should attack ever come upon us. All I ask is the chance to prove myself to you, in all things, not just domestics."

Chapter 11

"What is your difficulty with Caelia, Gerard?" Liam asked as soon as they were out of earshot of the door. "I have never heard you speak to a woman like that. Even Floree, that night in Camelot when she made that claim to Arthur. You were calm and collected that night. Here with Caelia, who is younger and far more innocent than the whore of Bedver, you come near to vicious when she speaks of swords. Why?"

"I am not unaware of how I am with her and I wish that I could tell you why, but I cannot." Gerard said, his voice tense. "I am sorry Liam. I know you are going to marry her, and I am sure that she is…lovely. She will give you what you want, what you lost will be replaced and I will stand at your side for the rest of your days as your friend, but do not force me to pretend a bond I do not feel."

Liam's feet thundered down the stairs before he stormed out of the house and into the yard. He could not understand why Gerard was so angry. He had not been like this years ago when Liam had fallen in love and married the love of his youth.

Gerard had stood at his side, danced at the wedding and had been the first to raise a glass to toast the announcement that a child, the child that died killing his mother, was to come. He had also held Liam's hand, after the joint death of those Liam loved. He had forced food and drink down his throat and sat with him beside the fire that burned everything she had owned that could be consumed by fire, everything he had made for his child with his own hands. Gerard had been there for everything that had caused him pain or happiness, so why was his closest friend fighting so hard against this second union? Especially when it held the key to achieving their return to Camelot.

He was still stewing on the problem hours later when he took his seat at the head of the table. Lionel was sitting opposite him at the foot of the table with Saffir, Emrys, Rion and Lucas around him. The chairs to Liam's left and right were empty, one would be filled with Gerard, as it was every night and the other would be Caelia. He would be between the two of them and the one who would enforce peace should they begin a war of words.

"You are looking grim, my friend." Gerard said, taking his seat and looking at the finer clothing that the others were wearing when he was still in his work clothes from the forge.

"And you are looking dirty. You could not pause to change your attire for dinner tonight? Her first dinner at Redbourne?" Liam said, offering him the jug of wine. "It would be good manners."

"Well, I got a little behind on my day helping to move her things upstairs, so I got caught up instead freshening up. My apologies if the lady finds my work attire offensive." Gerard said with his usual smile.

"If she does, she will have the good graces not to show it." Liam said in a dry retort.

"Ger do you really take issue with that lovely girl?" Emrys asked, Rion and the others stopping their conversation to listen to his answer. "What could you possibly have against her?"

"I do not know her well enough to have a preference or issue with her person." Gerard said defensively now that the other men were siding with Caelia. "I simply dislike any interruption to our daily life and the stress that the return to Camelot, for Arthur to approve of her, is going to bring to Liam and the rest of us."

"Being in the presence of King Arthur brings you stress, Sir Liam?" Asked the feminine voice that was growing to be familiar as was Liam's reaction to it.

Every man at the table turned to look towards the doorway and Liam sputtered a cough, nearly choking on his wine when he saw the lovely, lady-like appearance of Caelia. She was dressed in a midnight blue dress that showed off the sun-kissed cream of her skin. Her dark hair, shining in the light of the candles, was twisted in braids that were bound around her head and made him think of a crown for she looked every inch a princess in that moment.

"Caelia, I must insist that you call me Liam, please." He said with a smile while he stepped away from the table to meet her and escort her to her seat. "As for the King, we call him Arthur when we are all alone together as knights, there are no titles at the round table as there is no head or foot."

He took his seat and poured her wine and water. "Things are even more casual here, despite the shape of the table. We cannot all have the glories of Camelot, but we get along well enough, I think." Liam looked at the other men who nodded their agreement.

"Liam." She smiled so sweetly when she said his name. "That does not answer my question about the king and his company causing you stress. Are you concerned about this summons that everyone keeps speaking of? Am I not going to be found suitable there as well?"

Liam cast a quick glare at his best friend. He had, in less than a day, made the sharp, strong, young woman doubt her worth. No doubt it had ties to her family and countless times of being told that her personality, who she was as her honest self, were not good enough or was undesirable to many men in a wife. He would not have his favorite things about her, her fire, dampened by anyone.

"You are more than suitable my dear." He said quickly. "In fact, I believe that you are what has been missing, here and in Camelot. They may not know it yet, but you will be a breath of sea air in that landlocked place and they will love you for it."

"Thank you, Liam." She said, with a slight blush at his praise.

Liam ignored the look on Gerard's face and the surprise on Lionel's. They both knew that he was not a man to give compliment's lightly so it might seem strange to them. He felt every word of it though and hoped that he was right in voicing his feelings.

"You are definitely unlike any woman that I have met at court." Gerard said.

Even though Liam felt that his friend did not mean it as a true compliment the other knights raised their cups in a salute to Caelia. Even Lionel, who was not sure about this arranged marriage, had the good manners to join his brothers in the welcoming toast.

"I can certainly assure you that I am nothing like the, dull, complacent women of any court." Caelia said, a pride in her voice that Liam could recognize as she challenged the knight that was more than fifteen years her senior. "Though I am sure someone who is docile and obedient, as uninteresting as a tin cup would be much more to your taste Sir Gerard, I do hope that Liam finds me a bit more interesting than the women he found not worth marrying."

The room fell silent for a moment until Lucas, his desire to ride Caelia's horse shining in his eyes, started to chuckle at the surprise on Gerard's face at being spoken to in such a tone by the daring girl at Liam's right. His chuckle spread until every knight, including Liam, was laughing.

"If I did not know better, I would think you were quite familiar with the court of Camelot by that statement, Caelia." Lucas said, setting down his cup and getting to his feet to help Hilda who had just entered with the evening meal.

"It is good to hear you all laughing. Care to let me in on the joke?" The cook asked with a smile.

"If you had heard what Caelia just said to Gerard, about the women of court, you would be laughing too." Emrys said, elbowing the still serious blacksmith. "He cannot seem to crack a smile though. Still in shock there Ger?"

Liam watched the man carefully. He knew him so well that he could almost feel the thoughts that were churning in his mind. How could he retort without being rude to the future lady of the house and Liam's bride-to-be, but how could he stay silent and face the ribbing jests from the other knights?

"I think that you might find, Caelia, that your tastes and mine are not so dissimilar. I like a bit of adventure in a lover. One simply did not expect the same in a maiden barely old enough to wed. Tell me, how old are you, as of your last birthday?"

"Caelia is more than old enough, Ger. Let it be. The girl is more than you thought. Perhaps you struggle because she is quite like a female version of you?" He said, smiling at Hilda as she placed their plates down as well as a pair of pies in the center of the table.

"You are all still children to me and if you do not mind the manners that I taught you then there will be no dessert for a week. I do not care who started this bickering, it ends this instant or those pies go back with me." Hilda said firmly, her hands on her narrow hips. "Now I mean it. Make your peace for the day and do not ruin this dinner for Liam and the new lady of Redbourne. Do you hear me, young Gerry?"

Even Liam would have been brought to heel with that tone of voice from Hilda, the undebatable matron of many years. Gerard nodded and turned his attention to his plate, giving the tiny woman the chance to turn her eyes over each man at the table. Even Caelia got a portion of that weighted glare.

"I think we are all ready to behave like the adults we claim to be now. Thank you, Hilda. You are always the steady, calm voice, when we need it." Liam said, as she left the room without bothering to look back.

"I think if you two can play a little nicer with each other then we will enjoy the rest of dinner?" Saffir said with a rare smile and a raised glass.

"I agree." Gerard said, lifting his head to look Liam in the eyes. The affection and respect that had been built over a lifetime of friendship was still there, making Liam believe that, eventually, this would come to work. He could have his wife and children without losing his best friend if he was patient.

"My apologies to you, my lady, if my words have brought you to feel unwelcome. I would request your forgiveness. Redbourne has been without a lady for so long I seem to have forgotten how one is expected to behave." Gerard said, standing to give a slight bow.

"Of course, only if you will forgive my defensive retort. It comes from years of teasing from my brothers." Caelia replied, making Liam smile to himself when she offered a toast to Gerard. "To Liam, whose happiness we all desire."

"To Liam." Gerard replied. "As we have said all our lives together; from paddock to pasture."

After that, the rest of the meal and dessert could not have gone better if they had all known each other for years. Caelia laughed and teased the other men. Liam and Gerard even joined in though their eyes seemed to meet more often than normal, or perhaps he was simply noticing it more tonight than he had before. It felt like time had barely passed when the fire finally sank to embers and the weariness of the day sank in.

"I think, boys, that it is time that I escort my lady to her room, and you may all enjoy her company further in the morning." Liam stood and held out a hand to Caelia, helping her to her feet. "If you are quite ready, my dear?"

"Yes Liam." Walking toward the door she turned, not letting go of his hand, and said. "Thank you for a lovely evening. Indeed, it felt like I was home again, without the smell of my brother's boots by the fire. I hope you all sleep well. Goodnight."

Chapter 12

Liam and Caelia were silent ascending the stair and down the hall towards their rooms, it did not feel awkward, but comfortable to him. Once they were behind the closed door of their shared drawing room, that he had to admit did look stark and bare in the low light of the banked fire, he found that he did not want to leave her company. Perhaps she would stay and talk with him a while? That was what married and engaged couples did, was it not? Talked to each other alone?

"You did well, with the knights this evening. I suppose that you are used to keeping company with men? Though your brothers are married, are they not?" He asked, opening the drapes to let in the moonlight.

"They are, yes. Their wives are lovely women, especially if one is feeling ill or enjoys needle point."

He turned to see her admiring his battle sword that was resting on the mantle and was struck by the beauty of the woman he was alone with. He could not clearly recall the last time that had happened. Looking at her, reaching out to touch the sword that Arthur had given him the day he was knighted when they were all much younger men, it stirred a desire in himself that he had long thought to be dead. As lovely as she was, as physically attractive and desirable, it was the spark of awe that bordered on reverence that made him think that there could be something more than just the fulfilment of the basic vows of marriage. It might be possible, eventually, that they might come to love each other.

"I do not think that you are a woman for such things, are you?" He asked, stepping closer and lifting the blade from its resting place. "You are stronger than your age and stature implies. You enjoy the company and hobbies of men."

The last words brought a flash to her eyes and Caelia opened her mouth as though to protest. Liam stopped her words with a finger pressed to her lips, that seemed as soft as a flower petal beneath his touch.

"I do not mean it as an insult, please believe that." He whispered, even though they were alone in the room. "I quite like the idea that you are not a courtesan nor are you interested in becoming one. Though I do not think you would like the life of a squire much either."

"No. Not a squire." She shook her head and whispered.

Staring up at him he realized, for the first time, that her eyes were not a deep black as he had thought. The closeness and the bright light of the moon showed him that they were, in fact, the deepest blue he had ever seen. Like a sapphire, sparkling with an innocence that touched the cold, stoniness of his heart. She was lovely and though she might play the part of a rough and callous 'boy-at-heart', Caelia still had the hopes of any young girl, for love and romance, deep in her soul.

"Not a lady of the court though." He shook his head, standing the sword between them while his free hand stroked her cheek. "You are too wild for such constraints. Maybe this place, Redbourne, will become a new home to you? Maybe these stones will find a way into your heart along with the man that brought you here?"

"There might just be room enough and a little more." She said, a breathlessness in her voice to match the look on her face.

This was the moment, in the poetic tales, when the honorable knight would likely kiss the damsel. He was not, however, an honorable knight by the standards of Camelot. If he ever hoped to regain that honor, which was a major reason for the marriage in the first place, the biggest after the creation of children, he could not do anything that could be considered improper. Not again and not with this truly innocent woman who was growing to trust him.

Liam slid his hand down to take her hand in his and brought her fingers to his lips.

"I shall pray that there is, my lady, Caelia." Liam smiled as he said her name. "I shall see you in the morning. Do not be alarmed if I am not here. I often train with Gerard in the earliest hours. Since we were boys together. I will meet you at the table for breakfast though."

"I will see you then." She replied, turning to go to her door.

"Goodnight, Liam." Was the last thing he heard before she closed the door, leaving him alone in the moonlight.

"Goodnight." He said to the closed door and opened his own.

If he had been a younger man, he would have leaned against the bedroom door, desperate for a way to find the release that his body demanded. If he was a younger man, he would still be kissing those soft, inviting lips that he imagined would taste as sweet as the honey from the lavender flower that Hilda drizzled on the sweet things she baked for him.

There were, realistically, only two ways to deal with the feelings swirling inside him; physically or mentally. Stripping off his tunic and the shirt underneath Liam splashed cold water on his face and neck. He hoped the chill would be enough to push the thoughts of Caelia's lips from his mind.

When he looked at the bare reflection dripping back at him Liam wondered what the woman across the drawing room would think when she saw it for the first time? His shoulders were broad enough and his arms were well muscled, without the bulk of Gerard or Lucas who did more physical labor than any of the knights at Redbourne. Perhaps his waist was not as trim as the younger men, but there was less fat on him than there was on many men his age and the dusting of hair across his chest still had more black in it than grey. He was hale and strong, still as passionate as he had been in his youth, but with more experience now. She might find him as appealing as he found her and that was something he could build on. He did not expect love, not right away, but if there was attraction between them everything would be easier.

In bed, naked beneath the covers, Liam steeled his resolve to not give in to his lustful thoughts about Caelia. He wondered if she was asleep yet, or she was awake and thinking about him too? Was she in the same type of shift that she had worn the night before in the inn, when she had slept in his arms? Or was she beneath the covers, enjoying the feeling of fine linen on her bare skin? Would she sleep beside him in this bed after the wedding or would she keep to her own bed unless he requested otherwise? So many questions came to him, stealing moments of sleep as he pondered them. The biggest one of all, that troubled him to his soul, could Gerard accept her or would this be the final nudge that would send his best friend, right-hand man, far from his side where he belonged?

Still thinking about his dearest friend, Liam drifted off to sleep with more questions than answers on his mind. The smell of oak and fresh water whispered through the room, filling it with a smell that took his unconscious mind back to the night before he and Gerard began their journey as squires to the knights of Arthur's father, Uther.

They were nearly thirteen and felt that the boldest, most adult, thing that they could do was to go swimming in a forest pool in the dark hours of the night with only a moon to light their way. Sneaking out without getting caught had been simple, Liam later suspected that the older knights knew of their plans and made it especially easy for them, and the pair had made their way, giggling and trying to keep the other quiet, to the pool with its small waterfall and encircling willow trees to hide them and muffle the echoes of their last moments of childhood.

Gerard had been the first to strip completely naked and jump in the water with a wild holler.

"Ger? Do you not think that we should keep our breeches on? Is it proper to be swimming naked?" Liam asked, folding his clothes, and setting them beside the pile of Gerard's things.

"If you swim in them you shall have to sleep in them, cold and wet. Everyone will know what we did and then we will have to explain ourselves, at the very least. We may even be punished for it. Drop your drawers and get in already." Ger said, then dove under the surface.

Liam shook his head, removed his last article of clothing, and jumped in the water with a scream at the cold. It was only a few seconds after he had caught his breath that Gerard came up beneath him and pulled him down, deeper into the water. They struggled together for a moment before breaking apart and rising to the surface. Laughter bounced off the rocks around the waterfall and the curtains of willow branches while they splashed each other and jumped off rocks to see who could make the biggest splash.

The moved through the water like fish, their bodies brushing against each other before they would turn, and wrestle then break apart again. Often one dunking the other's head below the surface before diving away. Each time they came together Gerard's holds got tighter and more complicated. Even though Liam was the larger and older of the boys he was having a hard time escaping with breath in his lungs. It was as though Ger wanted to hold on and not let go. He wanted to keep Liam held tight, immobilized in his grip, for a little longer. Was he trying to prove that he would be just as good a knight one day? Or was he trying to kill him? The games had gone too far, and Liam knew he had to end it, head back to the castle and their separate beds.

"Ger? I think it is time that we head back to barracks. Everything gets started tomorrow and we need to be ready or Bedver is going to get the best posting." Liam said, starting towards the shore while Gerard climbed onto the rocks by the waterfall.

"Oh, come on Liam. Do not be such a ninny. We still have plenty of time and no one in their right mind is going to choose that pig, Bedver."

"I mean it. I want to go back."

"Then go back. I am not ready, not yet." He said, standing on the shining, wet, top of the large boulder at the edge of the pool with the waterfall pouring beside it.

"Ger. That is not safe." Liam called. Treading water, unable to look away.

"Hang safe. You only get one chance to really live." Ger yelled and took a giant leap.

Everything after that happened slowly, every second etching itself in Liam's mind for the rest of his life.

Something was wrong with the way that Ger launched himself from the surface of the rock, the angle was wrong, but he could not have known it. Liam could barely see it from where he was treading water. When Ger's head hit the water and his body kept sinking below the surface Liam burst into action.

He dove to take hold of Gerard's unconscious body and dragged him to the edge of the pool. There was no point in calling for help, the same branches that had offered them tranquility would block out any cry he might make.

"Damnit Ger, you are a bloody fool." Liam cursed at his friend, struggling to get his unconscious body out of the water. "You had better not be dead or I swear I will have a druid bring you back just to kill you again myself."

Laying Ger flat on the ground Liam tried to hear if he were breathing but there was nothing he could discern. He turned him on his side to let water slip from his mouth, pounding his hand onto his back to try to wake him up, but there was no reaction.

"You cannot do this to me. Wake up!" Liam was starting to panic. This night was supposed to be fun, not deadly.

"If you will not take a breath, I shall give you mine."

He took a deep breath and lowered his mouth over his friend's and blew into Ger's mouth only to have it flow out his nose and touch his cheek.

"That will not work, unless..." Liam closed his eyes, pinched Ger's nose and tilted his head as far back as he could. "It must reach your lungs."

He blew again, expelling not only his breath but his hope with it. Liam felt Ger's chest rise and for the briefest moment there was a pressure against his lips. Liam's eyes flew open, and he paused, staring into Gerard's confused face before sitting back with a smile.

"You idiot."

Liam sat upright in his bed, staring around the bedroom in Redbourne. Where had that dream come from? He had not thought of that night by the pool in years. They had gotten back to the knight's hall before anyone knew that they were missing and had never spoken of what had happened that night; the fall or how Gerard had woken up. Why would it come back to him tonight?

Chapter 13

Caelia woke after a deep sleep where her dreams were filled with visions, not of the romantic and courtly Sir Lancelot she usually imagined, but of the man who had ridden at her side for two days, held her in his arms and stared into her eyes in a room filled with moonlight, and still did not kiss her. She was dreaming of the man she was supposed to marry and thought she would never be able to feel for, Liam. He was even more handsome when he was relaxed in his own home than he was in the somewhat formal attire he had worn to retrieve her from her father's house. He smiled and laughed easily here and, as of last night, she wanted him to kiss her.

As she dressed, she was not so spoiled that she was going to wait for Lynn to wake her and dress her, she wondered if he did not like her or if he simply did not know that a woman, of any age, would want to be kissed by a handsome man in a moonlit room. He had been married before, so she had been told, how did he forget that kind of romance and affection? Or had he been like that with his first wife? Could she show him what she needed from him? Was she brave enough?

Stepping into the shared room Caelia was surprised to see it empty. Where was Liam? She had thought he would be awake and that they might have a walk alone together. It was unlikely that Gerard, with his dark and disapproving glares, would let her spend much time alone with Liam. She knew jealousy when she saw it, her brothers had all been quite popular with the local girls, but it made no sense coming from the blacksmith. She had no intention of coming between him and any of his brothers in knighthood. How could she show them that she was not here to destroy anything?

The sound of steel on steel ringing from outside gave her the answer. If she could join in some of the activities that they did together, it might help to build a bond. Riding and helping in places such as the barn and field would be easy, maybe even half expected because of how she grew up. Sword practice would be harder, though it would be a way to prove to Gerard that she could be a part of things while she showed Liam that she was capable of more than housework and that she belonged at his side.

Peaking out towards the sound Caelia saw the man she was to marry and the man that wanted to stop the wedding sparring in the small tourney field beside the barn. She quickly pulled on the boots that she used for riding and snuck down the stairs and out the door. There had to be a sword somewhere in the smithy that she could use to prove herself.

She was quick and stealthy while she found a small sword. Though it was not sharp and more like a long dagger than a sword, Caelia could move it well enough to suit her purpose for that morning. It might even help her to convince them both that she should have her own weapon.

Rounding the corner of the barn to face the tourney field where the sound of the blades was still singing out, Caelia stopped and stared, open-mouthed, at what she saw before her in the glow of the early morning mist.

Liam's back was to her and his broad shoulders were bare with sweat glistening across their span and down his back to a waist that was trim without a scrap of wasteful flesh on him. As he blocked and returned each blow that Gerard delivered Caelia was mesmerized by his motions. Barely able to hold on to the sword she had borrowed she stared even more when the men switched places and she saw Gerard's half bared body straining in combat against Liam.

The blacksmith's skin was tanned in contrast to Liam and every bit as impressive, though she was surprised to see scars on his body that were tattooed with ink like the ancient Celts. Was this why he was so angry? So possessive of Liam? They had fought together in wars past, side by side, but Liam had only one scar that she could see, marked with ink in the same way. She wondered which of these remarkably handsome men had saved the other? Were they brothers in blood as well as arms?

A laugh from Gerard when he landed the flat of his blade to Liam's thigh brought Caelia out of her musings and back to focus on her intention. She had to show them that she was worthy of becoming a part of…whatever it was that they were. Tightening her grip on the sword she waited until the blacksmith dodged away from a blow that Liam aimed for his shoulder and jumped out of the shadows, where she had been hiding, to catch his blade on her own.

"What in blazes?" She heard from her left where Gerard had moved as Liam stared down at her.

"I told you that I can fight, did I not?" She said with a wicked grin. "Do not stop. Let me prove it to you Liam."

She could feel his pause in the pressure from his sword on hers before he smiled.

"Show me what you can do then." He challenged her, disengaging their blades.

"Liam you cannot be serious. She is a girl with a sword that is not even sharp." Gerard said with exasperation pulsing in every inch of him.

"Then she cannot hurt me with it, can she?" Liam replied with an indulgent smirk that Caelia was determined to wipe off his handsome face.

"If I was trying to hurt you, Sir, trust that the sharpness of the blade would not stop me." She said with a smile, squaring off against him properly. "Shall we?"

"Oh, I do not think that you need a sword to do that Caelia." Gerard said, crossing his arms and leaning back against the barn. "But try not to injure him in this foolishness."

"I think she will do just fine and perhaps even have time to offer you a few lessons Ger." Liam said with a laugh that the blacksmith joined.

Caelia chose that moment to launch her attack.

"If he is up to it." She said with a focused smile

Swinging with careful precision the pair moved in a circle that seemed more like a dance to her than a swordfight. Their eyes locked together; she felt his brute strength in each measured blow. That he was holding back his strength she did not doubt. He was rugged and powerful in the light of the morning sun and she was out of practice. He could have easily disarmed and defeated her, but he allowed her to show what skills she had without a hint of mockery in his expression.

"I think the two of you might be better matched than you think." Liam said, blocking a thrust towards his side. "You are both a bit rash in your attack. If I could trust that you two would not try to kill each other I might suggest that you try to train together."

"I would rather train with you. If you are going to allow it." Caelia said, taking another swing that Liam blocked and countered, forcing her to take a few steps back towards Gerard.

Liam looked as though he was about to speak but a strong arm looped around her waist and pulled her out of the fight. Gerard's sword met Liam's while he held her tight against him.

"He is not going to allow it." Gerard snarled. "I am not going to allow this to happen. We will never get back to Camelot if you do this."

"Do what?" Caelia asked, stomping down on his foot, and ducking away from the pair of men. "What does my sword work here have to do with Camelot?"

"Ger, stop this." Liam growled, showing Caelia a taste of his temper. "None of that needs to concern her."

"You little…" Ger turned towards her with an angry scowl. "It concerns her as much as the rest of us Liam."

He dropped his sword and snatched the blade from her hand.

"I will not allow my work to contribute to this foolishness."

Though he was not much taller than her, in his anger he seemed to tower over her, intimidating more than he was threatening, his brown eyes flashing with a seething rage that made no sense to her.

"Then I will get her another, if you are going to be too pigheaded to be civil." Liam said, his voice low and dangerous. "There is no harm in this Gerard. Let her have something."

"I am. Trust that Liam." He snarled, lifting his own weapon from the ground with his foot before stalking back towards the house.

Taking a deep breath Caelia looked at Liam, who was staring after the man and not looking at her at all.

"I am sorry. I thought that if I joined in, if I showed that I can be just like another knight, that he might accept me." She said, touching Liam's arm so that he might look at her.

"Please do not do that. If I wanted to marry a knight, well, that is not allowed. I wish I could tell you why he is like that, but I have never seen him behave like this before."

He looked down at her, his hazel eyes sadder than she hoped to see after the match and how well she had done against him. The value he placed on Gerard, his opinions, and feelings, was more than she had thought. Somehow, she had to find a way to earn the man's respect if she could not have his friendship.

"If he were a woman, I would say that it was jealousy. I have no intention of coming between the bond of brotherhood that you share." She said, trying to find the courage she had felt earlier. "What does my being here have to do with Camelot and why would me knowing how to use a sword change you going back to there? Redbourne is your home, or are you, I mean we, expected to live there after the wedding?"

"Jealousy is what it looks like to me as well." Liam said with a sigh, touching her hand where it rested on his arm. "As for Camelot, it seems we are about to find out a little more."

He pointed to the horseman approaching the property. He had a royal banner and was moving briskly for the early hour.

"Sir Liam of Redbourne. You and your company are summoned to Camelot at the order of King Arthur. He expects you within the week." The messenger handed a sealed scroll to Liam.

"Will you stay and break the night's fast with us?" Caelia asked

"I will not. Thank you, my lady." He replied curtly and turned back the way that he came.

"He acts as if being here is an offence to him." She said, looking at Liam for an explanation. "Why would that be? You are a knight of Camelot, not an enemy to the crown."

"Yes. I am still that." Liam answered her, crushing the freshly read scroll in his hands. "You are to come with me. Get ready as quickly as you can please." He said, leaving her standing on the tourney field as he walked back to the house.

Chapter 14

He could have punched Arthur right in his royal face for sending this letter.

His highness had heard that Liam was getting married to a young woman and wanted to make sure that she was not being forced into the union. It was as though he thought that the one night, that night, meant that he had no honor, knightly or otherwise, and would force a girl to be his bride against her will. Did he think that any father that Liam would know could be so cruel as to force a daughter into something she did not agree to?

He stormed into the house and straight to his office to scribble out a reply. Lucas could take it after eating and would arrive at least half a day before Liam and Caelia would arrive. That should give Camelot time to get ready for them and for the social vultures to gather so they could make an evaluation of his choice in bride and his bride's choice in him.

Would Arthur deny his approval of the wedding? Or would some fool in the court decide to tell Caelia why he needed an invitation to return? Liam raked his hand through his hair in frustration. What would she think? Had he done enough, laid enough groundwork that she would believe him over the court gossips? Was he setting himself up for an even greater embarrassment and the loss of his wife before he even had her?

"Lucas?" He called out the door, knowing that if the young man were not yet inside for breakfast that someone would find him soon. Liam sat at his desk, trying to think of the best way to handle what would be waiting for them, for him especially, once they arrived at court.

Court was not a place for a girl fresh from such rural living. She may be an adult, but the drinking and debauchery that went on where Arthur could not see was not suitable for an innocent girl. In years past he would have been at the head table, at the left hand of the king with Galahad beside Caelia. There would have been no safer place for the feisty girl. He could only guess where a disgraced knight of his standing would be seated. It would take all the knights working together to keep her safe in that place and to keep the likes of Bedver away from her. Liam had no doubt that his enemy would do anything to hurt him and that included bringing harm to Caelia.

"Troubled by the little woman and her swordplay Liam?" Lionel said, pausing outside the door with a few papers in his hands.

"What? No. The swordplay does not bother me. She is actually quite good though her block needs a bit more work." He tossed the crushed scroll across the desk. "Arthur is what concerns me. I am, on his orders, to bring her with me to Camelot. He wants to meet my bride and make sure that I am not forcing her."

"But you are, in a way." Lionel said, holding his hands up when Liam glared at him.

"Watch your words. I have not forced anything."

"Did you ask her to marry you? Or was she told that she was supposed to?" Lionel said, calmly setting the scroll back down.

"Her father did that, not me." Liam said defensively. "I intend to ask her, before the ceremony happens."

"She is a smart girl and knows that there really is not much that she can do to refuse. You might want to make sure that she is willing, not obligated, to be your wife. Show her some romance. Be the knight in the stories." Lionel suggested.

"When? I have no time. We are to leave in the morning." Liam cried in frustration.

"Then use tonight wisely. Use the trip wisely. I will come with you and so will Gerard. Let her pick someone too since we cannot all come back with you."

"Actually, we are all commanded to attend. I have a feeling that he wants to question all of you." He said, running his hand through his hair and down his beard. "This is going to be difficult. Ger does not like her and she borrowed one of his swords without asking to pull that little exposition in the tourney."

"Damn, the girl is certainly bold. I cannot deny that, though it was foolish I can understand the need to prove herself." Lionel said with a smile. "I think I like her a little more for that."

"Well that is something then." Liam said, standing from the desk. "I suppose it is time to join the others and explain all of this. They will want to prepare for a few reunions I imagine."

"One or two I imagine. Gerard especially." Lionel said, putting his arm across Liam's shoulders. "Do you remember that blond princess from the northern kingdom of Gore? The one with the twin brother?"

"Yes. He used to spend a lot of time with them, the only woman I ever saw him enjoy the company of." Liam said with a smile. "Why?"

"The last letter I received from Hector told me that the twins have been part of Arthurs court for the last two years." Lionel said, stepping with Liam into the dining hall where the others were already eating, including Caelia and Gerard.

"What twins?" Gerard asked, his head turning at the word. "Elin and Banning? They are at court?"

"Yes, they are, apparently." Liam said, taking a seat and patting Caelia's hand. "The king has sent a summons not only for Lady Caelia and myself but for the entire company, to return to Camelot. He would see us all as soon as possible." He smiled when the younger men chattered excitedly to each other. "Which means, of course, that we are to leave in the morning."

"I am not sure that I have anything suitable for the court of the king. I will have to spend the day altering dresses so that I do not embarrass you in front of the king and queen."

Emrys chuckled and called from the far end of the table. "Caelia, there is no man at this table who would have known the quality of your dresses if you had not told us. You will look beautiful no matter what."

"The boy is not lying." Liam said with a smile, raising her hand to his lips for a kiss. "You will look wonderful, but if you want to spend some time on dresses then I am sure that Lynn will help to pack your things."

He was rewarded with a beaming smile from his bride. She truly could have gone to the court in sackcloth and she still would have been the most beautiful woman there.

Looking to his left Liam could not believe the change in Gerard's expression. The sour, angry glare was gone and in its place was a happy, almost dreamy smile with a light in his eyes that was positively boyish.

"Looking forward to reconnecting with someone special Ger?" Liam teased, nudging him with a grin. He hoped that the princess might still remember his friend well so that he could find some understanding for what Liam was doing.

"Elin and Banning are good friends. I have not spoken to either of them in years. Seeing them will be good, incredibly good." Gerard said, looking at the table with a touch of color to his cheeks that Liam could not remember seeing ever before.

"Elin is a lovely woman and, from what I hear, the pair of them refuse to let the other get married. Do you think because she still carries a torch for you Gerard?" Emrys asked, causing all eyes at the table to turn to the embarrassed man.

"I am sure that is not the case. She can have her pick of any suitor and deserves much more than a lowly knight." Ger said with a smile. "Though there are many fond memories of time with her and her brother."

"Then you will have to make sure to find time with your special friends Gerard." Liam said, his tone hinting that he would like to meet them himself.

The other men turned their attention to the meal and as they finished Liam assigned them tasks to see to as soon as they had prepared for the trip. There was a lot that needed to be done if they were to be gone for a week or two, depending on what the king had to say to them all.

"I'll be sure to prepare the swords as well, Liam." Ger said, standing from the table when was just the two of them with Caelia. "I am sure Lancelot will want to go another round with you. Just make sure that your bride knows the expectation of the court regarding the behavior of its ladies." He said pointedly before heading towards the stairs to retrieve the weapon from the mantelpiece and leaving Liam alone with Caelia.

"I hope he will eventually accept my being here." Caelia said, taking his hand when he offered to help her stand. "I truly do need to adjust some dresses to make them ready for court, if there is nothing else you need me to do right away?"

"You can do whatever it is that you need to do." Liam said, keeping her hand in his while they walked. "Do you need anything to make the work easier?"

"I can ask Lynn for some ribbons and beads. Perhaps, if there is time, I might be able to purchase a few things in the city?" She asked him with a shy smile. "I do not have anything with which to alter my two best dresses."

"Not the one that you wore last night?" He asked, looking up at her as she climbed the stairs. "That deep blue dress is utterly perfect. Please, do not change a thing about that dress."

"I was going to add a beaded belt, but if you like it so much then I will leave it as it is."

Liam realized that this was her way of seeking his approval, of trying to please him.

"That sounds lovely, perhaps I can buy you a silver one though, in Camelot. If you promise not to change the neckline. I love how that dress looks on you." He said, letting go of her hand.

"I promise not to change it then, since you like it so much." She flashed him a smile and hurried up the stairs, leaving Liam behind.

He must have been watching her more intently than he thought because he did not even notice Gerard come back down the stairs with a sword in his hand,

"What are you staring at?" He asked, slapping a hand to Liam's shoulder.

"Huh? What? I was watching my future wife. She seems excited about this trip, which is good." Liam replied with a shake of his head.

"It is good, until someone tells her why we're here and not there. What happens then Liam?" Gerard said, resting the blade of the sword on his shoulder. "Do you think she will be smiling when she finds out what happened? When the whispers start about you, her shining hero?"

"I am not a hero to anyone, especially not her." Liam growled as they walked towards the door. "I want her to be happy, Ger. I want her to love me, someday. I miss that. The feeling of being loved, knowing that the other person is not going to judge you for the mistakes that you make, is something I need. I know you do not want such things in your life, but I find that I do, again. You cannot understand what it is to miss that."

"I never said that Liam." Gerard said, stopping with his hand on the door. "I have never said that I do not want love in my life. I may not know what it means to miss that kind of love but that does not mean that I do not want it as much, or more, than you do."

"I am sorry Ger. I have never heard you speak of love as something you were looking for."

"I want the great love of my life to love me too Liam. I want our life back the way it was before we were cast out of Camelot."

"Then join me in the prayer that this summons is the next step to getting our life, that life, back. Then perhaps you will get your chance at love too."

"Perhaps." He said, heading off to the smithy to ensure that their swords would be ready for the journey.

"I hope so. My dear friend." Liam said, closing the door and heading to his office to meet with the steward about the needs of the property. "I truly hope so."

Chapter 15

Caelia could hardly believe that they were going to Camelot in the morning. She had known that it would happen eventually. Marrying one of King Arthur's Knight's came with the knowledge that the king would have to approve the match before the wedding could occur, but she thought they would have more time before the summons came. She could barely remember all the names of his companion and had barely spent any time alone with him.

How would she answer any questions from the king? Would she even find a voice to speak to him? Arthur? What about Lancelot? The object of the dreams of every girl she knew and, even if she denied it to her friends, she felt a certain flutter at the thought of meeting the epic legend.

"Caelia? Would you like me to pin the latest neckline on this dark blue dress?" Lynn asked, interrupting her daydreams.

"Which one? The dark? Oh. No. Please do not change anything on that one. It is Liam's favorite, and he has asked that I not alter it." She said with a smile and a slight blush.

"Of course, we will leave it then." Lynn gave her a knowing smile and carefully folded the dress into her trunk.

"It will look lovely when you are walking around the court in Camelot, and though it is not the new fashion, I am certain that the Queen will offer you a compliment on it."

"I am not a woman who is worried about fashion, Lynn." Caelia said, carefully rethreading the needle to add some embroidery to the cuff of a dark red gown. "I want to make a good impression on those who require it and do my best not to embarrass Liam with backwards manners and lack of proper protocols."

"He knows that you would never do such a thing on purpose." Lynn said, trying to reassure her. "I am certain he is already planning on teaching you everything you need to know on the journey. Oh, that means he will spend some time in the wagon with us, or at least riding beside it so that you can speak to each other."

Caelia watched her new friend finish packing the trunk and shook her head.

"I am not intending to spend the ride in the wagon. I want to enter Camelot on my own horse, Lynn. I have dreamed of going there for years and I mean to do so astride a horse not docile in a wagon. I do not mean to insult you, of course, but it is not who I am." She said as they carried the trunk down the stairs together.

"You want to bring your horse?" Liam said, stepping into the great hall. "What are you doing bringing that down yourselves. Rion and Emrys could have managed that for you." He said with a frown.

"We are perfectly capable of moving it ourselves Liam." Caelia said forcing a smile instead of matching his frown. How could he have crossed swords with her that morning and still think that she could not do something so simple as move a trunk with Lynn. "Who do you think moved it down the stairs at my father's house? I did not have Lynn's help that time though."

"You moved that alone? With all your brothers at home?" Liam shook his head. "I swear manners are a forgotten grace."

"Of course. What else was I going to do?"

Caelia watched as he turned and slapped the kitchen door with his hand to summon two of the kitchen staff. "Take lady Caelia's trunk to the wagon and tell Lucas he can prepare to ride the new black in the stable, since the lady of the house wishes for the horse to be available to her on our journey and in the city."

Lynn went with the trunk, leaving the pair alone together, only a few feet apart but with a charge in the air between them that Caelia could feel like the air before a storm.

"I could have managed without a problem but thank you for that." She said finally, her smile wavering under the intensity of his stare.

"I am aware that you could have but you do not have to. Not anymore. Not under my roof." He said firmly with no hint of a smile though he was staring as intently at her as she was staring at him.

His eyes were beautiful, and she could not seem to look away. She had to think of something to say, anything to keep him there with her a little longer.

"Lucas is going to prepare Aldon?" She asked carefully, stepping up to reach for his arm.

"Aldon? My apologies who is that?" He said, arching a brow in a way that made her burst into a real smile.

He was almost boyishly cute when he was confused. She wanted to make that happen more often.

"Aldon is my horse." She said, taking his arm and gently leading him towards the door. "He is rather particular about who he lets near him, riding him can be difficult. Are you sure that Lucas is up to it?"

"He has a special bond with animals, it does not always translate well to people, but Lucas is especially attuned to horses." He replied, squinting slightly when they stepped out into the noon sun.

"What am I attuned to?" Lucas asked, appearing on the far side of the wagon where Lynn stood, blushing suddenly.

"Horses." Caelia said. "And apparently some people as well."

Lynn looked embarrassed and rushed towards the kitchen door while Liam had the good grace to cough and pretend that he did not suspect anything from their reaction.

"Oh, well I am good with horses." Lucas said, joining Caelia and Liam. "What horse are we talking about exactly? Not that big black of yours Caelia? I would love to try to work with him if you need me to."

She wanted to laugh at his eagerness. She wondered if he had already asked Liam to work with the stallion and had been denied. It would be surprising. Most men would have taken the animal as one of their own regardless of the proper owner.

"His name is Aldon. I want to bring him to Camelot. I thought we would have to tie him to the wagon when I was not riding him, but Liam seems to think you might be able to ride him at times. Are you interested in trying to ride him?"

"Interested? I am more eager to try him than I remember being to try a sword for the first time." Lucas declared, a broad grin on his face. "Liam has barely let me touch him."

Her eyes shone when she looked at her intended who gave her a small smile in return.

"He is your horse, not mine Caelia. Of course, he is cared for, but I am not going to give permission for him to be used or ridden without your consent."

"Thank you, Liam." She turned to Lucas. "I will introduce you to Aldon. He is more likely to allow you to ride if I introduce you to him."

It felt strangely normal to Caelia while they walked towards the stables. There was no reason that she should feel so comfortable with men that were strangers to her less than a week before. Perhaps it was the knowledge that they were all knights or maybe they simply reminded her of her brothers, with the exception of Liam and Gerard, but she felt as calm and happy walking to the large barn as she had the small one at her father's home.

"He is a wonderful beast. I cannot remember seeing his equal." Lucas said, opening the paddock gate for her and Liam.

"He is the result of my research into bloodlines. I chose both his sire and dam from my father's mare and the stallion owned by my friend's father. No one thought that it would yield such a wonderful colt except for me."

"You were behind his conception?" Liam asked, watching Aldon trot across the yard towards them. "You studied horses for the purpose of breeding him? I am impressed."

"Because I am a woman?" She asked, stroking the long mane. "I should braid this on the way. I do not want him to look ragged when we arrive." She was hoping that the idea of Liam being forward thinking was not about to be dashed.

"He will look magnificent because he is himself, like his mistress." Liam said, running his hand down Aldon's neck until it covered hers, sending a flutter to Caelia's heart. "I am impressed because it is hard for anyone, man or woman, to be able to look at an animal and know the right match for them, who will be best for them. It is a rare talent and should be… nurtured." He said with a low voice, taking her hand from Aldon's mane and holding it, staring down into her eyes in the shadow of the stallion's head.

"Rare talent." She repeated, dumbstruck by the hazel eyes and soft smile. Would his beard be soft when he kissed her? Or bristly like a horsehair brush? Suddenly that was all she could think about: his beard on her chin when he kissed her, which she could hardly wait for. "How would one nurture that, do you think?"

"I can think of a few ways." Liam murmured and lowered his mouth to cover hers.

Her eyes closed and Caelia stopped breathing. His lips were soft, gently pressing against hers. The hair of his mustache tickled her slightly but wasn't wiry or hard. She… liked it. She liked this kiss, from this man. The hand that wasn't in his slid up to his shoulder, holding tight in case she fell in a swoon as the girls in her books did.

"I think he likes me." Lucas said loudly, completely destroying the moment and leaving Caelia trying to catch her breath.

"What makes you say that?" Liam growled, letting his forehead rest against Caelia's for a moment before he straightened and turned to face his friend, graciously giving her the chance to compose herself.

"He is letting me touch him now. He did not let me before." The younger man said excitedly. "I think you were right Caelia. Having you near was the key to getting to know him."

"Amazing how he is more comfortable around a giant excited toddler when the only rider he has ever had is next to him." Liam chuckled.

"You are a little more…energetic than I am." Caelia said, stepping around Liam to rub Aldon's nose. "He does seem to be alright with you touching him. That is a new thing, and it is good."

Liam's hand was on her hip while the three of them stroked the big horse, getting him used to both men being close. When he nudged Liam hard enough to make him step backwards, they all enjoyed a laugh until Gerard called from the fence.

"Liam? A word please." His face was neutral until the big horse stepped over to the fence and waited for the blacksmith to pay attention to him. "Hello big fellow. Carrots later?"

Liam pressed a kiss to her temple when she burst into a smile to see her distrusting horse liking both the men that she was trying to win over.

"I will leave you with Lucas. Try to keep him in one piece if Aldon will allow it." He said then joined Gerard. "Trust that you would be liked by another stubborn beast."

They went to the smithy and Aldon rejoined Caelia and Lucas with a prance in his step as though he had understood the other man's promise.

"Shall we see if his trust extends to riding?" She asked him with a smile. This all might work out with Liam's best friend warming to her, eventually.

"Yes. I think it will be fine. You want him to come with us, to Camelot?" Lucas asked, pulling Caelia back to the moment.

"Yes. I would like to ride him into the courtyard at Liam's side." She admitted, scratching Aldon while the young man prepared to mount him.

"If you do, which I think is a good idea for Liam's image and your own confidence, every knight will be jealous, even more than me."

"Even Lancelot?" She asked, watching her horse carefully when Lucas settled in the saddle. He seemed anxious but not as bad as when it was her brothers or father.

"Oh, especially him. He has a special liking for big chargers like this handsome boy."

"Then it will be even more fun. Why will me riding be good for Liam's image? He is a close friend to the King. Everyone knows that." She looked at him, stepping back so the Aldon could begin to test his new rider.

"Yes, he was. I mean, he is. They just have not spoken, face to face, for some time. It will make a good impression on the entire court to see you and him arriving side by side. They are fans of the romantic and that will make it look as though you are in love instead of an arranged marriage." Lucas said before nudging the horse forward and away from her for a lap around the paddock.

"Of course." Caelia said to herself, slightly crestfallen at his words. "Just an arranged marriage." Perhaps the kiss, her first, had not meant to Liam what it did to her.

Chapter 16

Laying in bed that night Liam could not sleep. Thoughts of the kiss with Caelia keeping him from finding any rest. He could have pummeled Lucas for breaking up that kiss, over a horse. It had been unexpected and sweet, just like Caelia herself. It was the kind of kiss that could keep a man up all night and send thoughts of keeping her up with him straight to somewhere other than his brain.

If there had been any doubt about marrying Caelia, any worry that he may not find himself attracted to her, that there might not be a spark between them, it was gone now. He would marry her as soon a possible and begin their lives as husband and wife with a smile instead of a sigh of resignation.

He did not care that Gerard was worried about taking an unschooled girl to the highest court in Britain. This was going to happen, and Liam was going to have another chance at the happiness that had been stolen from him and no one was going to ruin it. Even his best friend.

Ger had used the slim excuse of needing him to inspect the sword he had made to be given to Arthur as a gift. There was nothing wrong with the weapon. It was a beautiful piece of work, as was almost everything Ger put his mind to creating, and Liam suspected it had been a ruse to get him away from Caelia. He would be sure to speak to him about it on the road or in the inn on the way to the capital.

There could be no chance of his reluctance to accept her being brought to the awareness of the king or, heavens forbid, the queen. There would be questions, including speculation towards the validity of their relationship, and Liam could not have that happen, especially after that kiss. He settled in bed, trying to calm his mind with the decision that he would do all he could to encourage the affection that Caelia had started to show. It was possible that he might, someday, develop a deeper affection himself, but for now he knew that he wanted to marry her and that he would not be as miserable as he had thought. These thoughts were enough to calm him to sleep, knowing that the journey beginning in the morning was the first step on the road to his return to his proper status in Camelot.

Dawn came much too early, but Liam woke determined to set his relationship with Caelia and her relationship with not only him, but Ger, on the path that it needed to be on. He was almost whistling, his feet thumping down the stairs, sounding like the ceremonial drums in the throne room. When he arrived at the bottom, he was surprised to hear raised voices from the dining room. With a stern expression he stalked towards the sound. Nothing was going to delay this trip or impede his goal, especially not a foolish argument.

"What is going on in here so early?" Liam asked the rowdy discussion around the table. He had been prepared to find an argument at the table but was shocked to find laughter. Jokes were being flung back and forth to accompany tales of past tournaments and duels in the halls and gardens of Camelot.

"Just a few stories to get everyone excited about the return to the city." Lionel grinned from the far end of the table. "Sit down and join. You would have a few tales to tell I am sure."

"You should have seen Sir Kay's expression when Gerard spun and knocked the sword across the room." Saffir continued, his dark features animated as he recounted the details of the match.

"Was anyone struck by it or was Sir Kay able to regain his weapons to continue fighting?" Caelia asked.

Liam could see the excitement in her face and decided to answer before one of the others could.

"Ger was lucky that no one was hurt." He said, sitting down and reaching for the nearest bowl. "However, the entire thing slid beneath the skirt of the notorious court flirt, Lady Ellen."

"The woman had her eye on Gerard and had for that entire week." Emrys added. The entire table laughed when Ger shuddered.

Liam clapped a hand to his shoulder. "She was determined to get you in the garden that night and the stunt with the sword almost got it for her, do you remember?"

"Kay certainly tried to make it happen. That woman was odious and wanted much more than a walk in the garden." Ger grumbled, finishing his plate, and getting to his feet. "I will bring the horses and wagon to the door. Rion? Lend a hand since your plate is empty too. Unless you intend to attempt to beg Caelia's sweet roll from her before she eats it?"

Liam could hardly believe that Ger was including her in his teasing but the way she playfully snatched her roll from the table said that she was enjoying herself with the men.

"I would like to be out the gate within the quarter hour." Liam said, chuckling when Emrys snatched the bread from Caelia and threw it to Rion as he left with Ger. "You can have mine, Caelia. None of them would be so foolish as to try and take it from you."

"Thank you, Liam. I would not want to deprive you of it." She cut it in half and offered a piece back to him. "Share it?"

He took it with a smile and nod to her.

"You are most thoughtful. Is everyone ready to go? If not go do whatever it is that needs doing. I do not want to waste time."

Saffir and Lionel left the table, Liam, Caelia, Emrys and Lucas were the only ones left.

"Lynn is making sure that the wagon is ready, but I would like to ride Aldon, at your side, as we leave." Caelia said, a hopeful smile on her face.

"I suppose so." Liam smiled. "I would ask that, for his sake, you do not make Lucas wait too long before giving him the chance to ride Aldon. The man has been beside himself with excitement since yesterday."

Lucas grinned and headed towards the door. "I really think Aldon is starting to like me."

Emrys followed him "That one would think any girl that smiled in his direction wanted to marry him. I am sure that he is going to think that animal adores him by suppertime."

"They are good men, though a bit foolish at times." Liam said, offering his arm to Caelia who took it with an eager expression on her dainty face.

"They seem to be. Emrys, Lucas and Rion remind me of my brothers actually."

"Your brothers? That is good. I hope they will look after you as brothers should. It is likely that in the city I will have to leave you alone, a few times, to have meetings with the king and other knights." He said, walking towards the open door slowly. Watching her face for a reaction was hard to do without getting lost in her eyes.

"I am sure that I will be fine. There are many other ladies at court, so I have been told. Even a few of nuns from the convent my father insisted that I visit last month have been known to visit the court. Cador likes to joke that they are trying to convert Merlin himself." Caelia said with that warm laugh that he liked to hear.

She could not know how impossible of a task they would have trying to convince that ancient druid that the church, with it's singular God and many new rules, would be better for him than the ancient ways with their magics. Though they were all encouraged to embrace the new religion Liam was not willing to abandon the old ways and how they welcomed everyone with a good heart.

"I think I would like to see that conversation happen. I do not think that you are ready to be alone at court so I will make sure that one of them is near enough to help you if needed, until you are comfortable." He smiled at her. "Does that sound acceptable?"

"A chaperone? Are you concerned about my behavior? That I will embarrass you?" She asked, waving to Lynn in the wagon. She sounded as though she was trying not to get upset so he took the hand from his arm and brought it to his lips.

"Caelia, I have no such concern. You are lovely and kind-hearted, which is rare in even the most chaste of courts, which Camelot certainly is not. My worry is not that you would say the wrong thing but hear it."

When she smiled with a blush on her cheek, he waved Lucas over with Aldon and lifted her to the saddle before she said anything.

"Take care of things Hilda." He said to the fearsome pixie of a woman standing in the doorway. "We will see you soon, hopefully with the blessing of the king to return things to previous standing.

He deliberately ignored the questioning expression on Caelia's face while they rode out the gate and down the road towards the city where his greatest triumphs and failures had both occurred.

It was not long before they continued their tales from the breakfast table. Each man seemed more determined than the last to have the best story. Liam was pleased that even Gerard joined in the stories and teasing as though all was well in the world. There was no tension between them, for now at least.

"You have told stories of Sir Kay and Gerard, and Emrys fighting in the palace. They have all been wonderful stories, but I want to hear about Liam. Do any of you have a story about him to share?" Caelia asked, bringing her horse up beside his. "I have a feeling that there are a good many tales that I should know about the man I am to marry."

Each of the knights turned their eyes to look at Liam, silently asking permission. Lionel and Gerard were practically laughing at the way he was flustered by the request for stories about him.

"I do not know that there are many stories that would be interesting. I am afraid I might be considered...dull during my time at court." He said with a sheepish smile, racking his brain for a story he could tell her that might impress a young woman.

"I would never call you dull, Liam." Ger said, bringing his mount up on Liam's opposite side. "There were certainly some adventures, swordfights and battles you were a part of. The time you crossed swords with the King of Gore on the staircase because he made a rude remark about the Queen?"

"He is the father of the twins?" Liam asked, then smiled at the memory. "Yes. He had said that she was a simpleton and refused to take it back. He needed to be taught a lesson."

"You taught it to him?" She asked, with what sounded like adoration in her voice.

"He did." Ger said enthusiastically. "Not many people knew how fierce Liam's temper can be when he is truly riled, but no one who saw that match could soon forget the force of it."

"I would not exaggerate so greatly Ger." Liam said with a modest blush. "I could not stand by and let a man, of any standing, insult a woman I hold in the kind of regard that I hold our Queen."

He watched Caelia think about what he had said. Did she want him to be defensive of her? Protective? She would quickly see just how much he valued her if someone treated her badly, or if any man laid a hand upon her. A part of him almost hoped that someone was foolish enough to try so he had the chance to impress her with more than charm and a smile.

"Do you think there will be a chance to meet Lancelot?" Her sweet voice interrupted his train of thought, sending a rock to his stomach with her request for an introduction to his rival.

"I am sure that he will make himself available to meet, yet another, young woman who admires 'the legend of Lancelot' and wishes for a dance." Ger said with a smug smile. "He usually does, right Liam?"

Chapter 17

Liam smiled when Caelia seemed amazed at the stories of the men around her. Each of these knights were heroes just as honorable as Gawain or Kay. Even Lancelot himself could hardly boast of grander feats than the men around her.

She seemed to be especially interested in the stories of his earlier adventures. He did not want her to think he was vain, so he was quick to share credit for wise decisions and include the others in the glory that hard fought battles had earned him. Gerard seemed especially happy to tell her tale after tale of how they had fought together, often separated from the others. It likely sounded to her as though they were fearless warriors, destroying the enemies of law and order with smiles on their faces and laughter in their hearts. He did not want to disillusion her by telling her how terrifying those battles were in the moment.

"Have we bored you into silence Caelia?" Lucas called from the wagon where he sat with Emrys and Lynn.

"I told you lot that a lady would not be entertained by these stories for the entire trip." Rion said with a laugh. "Perhaps Saffir should sing?"

"Why would you want to torture me Rion?" Caelia teased back. "I had thought that we were friends, but you make this suggestion to me?"

"I feel as though one of my brothers may have, unfairly, told you that I do not have a pleasing voice, Caelia." Saffir said with a smile. "Though honorable, I can assure you that they lie horribly."

"I can honorably tell you that your assumption is correct." Liam whispered. "No one ever asks him to sing a second time…or a second verse."

Caelia laughed softly, her face telling him she enjoyed the joke between them. He was beginning to look forward, more and more, to making memories with her that they would be able to laugh about in the privacy of their rooms. Memories that no one else would have or share until they had children to share those moments with. The sudden thought of children with Caelia brought a broad smile to his face that she mirrored when she looked at him.

Their daughter should have her smile, and her eyes, she would be the apple of his eye as their son would be his joy.

Liam's mind raced at the realization that this was what he wanted. It did not matter that he was not yet married to the woman or that he did not know how she felt about children. He would convince her, change her mind, and awaken her body, towards the possibility that they should try, as soon as decent, to build a family together. Their family. He thought he had given up on the idea but found that there was new hope building on the foundation of her smile.

"I would, however, like to hear that sound more." He said, bringing his horse closer to hers so he could reach for her hand.

"Which sound? Saffir's singing?" She asked.

"No. That is nearly treasonous." He chuckled. "I meant the sound of your laughter. I like it very much."

"Thank you, Liam. I will not hold back if the mood strikes." She said, letting him take her hand in his as they rode.

"Please do not." He replied.

The sound of the other men died away while they rode in silence, enjoying the simple contact. Liam could not tell if they had fallen behind or if their noise simply made no difference when he was focused on her. It was easy, calm, and quiet as they rode for what seemed like only a few minutes before Gerard rode up beside him.

"While I do hate to break up the sweet little romantic interlude that has been going for hours, did you two even eat today?" He asked, smirking slightly. "I need to steal Liam away so we can ride ahead to the inn and ensure that we have rooms for everyone."

"Of course." He said, turning from Ger back to Caelia. "You will be alright with the others while we take care of this? It will not be long."

She nodded and looked back at Lucas.

"I am sure that we will all be fine. Poor Lucas is waiting not so patiently for a chance to ride Aldon and this would be a perfect time to let him do that."

Ger, damn his eagerness, nudged his horse forwards and Liam's followed it's lead as the pair were as close as the men who rode them. He had hoped for the chance to kiss her again, but there was no time.

A glance over his shoulder showed him Lucas letting Caelia get down from the big horse by herself instead of helping her, then getting on the big creature without assisting her to the wagon. He was going to have to talk to him about that kind of behavior in the morning.

"I am certain that she will be alright for less than an hour without you holding her hand, Liam. Come on, we will miss out on rooms if you do not hurry, or you will fall off the horse."

"Shut up you fool." He growled in retort. "Or I will make sure that you spend as much time on the dance floor as I can arrange for you. I am sure that a wide variety of maidens and their widowed aunts would enjoy the chance to dance with such an eligible bachelor. Last time I heard Gerard of Bast was still considered to be quite a catch at court."

"You can forget that and stop making enquiries about my social status." He grumbled, good-naturedly. "I am not dancing with anyone's widowed aunt."

"Neither am I, not this time." Liam could not help but grin. Dancing with Caelia would be heavenly. Staring into her eyes in the sparkle of the candles and glares of the women he had rejected before the offer had come from her father.

"I expect that I will be spending a lot of time dancing, but there will be business too." He said, watching his best friend carefully. "I need you to look after her for me Ger. When I am not there."

"Liam." Ger shook his head. "That is a task better left for Lucas or Rion. They are her age. They get along. It would be easier."

"They will be looking for their own partners or distracted. I know that if I ask you to keep her safe from the court and our enemies there that it will be done."

"Dammit Liam." He stared at him, seething in the saddle. "I have people to see too. You know that I will do it. If you are asking, I will do it but there are people waiting to see me too."

"I swear to you that you will have time with the royal twins, Ger." Liam held up his hand as they approached the inn. "All I am asking is that you do not let anyone touch her, scare her or hurt her. The evenings will be parties or if not, she will be in our rooms. I don't want her to refuse the marriage Ger. I want to marry her, and I want you to stop hating her for that."

"You want this? It is not just about Arthur and the court?" Ger said, pulling his horse to a stop. "Liam? Do you care about her? Not just because you are morally obligated to say it?"

The two men stared at each other, Ger questioning and Liam trying to find the right words.

"I care enough Ger." He said, hating the tension between them but this had to be cleared between them when she wasn't around. "I want her safe, especially from those that would gossip about the past. I trust you more than anyone else alive to do whatever is needed to make sure that she is looked after. Will you do this for me Ger? I need you"

"You know I will. There is no other man I would chaperone such a charge for, but when have I ever said no to you?"

The words were almost spat even though Liam knew that the man across from him would take a sword for him, jump in front of an arrow to save his life and that Ger would, without a doubt, make sure that Caelia was safe.

"Thank you, Ger."

"You will have to tell her, Liam. She will be furious if she finds out that you went through all this trouble to hide it from her. Women hate lies more than almost anything."

"I hate that I have to do it Ger, but I will tell her. I want to do it myself not have her hear the version that has been twisted by the court and those that hate us." Liam said quietly.

"Then do it before they get the chance." Ger said. "You might not listen, but that is my advice."

"Gentlemen, welcome." The voice of the inn keeper broke the tension and allowed them both to leave words unsaid that they might regret later. "Do you need separate rooms, or a shared accommodation?"

Ger walked off with the inn keeper to arrange the rooms, leaving Liam to consider his words carefully. He knew that he had to tell Caelia about the banishment and that he should do it as soon as possible. He should have done it already, but the growing adoration in her eyes would change the moment that she knew, and he was not ready for that to happen. Not yet.

He was still pondering how he would explain the story to his fiancé after they had all eaten and were making their way to the rooms provided for them, when he found himself standing in a doorway with Caelia. He glanced inside and saw Lynn turning down the bed and searching through a trunk, probably for a nightdress.

"I see you have a more appropriate bedmate." He said, hating that he felt as awkward as a teenage boy.

"Yes. The innkeeper said it is the best he has to offer. May I ride with you again tomorrow? To enter the city?" She asked, looking up at him with candlelight sparkling in her eyes.

"I would like that. I would like that very much." He said quietly, the corner of his mouth lifting in a smile when her entire face lit up. "I know the perfect place to switch from the wagon to Aldon." He hurried his words when she looked at him quizzically. "It is a tree that I used to spend a lot of time in, when I wanted to be alone. I would like to show it to you. I thought that perhaps that was the kind of thing that a man might show his young bride, a place to meet for a romantic moment, secret for the two of us."

"A secret place? For us? At the edge of Camelot?" She asked, taking his hand, and raising it near her face.

"Yes. Just for us." He whispered breathlessly just before she pressed her lips to his knuckles. "I have never taken any other woman there, but I want to share it with you."

She laughed lightly, thrilling him again.

"We will be with the rest of the group. They will all know where it is."

"They will not know that it is special, that it will be our place." Liam said confidently.

"Everything is ready for the night, if you are, Caelia." Lynn said, interrupting the moment they were sharing.

"Thank you, Lynn." Liam tried not to growl. He liked the girl, but she was getting in the way of him kissing Caelia.

"I am ready Lynn. Thank you." She said, stepping away from him into the room and leaving him wanting more of her, more of her kiss and that dazzling smile.

"Until tomorrow, my lady." Liam said, giving her the slightest of bows while the door closed, leaving him alone in the hall with a deep sigh. "My lady."

Chapter 18

In the morning Caelia was certain, as she dressed, that Liam would have kissed her again in Lynn had not interrupted them. She had not thought that he could be so thoughtful and romantic as to choose a special spot just for them. If she were honest with herself, she would have expected him to tell her to stay in the wagon, but her Liam was full of surprises. Her Liam. She like how that felt to say to herself. Did he think of her like that as well?

By most men's interpretation of the law she was practically his possession now that they were engaged if she tried to leave him he could use the night they had shared a bed as a way to keep her, but he would not destroy her reputation and bring dishonor on her father by using a lie. Knowing how honorable he was made the idea of being 'his' woman even more appealing. That was a part of why she wanted to ride into the city at his side.

Though there would be no fanfare or fuss made about their arrival anyone who did see them would know that she was the chosen bride of the great Silver Knight of Camelot. That was the thought in her mind while she descended the stairs to find Lionel waiting for her and Lynn at the bottom

"I am here to escort you to breakfast. The others are already there waiting and trying to keep the seats in all this bustle."

"Thank you, Lionel. It looks as though this is a well-liked place to eat, even if one did not spend the night." Caelia said with a smile, scanning the room for Liam but she could not see him

"I would have to agree with you Caelia. If all this tastes as good as it smells I will understand why Ger and Liam did not want to rush their food this morning. They lingered over it so that is why they are still in the yard training."

"He is not here? Oh." Caelia felt slightly deflated but joined the other younger knights at the table and ate her food thoughtfully.

"Did you need to ask him something?" Emrys asked her, a teasing glint in his eyes while he bit into a piece of bread.

"No. I think she wants to watch him and Ger pretend they want to kill each other again." Lucas laughed. "Though I doubt there would be a spare sword you could lay your hands on to join them today."

"What do you mean?" Saffir interrupted, joining them from outside. "Caelia does not have a sword, does she?"

"Would that be a problem for you Saffir?" Caelia asked dryly, noticing the way Rion and Emrys both raised their eyebrows at her challenging words. Lucas and Lynn seemed to be busy in their own conversation, leaving Caelia on her own against the knight.

"There is no need for a lady to have a sword, especially the wife of a knight who is as capable as Liam and who has so many of his brothers around him at all times." Saffir said in reply. "They are not toys, to be played with, but are tools for work a woman does not need to do with a man around."

She wanted to rail at him for the small-minded answer, but she suspected that would only make him say that women were too emotional to handle a blade. A part of her wanted to challenge him to a duel, but he was a knight, even if he was a fool, and there was a good chance she would get hurt.

"What about when he is not around?" She countered, carefully sipping her drink. "Have you ever seen a village ravaged by the victors in war? Have you seen what happens when the men do not return from battle? Those unable to wield a sword still die upon their blades."

"Their men failed them, but it would have happened all the sooner if they had left their weapons at home instead." Saffir shook his head dismissively at her.

"Yet there might also have been survivors if those they left behind had been armed." She said, standing from the table and looking down at him. "Survivors who could honor the dead better than a stranger who happened upon the carnage by accident."

"If their men had been better with them then they would have lived. Their deaths are a shameful wound on the nation, but it is their men that failed them, not their training." Saffir said confidently while he paid the woman who came to clear the table.

"I hope no one you love ever has to fight for their lives without the basic knowledge of how to do so." Caelia said, storming out of the room. How could he not see that, like reading or any other skill, the ability to defend the home was not just the job of a man. It was something she was determined that any child from her marriage, boy or girl, would learn.

If this is how every woman at Redbourne had been treated then she would have to find a way to train them, just in case, even if it were in secret.

Stepping out into the morning sun she smiled, briefly, at Liam. He was finishing his training, pulling Ger up from the ground, and flashed her a grin of his own.

Would he let her do it? Let her teach the women to fight? Maybe, after the wedding, he would help her or at least encourage the effort.

"Ready to go?" Emrys said, pulling up to the doors and helping Lynn up into the cart behind him while Lucas and Rion went to get the horses from the barn. "You will arrive rested and ready for the court and city. Try not to let Saffir get to you. He means well but is not known for forward thinking."

"That is why I must let him get to me. Why I must argue. If I do not then he will continue to think he is right when I know, and I hope that you do too, that he is wrong in this." Caelia said angrily. Her mood was soured by the knight's attitude, but the thought of entering Camelot at Liam's side after he showed her 'their' special spot helped to raise her spirits and shift her focus, for now.

"Suit yourself, but he is stubborn and loves to argue." Emrys said, starting the wagon down the road.

Lynn seemed lost in her own thoughts which suited Caelia's frustrated state of mind as she stared at the countryside passing by with considerably less enthusiasm than the day before. What if all of them thought like Saffir? That women should not learn to fight at all? She could understand, to a point, not having their own swords or training like the knights did, but not keeping them helpless on purpose. Could Liam think that? Did he think that she would set aside her own desire for greater skills?

"Caelia? Is everything alright?" Liam's voice interrupted her worrying. "Should I get Lucas to bring Aldon here for you? Though he is enjoying the spirited stallion I would rather see your smile than his."

"Thank you, Liam." She forced the polite reply instead of peppering him with questions about the issue on her mind. "No, Lucas can keep riding until we reach that spot you had mentioned. It is good for Aldon to get used to other riders."

"Only if that is what you want. He is your horse and yours alone." Liam said, resting his hand on the side of the wagon near her head.

She wanted to rest her head on his hand, or his shoulder, and tell him everything that was upsetting her. His closest friend did not want her at Redbourne and Saffir thought that she and all women should defenselessly rely on men for all protection when it was men that were the cause of their pain. How could she expect him to take her side in any of it?

"I think I will stay and keep Lynn company. There is a special someone I think we need to discuss." She tried to keep the smile on her face that turned genuine when her friend started to blush. "Lucas was especially attentive this morning."

Liam chuckled, the deep rumble sending a wave of warmth through her that was new and made her think of holding hands and kissing and...something more.

"Well, far be it from me to get between ladies and the talk of romance. I can only hope that I measure up just as well as Lucas's attentive breakfast conversation." He said, patting her hand before he nudged his horse to catch up with Ger.

"Is he really romantic Caelia?" Lynn asked with a wide-eyed smile. "I always thought that he would be."

"You have thought about Liam like that?" Caelia asked with a look of surprise.

"When I was younger, I thought he was the most handsome man in the world. You must have been amazed when you found out that he was the man you were to marry? Was he dashing and wonderful?"

"He was, I think, more annoyed than anything else." She cringed inwardly at the memory of just a week ago and the different way she viewed the man now. "I think he is quite wonderful though, more romantic than I thought he would be."

"Annoyed? With you? But he looks at you so tenderly, how can that be?" Lynn asked, taking out her stitching after a wink from Rion sent a blush to her cheeks.

"It was not a good moment when he walked in on the conversation that I was having with my father." Caelia admitted before telling her friend how she had been opposed to the idea of any marriage, especially one to a man so much older than herself.

"You no longer feel that way though, do you? About Sir Liam?" Lynn asked.

Caelia could hear the genuine curiosity in her voice and wondered if others at Redbourne missed the calming influence of a 'Lady of the House' would have on the knights and, most of all, on Liam.

"No. I do not think that it will be a bad thing at all to be his wife." Caelia said with a soft smile, looking up the road at

Liam and Gerard laughing at something she could not hear. "Not a bad thing at all. It may take some time for us to all find our way, but it will be worth it. I will love him, some day."

That seemed to satisfy Lynn's curiosity and they spent the rest of the day discussing how the drawing room at Redbourne could be redone and what they might see in the city. Caelia did not even realize that the afternoon had draw late until the entire party came to a halt in a grove of trees that was just off the road.

Looking around she was amazed at the lush green of the trees and grass. It was like being inside of a piece of glass. She turned around slowly, drinking in the beauty around her until strong arms encircled her waist, stopping the turn.

"It is unbelievably beautiful; do you not agree?" Liam whispered in her ear, his beard tickling her neck to make her smile broader.

"Yes. I have never seen anything like it before." She whispered, leaning back against the strength of his chest. She would have never thought that such a simple touch could melt her all the way through her bad mood. "Is this the place you wanted to show me?"

"Sort of." He said, lighting a lantern, taking her hand and leading her away from the others who were changing into fresh clothing that was nice enough to be presented to the King and Queen if they were summoned right away to the palace.

"I have your dress and cloak." Liam said, sensing her concern as they stepped out of the view of the others. "This is much more private than the side of the road."

"In the middle of a forest?" Caelia asked with a laugh.

"Not for my wife." Liam grinned. "A private dressing room, created by the old gods themselves."

He lifted the lantern and held it close to the tree, revealing a hollow interior. It was rubbed smooth and there was even a small seat carved out of the wood.

"I spent years on this and never shared it with anyone." Liam said.

She could hear the pride in his voice and could not deny that it was well deserved. This was an amazing secret and the drooping branches and knotted trunk made sure that the entrance was, indeed, a secret.

"Not even Gerard? I am honored." Caelia said, stepping inside and touching the walls.

"He knows about it but has not been inside." Liam said with a shrug, handing her the lantern and her clothing. "We can come back another time, we should get into the city before the main gates close for the night. I want to ride down the main street with you before they are deserted. Camelot in the lamplight is wonderful."

Quickly changing and running her fingers through her hair Caelia wondered if there would ever be a secret between them that did not include Gerard.

"Then we should hurry, Liam, I do not want to miss something so lovely."

Holding the lantern and shaking out the skirt of her dark red dress she stepped down from the tree to find a transformed Liam staring at her. The dashing figure in a grey that as so dark it was almost black, with silver decorations and accents that flashed in the flickering light, was a far cry from the man that had looked more like a farmer than a knight only moments before.

"I would not miss the loveliness that stands before me." He said, after a few moments of silent staring. "How beautiful you look. I do not think there is a color that does not make you look divine."

Caelia took his offered hand and was about to reply when he suddenly turned and pressed his lips to hers with even more force than he had used the morning in the training yard. His tongue swept between her lips while his arms wrapped around her.

Surprise gave way to delight and she gave in to the kiss with a moan. Her hands slid up his back to his shoulders as he deepened the kiss. It was beautiful and more romantic than she could have imagined.

"Liam? Caelia?" Ger called, stomping through the brush, and calling for them both. "We are ready to go. You said you did not want to be late. Shall we go."

"Damnit." Liam growled, pressing his forehead against hers. "We should go."

"Of course. People are waiting." She said, stepping towards the rest of the group.

"This is not over Caelia. We will finish this later. I promise."

Chapter 19

Riding towards the gates of the city, beside Liam, with the other knights riding behind them in finer attire than Caelia had ever seen, was an amazing feeling. She felt like the leading lady in a fairy-tale. With the handsome man beside her, reaching for her hand, as if that would be enough for either of them in the wake of the kiss in the forest, she could not help but smile with genuine happiness. It felt, in that moment, that anything, any problem, could be solved if they tried hard enough.

"We are just in time Liam." Gerard said with nod, riding back from the gate. "Gawain left word that we are to head directly to the palace upon arrival."

"Arthur does not waste time, does he?" Liam said with a shake of his head, the smile that Caelia had been admiring slipping into a thin line of grim resignation. "Are you ready to meet the King, Caelia?"

"With you at my side I think I am ready for anything the city has to show me." She said with a nod, nudging Aldon forward towards the open gates. "Who could be afraid of a king with one of the greatest knights in the realm at my side?"

"Your confidence in me is reassuring." Liam said, leading the group through the gates and into the greatest city since Rome. "Let us hope that Camelot does not disappoint."

The sight that greeted her eyes was unlike anything she could have imagined. There were more people, even at this late hour, than she had seen in any one place before. The dozens of lanterns hanging from posts encircled the square inside the gates illuminated everything and lit several paths away from the market in many directions. It was magical and modern all in one place, as if the old gods and the new had come together to create a place of unity and light.

"Something special, is it not?" Liam asked her while they rode, slowly, through the crowd.

"I could not have dreamed it would be like this. Which way do we go? How does one stop from getting lost?" She replied breathlessly. She could hardly sit still, the bustle of the closing of the market was captivating and everywhere she looked there was something new that she felt she just had to see closer.

"One takes a guide that knows the city or else there is a near certainty of getting lost." Liam said, leading the way to the largest of the lit roads. There were more lights here, on both sides of them. "This street, however, will always lead you to the palace. So will most that head up the hill, but this one is called 'The Queen's Path' and goes straight to the doors of King Arthur's palace."

The all moved up the path, the press of the crowd growing less with every light that they passed until they were completely alone with the sounds of the market far behind and only a few household noises to break the silence.

"Why do they call it the Queen's path?" Caelia asked, looking around at the flowering bushes lining the path.

"This is the route that Guinevere took when she arrived at Camelot to wed Arthur." Lionel said. "There was much less town here then and none of it was on the hill. There were easier ways she could have taken, but she had her eyes on the palace and was not going to be deterred."

"No man, woman or wizard was going to get in the way of her getting to Arthur." Gerard said with a laugh. "It was amazing to see how determined she was to get to him, on her own."

"She wanted to show that she was willing to work on the relationship, the marriage and the kingdom." Caelia said, feeling a slight kinship to the admired Queen with her own desire to make the marriage she was facing work and thrive. "I can understand that."

"Is that so?" Gerard asked, the weight in his tone making her look at him, across Liam's horse.

The look in his eyes was filled with the dislike she was growing used to from him, but even more so it was filled with skepticism. He did not believe that she was as willing as the Queen to put work into a marriage that she had not, originally, wanted to be a part of.

"Yes. It is Gerard. I can understand that a woman, who wants to make her marriage work, who cares about her husband, is willing to do anything to make it work. To take the hardest path, to impress those who think she is not worthy. I can understand that fight and respect her choice. This street is something special I think."

She was so busy staring down Gerard that she almost did not see that Liam was looking at her as well.

"Was that too forward? Aggressive for the court? My father told me that I would have to bite my tongue, or no man would want to marry me." She said, suddenly nervous that Liam would change his mind when he found out that she was this strongly opinionated.

"I would not speak so forcefully in the first meeting with the king." Liam said, a smile teasing at the edge of his lips. "Though I am sure that, since it is in support of his wife and marriage that he would appreciate the sentiment."

Caelia smiled, ignoring Gerard's eye roll then took a deep breath as they arrived at the archway into the palace courtyard. She was about to have an audience, with Liam, with King Arthur himself and she had just snapped at one of his knights as though he was a degenerate.

Walking through the halls of the palace, Caelia was awed into silence. There was something about the calm, quiet that stilled her curiosity. Alone with the knights, Lynn had been ushered off to the rooms that had been set aside for them in this majestic place. She felt small, provincial, and decidedly uncomfortable.

"Liam? I am nervous. I am going to say the wrong thing and offend the King or the Queen. I am not refined or ladylike, especially when I am like this."

"Relax my dear." Liam reassured her. "Despite the quiet and the formality of the moment we are not on trial and Arthur has been my friend most of my life. There is nothing to be afraid of, except perhaps the wizard."

"Oh, fuck the wizard." Gerard said. "The man is creepy. He looks at me as if he knows my deepest darkest secrets."

"I do not think that Merlin would like that Ger." Rion teased. "He had a lover once, a woman."

"Did you ever stop to consider that perhaps he actually does know your deepest and darkest secrets, even the ones you do not tell, to Liam or the rest of us?" Lionel said with a smirk when Gerard's eyes widened with panic.

"Keeping secrets Ger?" Liam teased with a smile.

"Nothing worth the attention of that blasted wizard." He grumbled then stilled as the guard knocked on the door.

"Enter." Came a deep voice from the other side and the door opened to reveal the throne room of Camelot. The King and Queen sat upon the dais, waiting for them in the, all but empty, room. The third person in the room was a knight, in full armor that Caelia guessed must be Lancelot.

"Do not just stand in the doorway like Frenchmen." The King called, getting to his feet, and coming down the steps. "Come and greet your king like his loyal knights and your friend like it has not been eight years since we have last laid eyes upon each other."

"Your Majesty." Liam bowed his head, stepping into the room with the others. "Arthur."

Caelia could hear the grin in his voice while she watched him stride towards the king, who met him in the middle of the room to clasp arms before pulling each other into a warm, brotherly embrace.

"It has been far too long, old friend." Liam said, releasing him so that Arthur could greet the rest of the men, giving Caelia the chance to see the legend closer and see why every woman in the realm got a dreamy look in their eyes when they would speak about meeting him.

He was tall, taller than Liam by a handspan at least. His smile was broad, with a lift to one side that made her think that any moment he could burst into laughter. When he did the sound was rich and smooth, making her want to hear it again, especially when the Liam joined in. Light brown eyes sparked beneath a thick head of dark brown hair, so dark it was almost black in the candlelight. It was cut close to his head, unlike the full, shoulder length hair of Lancelot, who was approaching with a smile on his face that made Caelia blush.

If ever there was a man that looked like a fairy-tale brought to life it was him. He looked almost unreal though he was only a few feet away and thus obviously a real person. He was as fair as Arthur was dark and as Liam was silver. Two months ago, she would have been in awe of the beauty of Lancelot. The bright blue eyes and golden hair touching his shoulders had once been the ideal that she had aspired to. None of the young men near her father's home could measure up to the dreams she had of the man approaching and holding out a hand.

"Liam. It is good to see you, you as well Gerard. I did not know that you had used these years to hunt down the loveliest gem of a woman in the countryside. I insist upon an introduction immediately so that I may commission the bards to begin a song praising her beauty this very night."

"Pardon?" Caelia said, eyes wide at the flattery. She turned to look at Liam as Lancelot took her hand and pressed a kiss to the back of her hand.

"I am Lancelot, m'lady, and your name is?" He said with a voice as smooth as honey.

"My name is…"

"The name of my fiancé, is Caelia." Liam said, returning to her side and removing her hand from that of Lancelot. "The bards can wait and so can you. We have been on the road since dawn, she does not have the energy to deal with you Lancelot."

Though he was smiling Caelia could hear what sounded like tension in his voice. Did they not get along? She had thought that the two of them had worked together with the king for the good of the kingdom, but the look shot between them was anything but friendly. She was about to say something when the king turned from talking with Gerard to join them.

"This is the young lady that melted that sterling cold heart of yours? I think I would like proper introduction Liam." He turned to her and took her hand, barely brushing his lips to the top of her fingers. "You are most welcome in Camelot, Caelia. I hope, when we are alone in private company like we are now, that you will feel comfortable calling me Arthur as your husband-to-be does. We are old friends and I am happy to bring you into that circle. We like circles here, do we not? Gentlemen?"

Though she was certain that there was no one better for her than Liam it was impossible not to be charmed by the magnetism of Arthur. She could understand the swooning women in the tales and poetry now that she was face to face with him. He had something that made her want him to ask her for a favor simply so that she could agree to do it and make him smile again.

"We do indeed, Arthur." Gerard said, while the others chuckled. "Round is right, is that not what you used to say?"

"I am honored, majesty." Caelia managed to say, still dazzled by the handsome king.

"Call me Arthur. Come, let me hear you say it and then I will give in to the look that Liam is giving me and let you get to your rooms." He said with a charming tease.

"Thank you, Arthur. I am happy to be here. I am sure I will be more entertaining company after some rest."

He and Liam were about to speak again but the soft voice of the Queen silenced the room immediately.

"Let them go rest Arthur. There is plenty of time now that they are here." Guinevere said, standing from her throne and, with a smile to Caelia, she exited the room.

It was less than a moment after that the door they had entered through opened and Lionel began to usher them back to the hall.

"So, did the fabled King Arthur and Sir Lancelot meet your expectations Caelia?"

"Oh yes. This place, the king, are all so awe inspiring." She replied with a beaming smile. "So much more than I even dreamed."

Chapter 20

Liam could not believe the gall of Lancelot.

He was flirting with Caelia right in from of him. She was embarrassed and had looked nervous at the inappropriate attention. The man was incorrigible and had less tact than a squire. If it had not been for the way that Arthur laughed, as if it were an amusing jest instead of an insult, there would have been an incident that would have him banished all over again. As it was Liam was worried that Caelia would feel uncomfortable at court now. Lancelot was not even the worst of the men that would make a pass at her.

He could not help but cringe inwardly, walking with Caelia's arm tucked into his when he thought of Bedver trying to get close enough to talk to her. Using his considerable charm he would try to tell her what he had told Arthur that night eight years ago and, if she had any wine or if Ger failed, somehow, to keep them apart it could ruin everything he had been working towards and everything they had begun to build.

He was not so foolish as to think that the young woman was going to fall madly in love with him in the space of weeks, he was not amusing or charming in the same way Rion, Emrys and Lucas were. Even Lionel, for all his bookish behavior, could be as charming as one would expect a knight to be. What did Liam have to offer in comparison to the charm of youth? Especially if she thought him the monster that had been cast out of the court eight years ago?

Nothing. So that could not happen. They could not fail in the mission to keep them apart until he could tell her.

He should tell her tonight. Before she went to sleep. Liam knew that he should take her on a walk to the most romantic of the palace gardens and tell the girl that he was falling in love with that he had been banished from Camelot, the place he loved only second to Redbourne Hall, under the accusation of raping a serving girl that looked like his dead wife.

How could he look into those beautiful eyes that adored him only hours ago and tell her that he was the worst kind of man, in the eyes of all those that she would be meeting. Would she believe his innocence? Would she believe that he was still the man she was coming to know? Coming to trust? The man he hoped she could come to love?

He had to know and yet he was afraid of the answer.

He was not ready to see the light in her eyes fade because of him, but there was truly little time left before someone else told her and she would hate him for hiding it from her.

"Liam? Are you still with me?" Caelia's voice interrupted his spiraling thoughts. "You seem so far away."

"Only thinking of tomorrow and the way that the court is going to be amazed when they see you." He replied, patting her hand. "Do you want to bathe and rest or would you like to go for a walk in the garden?"

"We cannot go to the court hall?" She asked with a note of excitement in her voice. "I have been presented to the king and queen already."

"That was in private, the ceremonial presentation is tomorrow and until then you cannot. I do not want to go without you so I thought a walk could be nice."

"What about just sitting by the fireplace and you can tell me your own stories of this place?" She asked with a smile he thought might be hiding disappointment at his words.

"That would be lovely, and I promise that tomorrow we can all join in the court activities." He said, grateful for her compliance.

Though it would have them alone together for the rest of the evening Liam was grateful for the time to build her trust before he broke the news.

"You are not going to join me, join us, in the barracks Liam?" Ger asked him with a surprised look on his face. "It has been eight years. There are old friends to see, to catch up with."

Liam was torn. He looked through the door to see Caelia perusing the room, excitedly exploring each luxurious item that was grander than anything she was likely to have seen before. She was so innocent compared to this world, it was all a dream or fairy tale to her. He was going to have to change all that, but tonight he could give her a touch of the romance she deserved or he could go with Ger and find out what kind of reception could be expected in court the next day.

"They have waited this long they can wait one more night. I am going to spend the evening with Caelia. She needs to know what she is likely to find in the court, the reception she could receive as my bride to be."

"You could have a year to prepare her and she still would not be ready for all of that." Lucas added with a laugh, setting down the trunk he was carrying with Emrys. "I think these dresses would look better on Caelia than they would on any of us. They were delivered to the wrong room."

"Thank you, Lucas." Caelia said with a smile. "I am certain that you would look lovely in the light blue one, but I am glad to have them back."

"And on that note of gratitude, gentlemen, we wish you a goodnight." Liam said, shoving the trunk inside the door and closing it behind him. He smiled at Caelia, who looked ethereal in the firelight. "I am at your complete disposal, Lady of Redbourne. What would you wish of me?"

"You would really rather spend the evening with me, here, instead of drinking and enjoying the company of your friends?" She asked, opening the wardrobe door, and starting to hang up her dresses.

"Of course. There is so much more we can know about each other, about what our life together should be in the future." He said, pouring some wine and offering her a cup. "I can have someone come and do that for you. Lynn is not likely to be asleep yet."

"I do not mind doing this myself. I find it soothing, a way to settle myself in the space."

"Then pause and join me for a drink. I will help you after that." Liam said, holding out the cup and gesturing to a chair. "Come, sit with me. Please?"

Caelia surprised him by sitting, not on the chair across from him but at his feet, her arm resting on his knees, while she took a sip of the wine and looked up at him.

"Tell me about your time here. Something that the others would not think to tell me." She asked him after a few moments of peaceful silence.

"What kind of thing? Swordfights? Great debates around the round table? Policy discussions with Arthur and Lancelot?" He tried to think of any other stories that might be of interest to her.

"Nothing so grand. Tell me why you like it here? Why you wanted to come back? Why you left in the first place or why Arthur, I could not have imagined I would ever call him by his name, why he summoned you here instead of you coming when you wanted? What about when you were a boy, was it here under King Uther and his knights?"

"Those are a lot of questions." Liam said, chuckling as he took a sip of wine. "Why not let me tell you my favorite memory of this city instead?"

"That sounds lovely. Were you a young boy or a strapping knight errant on some important mission for the king?"

"Neither of those, though I had many such adventures and will have more in the years to come if all goes well. My favorite memory is something much simpler." Liam said with a smile at the recollection.

"Really?" Caelia asked, staring up at him eagerly while she sipped her wine again.

"Really and truly." He tapped her nose, wishing he could kiss her instead of simply talking. He should have married her before Arthur had even heard of any of this, then this could have been their honeymoon instead of a trial before going through with the ceremony.

Standing slowly Liam eased the chair back so that he could sit on the floor next to her.

"I thought that this was nicer than looking down at you. I would much rather sit eye to eye with you than put myself above you." He stroked a strand of hair that had fallen across her cheek. "You are truly lovely, Caelia. There is no woman in the court or all of Camelot that compares to your beauty. How can it be that you are here, with me?"

"Well, we are going to be married so that puts us together. You are a man of honor with an open mind, which is why I am happier to be here than I thought I might be. You are supposed to be telling me about your happy memory though, not making romantic eyes at me in the firelight."

"What about a kiss?" Liam said, leaning closer, his lips only a breath away from hers. "Since we are to be married? We should become as comfortable with physical affection as we are talking with each other. It is important."

"Is it?" She said, her voice a breathless whisper. "I must rely on your knowledge of these things Liam as I have no education in the matters of marriage and the intimacies of a husband and wife."

"I promise you that it is very important Caelia." He whispered back, letting a hand slide around her waist to hold draw her body closer. When her lips brushed against his he was almost undone. "Let me teach you. I will be thorough and gentle."

He pressed his lips to the softness of her mouth, silently pleading for her words that would permit him further allowances with his affections.

"Teach me, Liam. Please?"

Her simple request set free the fires of desire in Liam's blood and he pulled her into his lap, the warmth from the fire chilled in comparison to the heat growing between them with each kiss. Her hand threaded in his hair and his fully encircled her slender waist. They were as close as two people could be while fully dressed and it still did not seem like enough.

Though this passionate embrace could not be considered chaste, he would not allow it to go too far, despite his certainty of his desire for her. Some things, some acts, were best left for the wedding night when they were both as sure as he was now.

She was pressed against his chest. Her innocence was so obvious in the way her fingers trembled as they unlaced his shirt before she kissed his neck. It was the way she kept looking into his eyes, silently asking if what she was doing was what he wanted that touched his heart the most. She was so confident in every other moment, in every other choice that she made, the way she sought his approval along with his affection allowed him to see the vulnerability that she kept hidden from the world. Her openness honored him even more than her affection.

He let her set the pace, exploring as she gained confidence to match her curiosity. It was hard to restrain himself. He wanted to show her how much more there could be, how much pleasure they could find with each other. This was not the night for it though.

"Caelia." He moaned, cupping her face in his hands to bring her eyes to his. "I must insist, beg for a reprieve for the night. My control is only so strong when faced with everything that you are, everything that you offer."

"Liam?" She placed a hand on his cheek. "Have I done something wrong? Was this wrong?"

"No. Not at all, my dear. You are far more wonderful than I deserve if I am honest." Liam said, pressing a kiss to her forehead. "It is late, and we should both sleep now. I am afraid that if this continues much longer then neither of us will be ready for the presentation tomorrow."

"Court...the court of Camelot. In the blue dress that you asked me not to alter?" Caelia asked when he helped her to her feet.

"Your beauty will eclipse them all, including the Queen herself. I will be the proudest man in the land to be at your side." He kissed her fingers and then her lips once more before guiding her through the door to her room.

"I will be equally proud to be on your arm." She told him, closing the door between them.

"I hope that is still your sentiment by the day's end." He said to himself with a final look to Caelia's bedroom before closing the door of his own. "Or more than this engagement will be in danger of breaking."

Chapter 21

Caelia was utterly exhausted. She had lain up half the night thinking about kissing Liam; what it meant, what it had felt like, what it made her feel and, most of all, what it made her want to do.

She had wanted to do so much more than kiss him. When their tongues had danced together in the deep kiss Caelia had wondered what it would feel like to have his lips on more than just her lips and when he had moved to her neck she had thought there could be nothing more blissful than that.

She could not have been more wrong.

Liam had surprised her when he pulled her into his lap and the intimate contact had sent a new thrill through her. She would have never thought that she was a girl who would find herself in the lap of a man, wrapped in a passionate embrace before a fire, and yet it was the most incredible thing that she could have imagined. She had surprised herself when she had unlaced his shirt and pressed kisses of her own across his collarbone. The moan of pleasure he had given her made her almost as proud as she had been when they were sword fighting in the training yard at Redbourne.

When he had stopped the kissing, she had been afraid, at first, that she had done something wrong. Had she been too forward? Gone too far? She had even worried that he did not enjoy her touch, but before he shifted to stand Caelia had felt the size of his arousal, straining behind the laces of his breeches. That was when she realized that if they did not stop Liam might forget that they were not yet man and wife.

She had dreaded the wedding night since she had been told about the arranged marriage, but now, instead of fear, she was becoming consumed by an intense, wet heat low in her belly. She was not sure that she would have had the conviction to stop him if he had slid his hand under her skirt like she had once seen her brothers do with girls in the barn. He would make the night, when it came, one of best moments of her life, she was sure of that now and more eager than she could have guessed.

Before that could happen though, she would have to pass the test of being presented publicly at court. It seemed a nightmare, but at least she would not be alone. Liam would be at her side and the other knights from Redbourne would be there too. Would Ger speak against her and risk the displeasure of his best friend and leader? Would Liam speak in her defense if he did?

The relationship between the two men was still so confusing to her. She thought she knew about the relationship between men. Growing up with brothers and their friends had shown her everything she knew about men. She was used to their jokes and roughhousing. It made her laugh more often than not. When the knights did the same thing, even though they had swords instead of fists, it was thrilling but not in the childish way of her brothers. It was exciting, exhilarating, and dangerous. She loved it.

She had spent the days at Redbourne and the journey to Camelot watching how all the knights interacted with each other, trying to understand how each of them stood in the rankings of authority. It was the unspoken code of men to just leave the authority to be discovered. Women would state it, loudly and clearly, so that there could be no misunderstanding.

She knew that Liam and Gerard were the two men most looked up to and after them it seemed to her that Lionel, bookish but sweet, was the one that everyone turned to with their questions. Since he was the overseer of the Redbourne estate that made sense, but she wondered if there was something more to it than that. Perhaps, if she asked him, he would explain the dynamics of the group a little better for her. It would help her to try and win over Gerard as well as finding her own place within the dynamic of the estate that was now her home and the men that she should think of as brothers.

"Alright, my lady, enough daydreaming. We need to get you dressed for this fancy ceremony." Lynn said, pushing back the heavy drapes and tugging Caelia to her feet.

"Lynn, I asked you to call me Caelia. Please?"

"That is fine enough for at home or on the road but not here in Camelot. It would not be proper and we all much be on our best behavior. Do you not agree?"

"I suppose that is true, though it seems so horribly formal between friends."

"Formality is a very popular thing here, it seems." Lynn replied, opening the wardrobe, and removing the dress that had been chosen for the presentation.

As Lynn helped her into the dark blue gown Caelia could not help the feeling of anxiety that came when she thought about the ceremony that would be happening in only a little while.

Everyone would be staring at her and judging whether she was good enough to be the wife of a knight the king held in such high regard. How could a young woman who had no experience in the realm of royalty and the workings of the court understand what it took to help a man of such importance?

It was likely that, even now, Liam was in conference with the king and other knights making plans for their next mission or adventure. Would it mean that she was going to be left behind in the city or would she go back to Redbourne with any of the men that did not go with Liam? Although the city seemed like an exhilarating place, she did not relish the thought of being there without Liam to enjoy it with.

"There. That dress really does look lovely." Lynn said, finishing with the laces. "Now for your hair. Something simple and yet elegant?"

"I am not sure. I trust you to do what is best. I want to look proper, not as though I am making any assumptions about my reception or place among those that have been here longer."

"I would not imagine anyone would think you were putting on airs if that is what you are worried about." Lynn said with a reassuring smile. "There. A simple coronet braid with some of your hair still down your back will give you the look of a courtly lady while still having the air of a maiden."

"That is important here in Camelot. The proper impressions held by the proper people?" Caelia asked, smoothing the front of her dress carefully before heading to the door to wait for Liam in the joint drawing room.

"More so than other places, yes." Lynn said. "You look just as you should in this situation, and I am sure that Sir Liam will be proud to have you at his side."

"I am always proud to stand beside her." Liam said, turning from the window where he was standing with Gerard. "Today is certainly not an exception."

Caelia smiled when he crossed the room to place a kiss on her cheek.

"I am glad that you approve, Liam. This is the dress that you asked for and Lynn took special care with my hair."

"I never understood the importance of women's hair in the court." Gerard said, shaking his head. "But you look...good."

"Thank you, Gerard. I appreciate that." She flashed him a grateful smile, understanding that could not have been easy for him to say.

"She looks much better than good, though there is something missing." Liam said with a slight growl towards his friend.

"Missing?" Caelia panicked, looking down at the dress and feeling her ears and wrists to see if something was missing. "What did we forget?"

"You forgot nothing. I simply have this belt, that I bought for you this morning." He drew a belt of intricately linked silver chain out of his pocket. "I did say that I would get it for you. I hope you like it."

"It is lovely. I have never owned something so fine." Caelia said, a note of awe in her voice while she brushed her fingers over the delicate silver. "Thank you, Liam."

"I am pleased to be able to make you smile like that today." He said, quietly before he looped the belt around her waist and fastened it on her hip. "It finishes the look perfectly."

She gave Lynn a quick glance for her fashion approval then took Liam's arm.

"Then I am ready for presentation to court as long as you are with me."

"It is not as bad as you think it will be." He said warmly, walking down the hall towards the stairs.

The great hall was at the bottom and the assembled court would be waiting to see her, to see if she made a mistake or tripped on her gown.

"What if I say the wrong thing? Offend the Queen with an improper curtsey or say the wrong thing to the King?" Caelia asked in a whisper, her heart racing beneath the luxury of the velvet gown.

"You will do just fine. You are graceful and have an elegance that will see you through without fail." Liam said, guiding her down the stairs. "There is little chance you could offend Arthur. If you give honest answers to the questions that you are asked, which will not be many, then you have nothing to worry about."

"Except for all the people who are staring at me." She whispered as they reached the bottom of the stairs and the packed hall turned in unison to look at them. "It looks like a wedding, but it is not, is it?"

"No. I would like to think that we would have a little more notice if there was going to be a surprise wedding." Liam said, stepping on to the plush red carpet that ran the length of the room. "One never knows though. Stranger things have happened, so be prepared."

She knew that he meant to be comforting but it was a terrifying thought that she could reach the podium only to find out that she was to be married in front of strangers, without her father or bothers present to give her away.

Every step that took them closer to the King and Queen made her a little more nervous and even more excited. The final rows of people were men in long red robes that she knew meant that they were knights of the round table. She scanned the ranks but there was no sign of the other men from Redbourne. Liam was not wearing his cape either, was there something that she had missed?

She would have to ask him later, because now the King and Queen were only the dais steps away from them. It was time to make this engagement official or see it commanded to be broken by order of the king.

"Liam of Redbourne." Arthur's rich voice pulled her into the moment and away from her worries. "You return to court at the request of the crown to present the woman you intend to marry?"

"Yes. I answered your summons with my lady, Caelia." Liam said, his voice ringing out around the room. "She is a lady of integrity, honor and intelligence. I am proud to have her at my side, Majesty. As proud as you are to have Queen Guinevere at yours."

She thought that the statement was bold, possibly even offensive to the man before them and the woman who had stood beside him through wars and the journey to unite the island kingdoms under one banner.

"And what do you say, Lady Caelia, daughter of Hebron?" Arthur asked her, his voice sending shivers down her spine, especially when she caught the eye of the druid Merlin just barely in sight at the edge of the curtain. "Are you a lady, pure of heart and as honorable as a knight of my round table? Can you take care of him as we, the knights, take care of the kingdom?"

The silence of the room was as heavy as a winter cloak, so was the importance of the question King Arthur put to her in his rich voice that echoed through the hall.

"Yes, your majesty. I am able to care for my knight as you care for all of us. I will stand at his side, hold his hand and, when he needs me, be his shield against the harshness of the day."

She turned her head to look at Liam who was smiling at her with a warmth and pride that she mirrored back at him.

"If that is the depth of your feeling, then I see no reason to delay such a union." Arthur said.

Liam turned his head at the same time as she did.

"Majesty?" Liam asked, taking her hand in his and giving her a squeeze to calm her from an outburst.

"You are so devoted to each other that I see no reason for you to wait. Tomorrow at sunset, in my personal garden, I will perform the ceremony myself."

Chapter 22

"We are getting married tomorrow night?" Caelia asked for the second time since they had been escorted from the great hall. "There is no way to refuse?"

"How can I refuse the king? Why did he have to offer to do it himself?" Liam paced back and forth before the fire, waiting for Arthur and Guinevere to join them.

"My father is not here though. I wanted...I thought he would be here or at Redbourne when this happened."

There was a hint of sadness in her voice that stopped his pacing.

"Are you having seconds thoughts Caelia? It might offend him, but I can try to get Arthur to wait." Liam said, taking her hand and looking down into her eyes.

It would almost certainly go badly if he tried to get the king to stop the wedding, it was worth the risk if it made Caelia happy though.

"Not about the marriage, Liam." She gave him a weak smile. "I had just thought that it would be happening at Redbourne, not here."

The fact that she wanted to get married at his home was wonderful, even if it did not look like it was going to happen.

"You wanted to get married at Redbourne?" He asked, stepping up to her and taking her small hand in his. He had taken off the ceremonial gloves and tossed them somewhere on the floor in his anger and frustration with the king and could now feel the tremble in her fingers.

When she nodded yes Liam pressed a kiss to her forehead. "Then, when we get home, we will invite your father and brothers and have a beautiful celebration at the end of the summer."

"That would be lovely, thank you Liam." Caelia said with the beginning of a smile.

"Yes indeed, Liam, that does sound nice. Perhaps I will accompany his majesty to be a part of that as well." Said a familiar and unwelcome voice from behind him.

Liam closed his eyes and cursed inwardly at the sound of Bedver's voice. The man was not only insufferably arrogant but also the reason that Liam and the others had been cast from Camelot. It was his planning and lies that had ruined Liam's reputation, all due to jealousy that Arthur held him in favor as an advisor and friend.

"I doubt that you would enjoy the simple, uncomplicated country life, Bedver." Liam said, turning to face his enemy and fellow knight. "Perhaps it would be better if you stayed at court where things run more to your liking. The drama and intrigue you thrive on do not exist outside these walls."

"I think you underestimate what I enjoy, Liam." Bedver said, his eyes on Liam's sword hand while he walked up to Caelia and took her hand. "The country does have some lovely attributes that cannot be found within the city. I have heard that country girls are by far the loveliest, delicacies in all the kingdom."

When the snake in armor kissed Caelia's hand and she gave a slight bow of her head Liam was ready to strike him so hard his head would have spun on his neck like a child's toy. That would have caused a skirmish to break out between them, which would likely have been witnessed by Arthur and spun by Bedver to make it look as though he was overreacting, even though the man's tone left no doubt as to what he desired to do with Liam's wife to be.

He had to remain calm for a few more minutes and then he could spend his anger in the training field with Gerard.

"I prefer to think that the women of the country are… untainted by the grime and other filth of the city. An innocence to be preserved at all cost by any man who calls himself a knight." Liam growled, taking Caelia's hand back, grateful that she seemed to trust him enough to not comment on the animosity that had flooded the room.

Bedver's laugh sent a shudder down his spine even though it confirmed that he was right in wanting to keep the man as far away from Caelia as possible.

"I could not agree with you more, Liam." Ger said, entering the room beside the king and queen.

"I am also in agreement, since my wife was once a country girl herself." Arthur said with a tight grin. Liam knew him well enough to know he was less than pleased.

Hopefully, he had heard Bedver's slight and not just Liam's reply, but either way Liam would stand his ground and do his best to keep Caelia safe from him and whatever he had planned.

"One could never guess that a lady of such elegance was once a simple country girl with dreams of nothing more than a husband and family." Bedver said, verbally stumbling by mentioning the one thing all members of court knew not to talk about around the queen: children.

"Thank you for the kind reminder of that fact, Sir Bedver." The Queen retorted. "Since I do not yet have a family to consume my time, I would like to take young Caelia under my guidance to plan the wedding that she would like, since my husband surprised her with the change of time and place."

"Majesty?" Caelia asked, the smile on her face making Liam, Arthur and even Ger smile in return.

Her sweet unassuming joy at the offer from the Queen sent a wave of relief through Liam. At the very least the rushed wedding would be a happy memory for her, something special as it should be for every bride.

"I think you ladies will have a wonderful time and I look forward to seeing your beautiful creation of the day." Liam said when Caelia finally looked towards him.

Caelia placed her hand in Guinevere's with a nod of encouragement as they left the room already talking about fabric and flowers.

"Such simple things women find pleasure in." Bedver scoffed, watching them go. "Perhaps that is why I have never found just one to be satisfying enough."

"As if any woman of sense would find you worthy of her time." Ger said, folding his arms across his chest and glaring at the other man.

Bedver was not tall and his orange hair was not as thick as his waistline but both Liam and Ger knew that he was good with a sword and with a lance in the tourney lists. He was not the man that either Liam or the blacksmith were, he did not have the battle experience, but he was still dangerous.

"Oh, I assure you, Sir Gerard, that I have my share of attention from the fairer sex, your share too since you left court."

Liam stood next to Arthur, who was reading a scroll brought to him by a page, and watched as Bedver walked up to Ger and smirked, hoping to get a reaction from the other man as he had with Liam.

"In fact, there is a certain lady, with a twin brother, that I am greatly looking forward to enjoying the company of during the celebration of the next few days. I hope that does not leave you without a dinner partner or alone on the dance floor."

Ger's eyes flicked to meet Liam's and he arched his brow in reply to his friend. They knew each other well enough that something so subtle was as clear a signal as shouting or waving a flag.

"Unlike you I do not find the need to focus on only one person to entertain myself. Indeed, I have many companions, friends, and brothers-in-arms to enjoy. With the King of Gore arriving later this afternoon I doubt Elin will have time for anyone, especially you." Ger said with a smirk.

Bedver's face tensed as he tried to avoid frowning.

"The king is coming? How would you know?"

"Because, unlike you, Gerard actually listens when the lady speaks." Liam said, joining Ger with a disarming grin that would only serve to agitate their enemy more.

"Your majesty? Is it true that the King of Gore is attending tomorrow celebration?

"Yes. Did I miss something?" Arthur said, rolling the scroll and looking up at the three of them. "Why are you still here Bedver? I sincerely doubt that Liam would like you to join us in the training yard with Lancelot."

"Unless he wants to hold our cloaks, or go against Gerard?" Liam teased happily. "I do not see Bedver joining the likes of us as a good idea or being good for his pride."

"I do appreciate the invitation, Your Majesty, but I have things to take care of at your earlier request and I am sure that the Queen will have need of things from the market that I can acquire for her."

"Do what you wish Bedver. We have things to do." Arthur strolled out with the carefree attitude of a man who had no doubt that his wishes would be followed.

Bedver left in the opposite direction, leaving Ger and Liam facing each other.

"Which is more arrogant do you think?" Ger asked with a grin. "The King or the man who kisses his ass hoping that he will not be shit upon?"

"In most cases Arthur is always the top of the pile, but this might be one thing that Bedver can best any of us on." Liam said, shaking his head. "Shall we join his royal arrogance once again?"

"We shall." Ger said, tossing his arm across Liam's shoulder with the comfortable familiarity that they had shared all their lives. "Once again it shall be talent against privilege."

"And once again talent shall reign victorious." Liam laughed.

"Which means that we will be drinking on the royal purse tonight. Do you remember the last time we did that? Must be ten years ago. Does your memory go back that far, old man?" Ger said with a laugh, punching his arm before he jogged across the yard to the training circle.

"How could I forget?" Liam asked his back.

When they arrived at the king's private training arena Ger grabbed the top of the fence and vaulted over, landing on his feet inside the ring as he had always done since they had first been invited to it.

Liam decided against attempting the same and used the gate instead. He was surprised to see Lancelot placing a kiss to either cheek, then pulling Ger into a full embrace. When had they become so close?

When they had last resided in the city the two seemed more likely to come to blows than embrace each other so warmly. Ger had always been quick to agree with Liam about the man's arrogance and had joined him, more than once, in questioning the closeness between the senior knight and the king.

"Not that we have a stone to throw in that regard ourselves." Ger would always conclude.

"Of course not." Liam would agree. "Some could make a similar observation about you and I."

This would always be where they changed the topic of conversation, but today Liam wondered if it was because he did not want to risk revealing a closer friendship with the man he had thought to be far removed from his affection.

"Liam, good of you to join us. Congratulations on your approaching wedding. I tried to convince Arthur that it should be tonight, but he insisted that the women would need at least a day to get things in order." Lancelot said, giving him a kiss to each cheek but withholding the embrace he had given Ger and making Liam even more suspicious about their relationship.

"Caelia had hoped to have the ceremony at Redbourne, with her father and brothers present." Liam replied, removing his cloak, and drawing his sword. "I have told her that, at summers end, we will have a celebration that she can invite them to. It is important to make small gestures like that to keep a woman happy in the home. You understand of course, Arthur?"

"Indeed, I do. Perhaps Gwen and I will come, with Lancelot instead of Bedver I think." He responded, facing off against Liam with a confident grin.

"If you bring Bedver to my house I will make you sleep in the barn, with him, king or not." Liam laughed and engaged the king.

Regular rules did not apply here, it was the place where Arthur was just another knight, but still Lancelot did not engage Ger, instead the two men were to watch and ensure that there was no foul play. At least that was what they were supposed to be doing. Instead of watching the fight both men were leaned in close conference, whispering and chuckling.

"Liam? Watch your head man." Arthur called, when his blade glanced off the edge of his helmet. "I almost took it right off. What are you thinking of?"

Chapter 23

"What were you thinking of that Arthur almost took your head off? Liam you never lose concentration like that." Ger asked him later that night when they were alone in his room. Caelia was in bed after the private dinner they had shared with Arthur and Guinevere, so the two men were drinking to celebrate the eve of the wedding.

"The better question is what were you and Lancelot talking about so privately? And when did the two of you become so close? You never said anything kind about him to me before." Liam answered, tugging off his boots and setting them by the fire.

"You are getting married, again, tomorrow. What care do you have what relationship I may or may not have with Lancelot?" Ger said, pouring them another glass of wine.

"You know that they say that he is often in the bedchamber of the royal couple and that he has a room of his own that is attached to theirs." Liam warned. "At the very least you could get caught up in those whispers, it is also possible that you could get between a royal and their lover."

"We both know that speaking those rumors outside of the strictest confidence is dangerous, for us and for them, Arthur especially as King." Gerard said, handing him a cup and sitting across from him on a stool.

"I am not accusing the man of anything, merely trying to find out what changed between you and Lancelot and how I did not know about it." Liam said, taking a deep drink while he watched his friend.

"Why? Are you jealous? Old friend." Ger replied smugly. "Afraid that I might leave you? Or just that I might have secrets of my own?"

I never kept any secret from you. Certainly not like this. You and Lancelot...we both know what kind of man he is."

"You never kept secrets?" Ger laughed. "What about when you and Lionel were sending the letters looking for your little bride?"

"Leave her out of this. None of it is her fault."

"Do you care about her Liam? For herself or just the ability to give you a child to carry on your name?"

"I never hid the fact that this is what I wanted, never lied about it. I admit that I did not expect to fall...to feel for her but I do." Liam stared into the dark brown eyes filled with hurt and anger.

How could Ger expect him to give up the wish for an heir for Redbourne? Without one the whole property would revert back the crown and the people he had been caring for and that he now took responsibility for would be without a leader who cared about them more than their ability to turn a profit from the land.

"No. You just hid the timing from me and involved Lionel in the search instead of the man that knows you better than anyone. I helped you pick your first wife. Did you forget that part from all those years ago?"

Liam downed the contents of his cup and glared at him.

"Do not think I forgot anything to do with her just because I am getting remarried. I remember every blasted thing about her."

"And yet you never say her name?" Ger countered, pouring more wine. "Why is that?"

"I am done talking about this with you. If you want to pick a fight go find Bedver or Lancelot. Oh, wait, you are not fighting with him anymore." Liam smiled darkly. "You still have not said why."

"And you have not answered the question of your jealousy. I suppose you have no intention of giving me the satisfaction."

"I have yet to decide if there is anything worth being jealous over." Liam laughed when Ger coughed, choking on the wine.

"You ungrateful bastard." Ger reached for a pillow from the bed and whipped it across the room.

"You will spill the wine if you keep that up Ger." Liam said, dodging the throw. "Or I might throw my knife at you."

"As if you would risk it the night before your wedding." Ger chuckled.

"No. I cannot very well go to the ceremony with fresh wounds or a blackened eye." Liam grinned at him.

It was good to laugh with Ger. Despite his displeasure in the wedding they would still be friends and that was what mattered most. Liam was not sure if he could have chosen between his future and his best friend if Ger had truly pushed against it. The secret with Lancelot still bothered him and that fact bothered him even more. Why should he care? Especially tonight.

"You should get some sleep too. I doubt your bride would be impressed if you were too tired to dance because I kept you up drinking all night."

"So I should." Liam said, sitting down on the foot of the bed. "I do not think the Queen would be pleased either after all the work they put into this. She has gifted Caelia a dress and gave her free choice over the flowers from her own garden. I think we might be welcome back sooner than we thought. If all goes well."

Ger nodded, sitting on the bed next to him. "When has that ever been our luck? That things go well."

"Often enough that I can hope but not enough that I would forget to offer prayer for it." Liam replied, leaning his head back against the bedpost. "Will you answer the question for me then? Or do you choose avoidance?"

"I choose avoidance for now, unless you answer my question." Ger said, holding up the last glass of wine.

"Ask and see it answered." Liam said with a heavy sigh, taking the offered cup to wait for the question.

"On your last night as a single man, again, do you have any doubt or regret? Other than the timing of the ceremony which Arthur took from you. Anything left you have not done?" Ger asked, quietly, leaning towards him with an arched brow.

Ger's eyes were staring into Liam's with so much expectancy and weight that it took a moment to absorb the depth of what he was asking, what he needed from him.

"Just one thing."

He set aside the cup and took Ger's face in his hand and kissed him. It was a risk with a serious consequence if he was wrong. They were not children this time and there was no excuse, no playful reason or game that was being played. This was the only chance he had to show Ger that no matter what changed, on paper or in the eyes of the court, they were what they had always been and would be, closer than blood.

He knew that it was the wine giving him the courage, but the feeling was, strangely, right. There was not urgent desire like he felt with Caelia, instead it was a slow building steady burn that he had felt since that morning in the training field. Liam could not have explained how it felt to think that Lancelot and Ger had been together except to say that it felt similar to the day he had taken an arrow to his shoulder, narrowly missing his heart. That was how he felt with Ger, who had a hand on his hip and the other gently stroking through his hair as their kiss deepened, their tongues dancing together in teasing eroticism, he was so close to his heart but could not possess it.

Liam paused to take a breath, breaking the kiss to open his eyes and look at Ger.

"Are you alright, Liam?" Ger said, his voice shaking slightly, reaching a hand to stroke his beard so softly Liam could not help but lean into his hand. "This is…what is this? Good-bye? An attempt to keep me from…others? I am not leaving Redbourne or you."

"Not good-bye." Liam said, moving one hand to rest on Ger's shoulder. "We do not say good-bye. This is the last night, for a long time, that my bed will not have a wife in it. Do you want to stay? Keep me company and see the dawn together as we used to."

"Like we used to?" Ger asked with a grin. "You never used to do that. Did Lancelot scare you into that or your tiny little bride?"

He leaned forward and pressed a firm kiss on Liam's lips, far from the softness of a moment before, his tongue slid between them and swept against his own with the taste of the wine they shared lingering in its wake.

"Have I ever been scared of you?" Liam said, grabbing Ger's shoulders and pinning him back against the column of the bed.

"Not yet, but you might." Ger grabbed the front of Liam's breeches, using his thumb to loosen the knot, pulling him closer. Liam's heart began to race faster when his fingertips dipped inside the loosened material. The contact he made sent an undeniable shiver down his spine that stiffened his entire body.

"Your body says what you will not." Ger growled low in his ear.

"Then, perhaps, we should let them speak for us." Liam said, pulling his shirt over his head and standing straight, looking down into Ger's eyes. "As that night in Wales."

After pulling his own shirt off and tossing it to the floor with Liam's making a pool of white linen on the stone floor, Ger's hands moved up through the short hairs on his chest until they rested on Liam's shoulders.

"Perhaps we should." He said before shoving, hard, to send Liam to his back on the mattress of the big bed.

The light of dawn was just beginning to creep through the window, he had not drawn the drapes closed all the way the night before due to the wine he had been drinking with Ger. Ger? Where was he? He reached behind him to feel in the bed, but it was empty. Warm still, but empty. Rolling over to look Liam saw him pulling up his breeches and grabbing a shirt off the floor.

"That one is mine. Yours is the other one." Liam said, not lifting his pounding head from the pillow. "Where are you going?"

"I go back to my room, before the entire palace is awake and buzzing in preparation for...today." The last word was sharper than it should have been. "I would not want to have to answer questions as to why I was here all night."

"The answer would be simple enough." Liam said, propping his head on his hand and letting his eyes roam the inked markings on Ger's back until the white linen of his shirt covered him completely. "We drank too much wine and you fell asleep here. No one would think anything of it. You are going in anger. Anger that I do not understand."

"Yes, I suppose I am. You do not understand? Think of how you might feel when I spend the night in the company of Lancelot and Ba... others of like mind. You might be able to understand it then." Ger snapped, reaching for his boots.

"You knew what this was Ger. It does not change the day or what I will do. I am marrying Caelia today and there will be jousting and celebration and dance tonight."

"Tonight? You will bring her back to this bed? Hers is hardly big enough for the two of you even if you held her close to your chest."

"I will, as a husband should." Liam frowned, sitting up. "I thought this, last night, was what you wanted. I thought you understood."

"And I thought you had made up your mind at last." Ger shook his head and started towards the door. "Do not expect me to come to your bed and show her how to please you. I am not so understanding as Lancelot. Oh, and change the sheets before you bring her here. I would not have the scent of us in your nose while you are with her."

"Gerard, stop. You are not..." The door closed, cutting his words from their target. "Being fair."

Though, perhaps it was he that was not being fair. To Gerard or Caelia who had no idea about any of this. It could never happen again, but he had to know that he was making the right decision. Despite his feelings for Ger there was nothing that would change the events of the day. His feelings for Caelia would continue to grow and they would truly be a loving couple by the time the summer celebration he had promised her occurred. He would always love Ger but as a friend not a lover. He would not, could not, do that to either of them.

"I am not worthy of either of them, let alone both of them. May the gods help me." He muttered before closing his eyes and falling back into a sleep filled with sorrowful brown eyes that were sometimes Caelia's and sometimes Ger's. "Help me to keep my word and my friend."

Chapter 24

Caelia adjusted the sash of her dress and straightened the jewelry borrowed from the Queen. She could hardly believe the day was here. She was getting married. It was to a man that she was still getting to know but he was the only man that had ever sent her heart racing just to hear him laugh and when he looked at her every nerve in her body tingled. What would he look like dressed for their wedding? Shimmering in chain mail? With his sword at his side? Or would he be in formal silk like a courtier? Would he like the dress?

"You look lovely, Caelia." Guinevere said.

"Liam will be absolutely smitten." Lynn added, squeezing her hand.

"I think that he already is, but he is certainly going to love this dress. Are you comfortable? You will be in it all day, through jousting and dinner and, of course, dancing." The Queen said.

"There will really be dancing? All night?" Caelia asked, spinning one last time before the mirror, and stopping when she faced the other women.

"For hours after you go to sleep." Guinevere laughed. "The energy of the court can outmatch even the energy of youth. I am sure that there will be some that do not see their beds until the sun rises."

"Bed...I will be in bed with a husband." Caelia paled, the smile slipping from her face. "I have barely kissed him. I have barely kissed anyone and now I will, we will, tonight?"

"You are a true innocent then." Guinevere said, patting the seat beside her. "Your mother was gone before you were old enough to be told these things? I would invite you, both of you, to sit and I will tell you, what it is that you can expect tonight."

"My mother and my father, made sure that I know all of that." Lynn said, smiling at Caelia who was blushing. "I will leave you two ladies to your discussion and go to make sure that everything else is ready for the ceremony."

Caelia sat through the lecture from the queen with her eyes wide. She had known some of the basics from living on the farm and having brothers, but her sisters in law had never taken the time to tell her that side of marriage.

"I was prepared for cooking, cleaning, running a household and helping to run the estate. I had no idea about this…any of this. I do not know how to do it, how to let him do it."

"You thought what happened between a man and woman was simply kisses and the rustle of bed clothes Caelia? You are not so naive as that?" the Queen asked. "You poor girl."

"I knew there was more, or course. I just do not know how to give myself up, to surrender to him."

"Drink some wine at dinner then water for the hours of dancing." Guinevere said gently. "Then, when Liam comes to you for your last dance of the night, have one more glass. Drink half at the beginning of the song and the other just before you leave the ballroom. Being relaxed will make things easier and Liam is a good man. He will want to make it pleasant for you."

"Can it be? You make it sound painful and awful." Caelia twisted the lace on the sleeve of her dress nervously.

"My dear girl, of course it can. Not your first time, usually, but it gets to be an enjoyable thing. If you fall in love with Liam it will be even better between you. I did not mean to frighten you from it. You needed to know so that, should it go badly, you do not blame yourself or him. I doubt very much that the Silver Knight of Camelot would cause you harm or do anything you are opposed to. He is still a good man."

"Still? You say that as though there could be doubt? Why did Liam and the others leave Camelot eight years ago? No one will speak of it directly and yet I feel as though everyone but me knows a secret that I should be privy to. Will you tell me?"

"That is not my story to tell and the bells are ringing. It is time to go to the chapel. Lancelot will be waiting for us."

"Lancelot?" Caelia stopped as the closed the door behind them. "Why is he waiting for us?"

"With your father not here to walk you down the aisle I asked Arthur to choose a knight to fulfill the position. Bedver wanted it, of course, odious little toad that he is, but my personal champion was chosen instead. Unless there is someone you would prefer over him?"

"No. Who could be better except Liam himself." Caelia said walking beside the Queen towards the stairs. "As a child I used to dream I would meet Lancelot, I am sure that I imagined marrying him at one point. I never once thought that he would walk me down the aisle to my new husband."

"You and many other young ones have dreamed of marrying him." Guinevere said. "I do not think anyone else has ever been walked down the aisle by him. That makes you special."

"Any girl marrying one of Arthur's knights is special, my Queen." Lancelot said, joining them and taking Caelia by the arm after kissing the fingers of the Queen. "Gawain is waiting to see you to your husband and, when the music starts, I will see this young lady to hers."

"Thank you, Lancelot." Guinevere said. "Good luck Caelia. He is a good man and will be a good husband."

Caelia nodded and watched the older woman descend the stairs with an elegance she did not think she could ever master.

"She is amazing." She whispered, forgetting for a moment that she was not alone.

"She is many things, amazing is just one of them." The handsome knight replied, offering her his arm again. "Are you ready, young lady?"

"As ready as I can ever be." She replied softly. "Thank you for doing this. I know that you did not have to."

"It is my pleasure. Liam is an old friend. We may not always agree on things, but he was a good man to fight beside so I am happy to stand beside him, and you, now."

"I appreciate that. No girl in all the kingdoms is as well looked after as I am now." She said with a smile as they approached the door to the great hall.

"I suppose not. You are about to become one of us, one of the family of the Knights of the Round Table. That means something." He leaned over and kissed her cheek just as the doors swung open and the wedding music began to play.

"Now, we shall go make it official. I think Liam is done waiting."

She turned her head to look at the man waiting at the end of the aisle. Liam was smiling and she could see his eyes shining, even from the distance of the door. When they began the walk, every head in the room turned to look. Caelia tightened her grip on Lancelot's arm.

"They are staring." She whispered.

"Because you look beautiful." He whispered back. "Liam has not taken his eyes off you."

"Liam."

His name was like a prayer and a shield from the eyes of others at the same time. Watching him watch her approach gave Caelia a confidence that grew with each step. They could build something with the feelings they had for each other and the attraction would only grow with the intimacy they were about to begin sharing as husband and wife. Though it might not be the life she had imagined even a year ago Caelia was coming to believe that things might be even better than she could have dreamed.

"I bring you a bride, Liam, by the grace and with the approval of, not only her father, but of our King, Arthur Pendragon." Lancelot said then turned to face Caelia, but she barely saw him. "Caelia daughter of Sir Hebron, I present you to your intended, Liam of Redbourne. May the gods see fit to bless your marriage."

He stepped away and left Caelia at the alter with Liam right in front of her. He was mesmerizing in a black tunic, decorated with small white gems and round, silver medallions along the bottom. The black contrasted with the white shirt collar just barely visible and the silver of his beard, making him the absolute vision of a fairy tale come to life.

"You look absolutely beautiful, Caelia." Liam whispered in her ear as he took her arm. "Just as I imagine one of the angels of the new Christian faith would look if one came to earth."

"Thank you." She replied, turning with him to face the priest. "You look like the hero of a hundred stories."

"As long as I can be the hero of your story then I shall be a happy man."

"Let us begin that journey now." The priest said to them quietly before addressing the crowd in a deep booming voice.

Caelia could hear the sound of his voice but the words were a distant mumble while she stared into Liam's eyes. Never had the shine of hazel eyes seemed so warm to her as his did that day. She felt so much hope for the future that the duties of the night to come did not seem so daunting.

Before she had time to absorb everything around her; the words of the priest, the attendants that the Queen had volunteered for her in their matching dresses or the men that were standing with Liam, they were directed to face each other.

The vows they exchanged were brief and impersonal, the same she had heard at every wedding, but Liam's eye twitched at the mention of fidelity of heart, soul, and body. She wondered if that was a sign or just an odd coincidence. The priest's next words were the most important she could ever hear, and she blinked, looking at him in order to concentrate.

"Do you take this man as your husband, freely and with the honesty of your heart?"

"I do. Yes." She said, a slow smile spreading across her face again.

"Liam, do you take this woman as your wife, feely and with the honesty of your heart?"

"I do." Liam replied, giving her the slightest wink of his eyes.

Perhaps that was what the twitch had been trying to be? A wink to calm her nerves.

"Then, by the power of the crown and the church, I pronounce you to be husband and wife. Sir Liam, you may kiss your bride."

Caelia looked into Liam's eyes as he wrapped his arms around her, hoping that he could calm her racing heart but there was only excitement.

"Hello wife." He whispered before guiding her closer and lowering his lips to hers.

Caelia had expected a soft, gentle, courtly kiss, but instead there was an explosion of possessive passion pouring from her husband into the kiss they shared. He crushed her to his chest and swept his tongue against hers. Encouraging her to return the affection.

"Hello husband."

Her arms looped around his neck and she gave in to the thrill of the moment. The kiss was met with a roar of applause from the crowd, but it was only a dull buzzing to Caelia who was lost in the kiss. Completely, utterly, blissfully lost.

Chapter 25

They walked back up the aisle, arm in arm, with the attendants following behind them, and the faces that had seemed so daunting before were now smiling as though something had been accomplished by the words they exchanged, that suddenly made her worthy of their peership.

"They seem less intimidating now." Caelia whispered, leaning up to his ear.

"Or, perhaps, you are less intimidated by them." Liam whispered in response with a slight squeeze to her arm. "You are quite formidable in your own way. You do know that?"

"I am nothing of the sort. It is you and the knights that I now call family, that is what changed their perception of me. They would not risk offending you or raising the anger of you and the others." Caelia shook her head. He could not actually think that there was anyone in this place that would be intimidated by her, she was hardly anyone until moments ago.

"I promise you, my dear young wife, that you are who they are in awe of, not me or any other man."

"You flatter me, Sir." She said with a laugh that he joined, pulling her close enough that she could smell the oil he had used to shave. "You should do so again."

"I will, today and as often as I think you need it." Liam teased, giving her another quick kiss. "We would not want you to develop too large of an ego, now would we?"

They had left the hall and were making their way towards the stairs to the courtyard, where they would walk to the jousting tourney field to continue the celebration of the day.

The entire property had been decorated with flags of silver and blue and bushels of wildflowers. There were ribbons and bows lining the paths from the courtyard, inviting exploration beyond the well beaten path to the tourney fields. She wondered if Liam would join her if she asked him to go for a walk instead of heading straight to the fields.

"Looks like Arthur has a good tournament set up to celebrate the wedding." Liam said, with all the excitement of a young boy going to see the matches for the first time. "I, as the groom, am to fight the final match, against the victor of the day. After the games there will be dinner and dancing before bed and tomorrow will be the jousting and another dance. Do you enjoy dancing Caelia?"

Turning her head to face him, leaving thoughts of walking the ribbon lined paths behind, she smiled.

"Yes Liam. Almost as much as I love to read, I love dancing." Caelia said with a smile at his boyish behavior. "Do you? Do you enjoy dancing? Or shall I have to drag you out to the floor with me, hushing protests with a kiss as my mother used to do with my father when I was a little girl?"

"I enjoy it though I cannot say that I am particularly good at it." Liam replied with a teasing smile. "Though I would not object to being coerced onto the dance floor with a kiss or two, my little wife, a girl no longer."

He raised her fingers to his lips for a kiss that was met with a burst of applause from the crowd that had filled the stands they had just arrived at.

"I will not forget that when I ask you to dance with me tonight, husband." Caelia said, ascending the stairs to take the seat she was directed to next to the thrones of the King and Queen.

"That is if the winner of the tournament does not leave our 'old man' too sore for such things." King Arthur said, joining them with Guinevere at his side.

"You are older than I am, majesty." Liam said settling Caelia in her chair then joining the King and Lancelot at the edge of the platform.

"They are not competing?" Caelia leaned over to ask the Queen.

"They will, later in the day. It is customary to let the younger men and those not yet knighted have a chance to prove themselves first." She replied, a slightly bored note to her voice. "I am not usually here all day so if you would like to join me and the ladies after the opening round no one would think less of you."

How could she not want to enjoy the tournament that was being thrown to honor her marriage? That would be rude to the men fighting and the king who had planned the spectacle.

"I think that I will stay and watch, if it is all the same to you. I appreciate the offer to join you, thank you, but I have never seen anything like this before and I think I could learn something from the newer men fighting, some of them look a little closer to my own size."

"Learn something?" One of the older ladies in waiting said. "Do not tell us that you fancy yourself a swordsman? That would be unheard of at court."

The Queen and other ladies laughed, bringing a bright red flush to Caelia's cheek. She hadn't realized that Lucas had stepped onto the platform behind her until he interrupted the laughter.

"Actually, I have seen her with a blade in hand and the new Lady of Redbourne could easily defeat at least three men that are currently on the lists." He said with an undisputable tone.

"You cannot be serious. A girl on the lists of a royal tournament? It could never happen." The woman said snidely.

"I am quite serious. Sir Liam, and the rest of us, are immensely proud of Caelia's abilities and I think the court would be well served if more of you ladies joined her practice." Lucas said with a grin as he looked down at Caelia.

"I would be more than happy to teach you, once I have a sword of my own." She said with a smile.

"What is it that you are offering to teach the court already, my dear?" King Arthur asked, joining the group with Liam at his side. "Something interesting I hope."

"Caelia and Sir Lucas were telling us that the young bride of Sir Liam is an accomplished woman with a sword. I am not sure, but I think they are serious." Guinevere said with an uncertain smile.

Caelia wanted to tell the giggling women that none of them could hope to stand up to an invasion of the city and that, if they were lucky, they would die at the end of a sword if their homes were ever attacked. She wanted to tell them that there was nothing unladylike or unwomanly about being able to defend herself against men, instead she looked the woman beside the Queen directly in the eye as she took Liam's hand and said, as sweetly as she could.

"I am always serious when it comes to aiding my husband, instead of getting in his way when it comes to protecting our home."

She could practically feel the pride pouring from Liam at her words.

"This is not a day to be serious, it is a day for celebration. Come, you must start the tournament Caelia." Arthur said, drawing to the edge of the platform with Liam beside her. "Now pay close attention, tomorrow you will have to choose a champion, that is not Liam, to fight wearing a ribbon of your favor to display his status."

"I have to choose someone else to fight for me?" She looked at Liam who nodded. "That seems so strange when the best man on the field is obviously my husband."

Liam chuckled.

"Thank you for that, darling. I will only be taking the field today and as the events are in our honor it would be rude not to choose someone." He leaned closer to whisper. "You can certainly choose one of the lads from Redbourne and I am certain they would be happy to wear your favor for the day."

"If they make it through then I will certainly choose one of them. Do you think that they will?" She asked in a whisper, watching the men ride into the arena. "There is Gerard and Lucas and Lionel. What about the others?"

"I believe that they had a few things that needed to be done today. Rion has family in the city, Saffir is at his prayers and Emrys is visiting Sir Hector and will join us later for our dinner."

"I look forward to meeting Sir Hector at dinner then." She said with a smile, dropping the white cloth that sent the first two men in the lists charging down the yard. "In the meantime, I intend to fully enjoy everything about today."

"I will enjoy it with you and, hopefully, I will be the victor in my own match and thus impress you further."

"I am sure that you will." Caelia pressed a kiss to his cheek. "Now, how will our friends do?"

The men of Redbourne may have been gone from Camelot's splendor for several years but there was no doubt at the end of the day that there was no lapse in their skill. There was not man among them that lost their matches until they faced each other and then Gerard and Lionel faced one another in the second to last battle of the day.

"Gerard could easily take him, but he seems a bit distracted." Caelia said, on the edge of her seat to watch the two men fight. "Do you think something is wrong? You were together last night, were you not?"

Liam coughed, the cup of wine in his hand almost spilling.

"Pardon? Together? We had a few drinks together to toast today. I do not think that would be bothering him now."

Liam stood, kissing her with a smile on his lips.

"I have to go get ready for the final match. I fight Lancelot and then we will get ready for the banquet and ball." He told her with a smile that Caelia felt did not quite meet his eyes. Something was wrong, and she could not quite figure out what it was. "You and I will share the first dance on the floor with the King and Queen, so I hope you are not shy before a crowd."

"Though if you do fall. I will catch you before Liam has a chance and thus secure myself the second dance of the night." Lancelot said, joining Liam at the bottom of the stairs. "A good knight is always prepared to help a lady in need."

"I am sure that Caelia will not be in need of you so you should concentrate on other things, other people, who might need you." Liam said gruffly, stalking towards the tents where the men had been changing into their armor.

Lancelot looked at Caelia "Do not let his mood ruin the day for you. This rivalry goes back a long way. It has nothing to do with you."

Chapter 26

Liam wanted to drive his fist through the smug smiling face of Lancelot. He had spent the greater part of dinner trying to flirt with Caelia. This was after the match that Liam had won fairly and after a solid fight from both parties, which Lancelot then implied was a deliberate loss.

"Who could deny any man the victory on the day of his wedding?"

"The man who tries would be a fool if he thinks that I could not put him to his back any day of the year." Liam had growled, face to face with the favored knight. "I would advise that you do not forget that. Stay away from what is mine."

"Caelia or Gerard, Liam?" Lancelot hissed, passing him to join the king on the platform to applaud the victor.

If he could have gotten away with it, Liam would have driven the sword in his hand through the smug bastard's throat, but he had to play nice for the king and for his bride. How would he have explained his rage to Caelia?

He turned his head and saw that Gerard was at the gate to the field, his impressive arms across his chest while wearing a simple linen tunic that made him look formidable as a fighter and as rugged as a blacksmith could possibly look. Had he seen that exchange? Had he talked to Lancelot after he had left his room that morning? Is that what caused the cocky attitude?

Did Lancelot think he had won some unspoken contest simply because of the vows made that morning? Damn him to hell if he did.

Caelia rushed down the stairs of the podium, ignoring the decorum of the court when she threw her arms around his neck.

"You were wonderful. Like a storybook hero, but even better. Liam, I am amazed. I have never seen anything like that. Truly, the hero of the day."

He had been about to thank her for her praise, with some modest comment about his opponent, when she kissed him. The crowd around them roared and Arthur clapped his hands above them.

"I am glad that you enjoyed the show. It was not my best, though I promise the one at Redbourne at summer's end will be much better. Maybe I will match against Gerard for that one. What do you think?"

"I think that, no matter who you are facing, you will win because you are the very best." She took his hand with a smile. "Come, you need a bath before we dine with the court."

"No wise man argues with his wife, especially when she is as clever and beautiful as you are." Liam said, loving how she smiled when he winked at her.

So much about her was easy to love and he could feel himself falling. Their hearts would grow together as the intimacy of their lives built a rhythm. Just as a swordsman learned his craft from his losses as much as his victories, they would learn about each other. From fights and failures as well the moments of pleasure and bliss that they would share Liam was certain that Caelia would teach him as much as he would teach her.

"We will see you both at supper then." Arthur said with a laugh echoed by the entire platform though Liam noticed it was not joined by Ger who stood, arms still crossed, staring blankly at him while he walked towards the palace with his wife on his arm.

"At supper, your majesty." Liam replied with a small bow of his head.

He was surprised that Caelia was silent the entire walk, up until the moment that they closed the door to their suite.

"You were amazing against Lancelot." She said, turning to throw her arms around his neck. "I have never seen anything like that in my life. You could have easily killed him. I know it."

"Well, perhaps. Lancelot is incredibly good. There is no lie in the reputation of his skill, but duels were never his strong point. I would not kill him without great need and certainly not on our wedding day, not matter how much the man annoys me."

"If he annoys you then we will not talk about him." Caelia said with a smile. "You do truly need a bath if we are to dine with the king. You have a coat of dust on your face and I am certain that you are covered in sweat underneath all that armor."

Her hand was caressing his face while she talked and Liam could not stop searching her face for a trick or lie in her affection and eagerness, but she was as honest as she was lovely. She was his wife in all ways but one, for now.

He watched her enter the bathroom and smiled when she turned to face him.

"I think that the Queen must have known how dirty you boys get when you play with swords. She has already commanded a hot bath prepared for you. Come and enjoy it, you need to get clean."

"Would you help me?" He asked, stepping into the warm room, trying not to laugh when he found it filled with warm candlelight, even though it was the afternoon. "I think the Queen is intent upon melting us both."

"I think it is beautiful and romantic." Caelia said, turning to test the temperature of the water.

While she was turned away from him Liam started to unfasten the buckles of his armor, realizing that he had forgotten to have a squire undo the ones on his back he groaned. Was she going to be comfortable with this?

"Erm...Caelia? I need your help to undress. The buckles on my back are out of my reach. Can you unfasten them?"

She turned to look at him and Liam's breath caught in his chest at her loveliness. The light of the candles reflecting on the water gave her an unearthly glow and blood rushed through his veins. She was his wife now and he could, was expected to, seduce her, make love to her, and enrapture her completely. Looking at her in the light blue wedding dress, with her hair pulled off her face and still pouring over her shoulders, there was nothing else he wanted to do.

"I can help you with that." She replied, smoothing her dress before she walked towards him. "I can help you with a great many things if you will tell me what you need." She looked up at him, her eyes asking for him to tell her everything that he wanted from her. He wondered, briefly, what other men had been in her life before him. It did not matter, not really, because he was going to be the last. He would also be the first in one, important, way.

"I will guide you through everything that you need to know, Caelia." He said, taking her hand. "Undo the buckles, please, and help me out of this armor. I cannot teach you what you want to know while wearing it."

"You will teach me though? Carefully?" She asked, stepping behind him.

He could hear the unspoken question hiding in the one she gave voice to and Liam tried to temper his desire so that he did not move too fast, did not frighten her with the evidence of his passion. This should be beautiful for them both. Their first time together and her very first time, was a delicate thing, He had to make sure that she enjoyed it or she would not want more and he wanted her to be as passionate about their bed as she was about her swordplay.

"I will be a tender teacher, Caelia." His voice was a soft, deep rumble. "This is not something you need to fear, not with me."

He could barely feel her touch as Caelia unfastened the buckles but once she lifted the metal away Liam could feel the touch of her hand on his back. He didn't want to scare her. She was as timid as a deer and, to her, he might as well be a lion.

"Just set it on the ground. A squire will come later to deal with it." Liam said, his voice calm while his heart raced in his chest. The way her hand was teasing across his back would have been suggestive with a more experienced woman, but Liam suspected that his sweet young bride was as curious about him as she was about every new thing that she came across.

"There is an easier way to explore, if that is your wish." He said, turning around to catch her wrist.

"There is?" She asked with a smile that he thought looked eager, excited. "What do you have in mind?"

He pulled his shirt over his head and tossed it to the floor. He could not help the smile that came to his lips when she stared at his bare chest. Her eyes were wide and more than once Caelia raised a hand as though she wanted to touch him.

"You can." He took her hand and placed it over his heart. "I am yours to touch though it might be easier in the water. Will you help me again?"

She paused, he could see her thinking, trying to decide what she wanted to do. He was going to say something more, but a light came to her eyes, a surety.

"Help me out of this dress? It cannot be soaked with bathwater when we go back downstairs."

His entire body relaxed at her words.

She wanted to explore the budding sexual tension between them as well. His brain rushed back to the day, trying to think of how much wine Guinevere had given to Caelia under the heat of the sun.

"How much has my little wife had to drink today?" He asked, trying to sound casual while he slowly unfastened the lacing at the back of the dress. The soft material was as blue as the morning sky and made Caelia look unearthly in her loveliness. "I would not want you to make any decisions that you are not ready for. I have no expectation here."

He may not have an expectation but when she turned to look at him, pushing the dress from her shoulders and onto the floor, revealing the simple, low cut bodice that barely contained the surprisingly lush curves of her breast Liam had hope. Hope that she meant what she was implying, that she was ready for this.

"I am well aware of what I am suggesting, what I am inviting, Liam. I also know how to handle a few glasses of wine in the heat of early summer." Caelia said, setting the dress over the edge of the bed across the room before coming back to face him, her hands resting on her hips. "Are you my father to chastise me or my husband who wants to join with his wife? I know it is the first time, but I had hoped it might be something special and not made awkward by anything outside this moment."

Liam had been removing his belt when she had crossed the room with the dress, now he snapped the leather between his hands, making her jump and bringing her eyes swiftly up to his.

"I can promise you, little wife, that I have no intention of replacing your father."

He closed the space between them with only a few steps, encircled her waist and drew her against his bare chest before she had time to reply.

"No intention at all." He growled before crushing her lips beneath his own in a kiss that lacked any trace of courtly etiquette or knightly manners.

Chapter 27

Liam's reaction to her question shocked and thrilled Caelia.

While she appreciated the courtly manners and knightly honor, she wanted passion from her husband, not simply duty and responsibility.

"You surprise me, Liam. I had not expected...this." She said, gasping for breath once he broke the kiss to unfasten her shift and guided her hands to the laces of his breeches.

"You did not expect me to want you? Caelia? Have I ever given you a reason to think otherwise?" Liam replied, his breath hot on her neck as he melted her knees with hot kisses and drags of his teeth against her skin.

"You said you liked the dress, not the woman in it. I thought knights were all about honor and chivalry." She whispered in reply, trying not to stare down at what had sprung free when she had unlaced his breeches. "The poems and bards never mention passion."

She heard him chuckle before he kissed her neck, the soft hair of his beard brushing her beating pulse and sending a shiver down her spine.

"Forget the damned bards Caelia." He straightened and stared down into her eyes, brushing the strand of hair that had fallen into her eyes to tuck behind her ears. "Open your eyes to the real world. Knights, for good or bad, are men, real men. We are just as passionate, maybe more, than any other man in the world."

Caelia nodded, feeling a little like a student standing before a teacher, though she had never been undressed or wanted to be undressed before one of her teachers.

"If that is so, that knights are like just like other men, then what do knights do when their wife stands before them? When she is aching to know how a simple girl from the country can please one of the greatest knights in all the kingdoms?"

"You are anything but simple my dear." Liam said, kicking off his boots and leading her towards the tub. "To answer your question, I cannot speak for other men. I, however, intend to kiss my wife, embrace her as a husband should and do what I can to wipe all thoughts of poetry from her beautiful mind for a time."

She was going to protest. Love was poetic and beautiful and making love should be the same, but he gave her no chance. His mouth was back on hers before she could speak. Pressing, playing, possessively demanding a response that her body returned instinctively. She had kissed boys before, on a dare or after a dance, none of those could compare to this. Even the kiss of their ceremony had not left her breathless with a gnawing hunger like this did.

"Poetry? What poetry?" She whispered, wrapping her arms around his neck, and surrendering to the kiss, to him. "Show me."

"As you wish." Liam murmured in her ear.

His hands slid, slowly, up her arms until they reached the sleeves of her delicate linen shift.

"While this is lovely, and it truly is, and it makes you look more delectable than anything I have seen before in my life I want to take it off you. I want to see you bare and beautiful before me. Are you ready for that? For me?"

"I have waited all my life to be ready." Caelia said, blushing so deeply that she had to hide her face in Liam's chest.

For all the hopes and dreams of romance there had been nothing that prepared her for the real thing, for hearing loving words of admiration from a wonderful man. Was she truly ready to do her wifely duty? Despite the flood of warmth pooling between her thighs and the thundering of her heart she was unsteady in her decision.

His fingertips trailed softly up and down her spine, each sweep moving the dress further off her body and exposing more skin to the air warmed by the hot bath and candles.

"Do I embarrass you, Caelia?" Liam's voice was quiet and calm in her ear, the brush of his beard in her hair making her lean her head towards the soothing sound. "I know that I am not a dashing young hero, fresh from the glory of the battlefield, but I can give you what you need. My experience, my past, is a blessing. Let me show you? That is, if you have any desire for me at all?"

This beautiful man thought she was ashamed that he desired her? That he might not be what she wanted because of his age and wife that had died years before?

"Liam, dear husband. I blush for myself, for the foolish daydreams of a child that wither at the sound of your voice and fade to shadows with your slightest touch."

"I do not understand. You are embarrassed? By me but not of me?"

"That I thought I knew what love and desire were. I thought I was so worldly and clever, from all my reading. When you speak though, I realize that I know nothing, absolutely nothing. I also see that I want to learn."

His eyes locked with hers, calm and understanding, but with a fire burning in them. He nodded slowly.

"Let the lessons begin then, my dear."

She closed her eyes and stilled in his hands which were tugging the final resisting fabric down and away from her until she felt it fall at her feet. She was completely bare before a man, her husband.

Caelia stood as still as a statue, willing herself to open her eyes and see what Liam's face was going to tell her. Would he be bored? Lustful? Or simply indifferent to her nudity as a man who had been married and surely had lovers since? It was a torture either way, knowing or not. Just as she had steeled herself to open her eyes, she heard the soft sound of fabric falling to the floor. He had removed his breeches, matching her vulnerability with his own.

"Dear gods." She heard him mutter, making her raise her arms from her sides to try and hide herself while she lowered her chin to face the ground so she could force her eyes to open.

"Please. Do not do that. Let me look at you. Dear heavens, let me look at you."

Caelia slowly raised her eyes from the floor. Liam was standing only a few feet away, his entire body tense and focused solely on her. One part in particular was obviously begging for her attention. His shaft was hard and thick with the glistening drop of moisture at the tip catching her attention. Without thinking she licked her lips which brought a groan from her husband and his hand covered the head her eyes had been locked on.

"Do not hide it from me. I want to...learn." She said, her eyes darting up to his where her breath caught at what she saw.

He was staring at her, his eyes scanning every inch of her exposed body. He was drinking her in, every part of her. When he started to walk around her, she turned her head to follow his steps. It was unnerving that he was so silent, and she was just about to break the agonizing quiet when she felt the brush of his fingertip against the base of her spine.

"The lessons are about to begin, Caelia." His deep voice filled her ear when he finished circling her, leaving his hand on her bare hip. When he was back to standing in front of her, towering over her with his body pressing close, he cupped her chin and raised it until she was looking right into his eyes. "I am going to teach you how a man uses his body to love his wife and how a woman can use hers to return that love. I will not hurt you, asking simply for your trust and that you will tell me, honestly, if something pleases you or not, if it frightens you or not. Even if you think that it is what I want, you must tell me the truth. Do you understand this lesson?"

Caelia pressed her lips together, aching to kiss him or to touch him but that was not yet permitted if she guessed right by his tone.

"I understand, Sir." She said. The breathy sound of her voice was almost unrecognizable to her and she could tell by the faint smirk that Liam was just as surprised by it as she was.

"The next lesson is to learn to accept my compliments and enjoy that I mean them entirely. You are not to question them, in public or our bedchamber."

"But I..."

"Shh." He pressed the thumb that had gripped her chin against her lips. "No arguing a compliment. When I tell you that you look as beautiful as a goddess and twice as divine because I am yours and you are mine, you will believe it and, I hope, thank me for them."

"Like in court?" She asked, darting her tongue out to flick against his tongue.

"As in, when I have buried myself in you, spent myself within you, whether to bring a child or simply satisfy our own desires and I tell you that I have never seen anything, anyone, so stunningly beautiful. I hope that you will believe and understand me well enough to thank me for them."

She was shocked into silence. The firm set of his jaw, coupled with the softness of his touch while his hands caressed and explored her torso, left her doubtless to the sincerity of his words and the authority of the command.

"You really mean that? Thank you." Caelia bowed her head slightly, the overwhelming call to submit to the man before her, in this act at least, flooded her. She had been proud of her wildness, her stubborn, unbending independence, but Liam changed that.

Opening her mouth to ask for more, Caelia gasped when the rough fingertips that danced across her ribs. They were just below the curve of her breast without actually touching the heavy, aching flesh. Her body was burning for his touch, for the more intimate connection.

"Liam? Please?" She whispered.

"Touch me, Caelia. I am as much yours as you are mine." He said, an edge to his voice while he took her hand and placed it on his stomach. Her fingers crept up until they brushed the short, soft hair on his chest, letting it caress her fingers until her palm felt the thundering of his heart.

He was as excited as she was, even if there was no outward sign of it.

"Touch you here?" She asked, looking up at him before she moved her hand lower, following the trail of dark curls down, over his defined abs that reminded her of the Roman armor that Arthur kept on the wall in a hallway.

"Lower, sweetheart." He replied, his body tensing under her hand. "A little bit lower."

Was that bad? She could hardly tell except that his shaft was still hard and pulsing as her hand neared his hip.

"Lower? Here?" She asked, trying not to smile when his eyes closed with pleasure when she took his hard length into her timid grasp.

When she pulled her hand in a long stroke from his base up to the tip Liam groaned.

"Just there. Like that." He said, his eyes closed for another moment. "Just like that."

The surge of pride that she felt was dashed from her mind when his hand cupped her breast, kneading the flesh and sending a new sensation of pleasure.

"Oh. Oh Liam." She gasped, letting her head fall back to give him more access to her while she enjoyed the response of his body to her touch.

One of his hands continued its play while the other, on her hip, drew her closer against him. It made her stroke a little less smooth but gave him the chance to put his lips on her neck.

"I am going to make you weep with pleasure, just for me." He growled, withdrawing from her hand to bend and scoop her into his arms.

"But your bath?" Caelia laughed once he had deposited her on the plush bed.

"Damn the bath. I will have it cold if I must. This, you, us, is more important."

Chapter 28

Liam was struggling for control that he was quickly losing. Caelia was even more divine undressed than he had imagined. She was so light that, were she not naked and causing his cock to throb with her innocent sensuality, he would have thought that he was carrying nothing more than a bundle of blankets. Instead he had his new wife, so young and gorgeous that he knew he did not deserve her at his age.

He could barely recall the last time he had been with a virgin that aside from his first wife. There had been others since her death but not even one that meant anything to him. No woman had touched his heart like the one in his arms. Her absolute trust in him was a gift that he would treasure for the rest of his life. There would be no betrayals now that the vows were said. No more sordid nights or dreams of the past. He would be a model husband and model knight. He would be what she deserved.

"Now, you lay there a moment." He said, starting to turn away but stopping when she grabbed his hand. "Scared? Second thoughts?"

"No. I just want you to stay with me. Come to bed with me. That is what we are doing, what we are going to do, is it not?"

"Yes, Caelia." He smiled, stroking her cheek. "I just want to do one thing first and then I am all yours. I promise." He smiled and kissed the palm of her hand. "I want to make sure that no one is going to disturb us."

He could feel her watching him while he walked to lock the door and quickly splashed some of the bathwater in his face and a few other places that he wanted clean for her.

Returning to the bedside he smiled before getting in beside her.

"Now, where were we, my lovely bride?" He chuckled, pulling her close so they were in the middle of the great bed.

"Somewhere around here, was it not." He lowered his head to kiss her lips and then, slowly gauging her reaction, he took her breast to his mouth. The soft flesh flushed under his attention and, gods help him, she moaned with pleasure for the first time, for him.

The things that sound made him want to do, were too brutal and barbaric for the first time he made love to Caelia, but he would ensure that she felt his claim, nonetheless. Body and soul, then, eventually, her heart.

The loosened strands of her hair were spread across the stark white of the pillow with all the splendor of a star in the midnight sky. The dark locks felt like silk between his fingers, but it was her skin, that he could not help touching. Every new inch that he explored was more exquisite than the last. Soft hollows and curves that fit the palm of his hand as though she had been cut from the heavens, just for him.

"You are so beautiful Caelia. Utterly stunning." He said, using the hand that he had been leaning on to cup her face so he could lean in to kiss the sweet petals of her lips. "I am stunned each time I open my eyes and see that you are still here with me and I am not dreaming."

"I feel the same surprise, Liam." She murmured against his lips. "The stories, the poetry, they cannot compare to your kiss."

"There are many more kinds of kisses you know." Liam said, tapping her nose and then kissing her again, sweeping his tongue into her mouth. She moaned beautifully again, and he knew that he had to take the next step. How would she sound in moments filled with pleasure? How would she sound as she came apart in his arms?

"If you think a kiss is incomparable, let me show you a whole new meaning of the word." Liam said with a smile. She nodded as he moved his head lower to place kisses on her stomach and then her hips before dragging his tongue along the crease of her thighs. "Anything you feel like doing, touching, or tasting, do so. I would very much like to see the sensual side of you, without direction." He said before using a hand to gently open her thighs. He had managed to turn his entire body on the bed. He could have rested his head on her knees now and she could rest her head on his.

"What are you going to do?" She asked, her voice shaking just a little.

"I am going to show you one of the most beautiful, exquisite kisses that a man can give a woman. I want you to relax, feel everything and be completely free to respond or soak in every sensation that I am going to give you. Understand?"

She nodded, moving her hand slowly up his thigh, closer to his hip. The sensation was nearly enough to make him ask for her to touch him, take his length in her small but undoubtably strong hands, but he kept his focus on what he was going to give to her. The feeling of complete sexual release coupled with the safety of knowing that he would be there for her no matter what. They were bound by the laws of the old gods and the new Christian one that had come to the land and that was what was needed for the court of Camelot, but in his heart Liam knew there was more to it than that. Just as he knew that he needed Ger in his life the knight knew that he needed Caelia just as much. Together they would build something strong, unshakeable, and the world would be as it should.

"Do not worry about anything, just give in to whatever you feel. I have you, you are safe." Liam said quietly before kissing her delicately at the top of the curls between her legs, taking his time, inhaling the sweet scent of her feminine core. "You smell like heaven."

"Do men like that? The smell of women?" She asked, making him chuckle as he nuzzled between her folds.

"Oh yes. Men, most that I know are utterly intoxicated by this. It makes us want to do things, things that would make you blush if I were to say. Let me show you instead."

His fingers moved through the dark hair of her mound, surprised to find heated moisture waiting for him. She was already aroused, by him.

He had worried that her fascination for poetic heroes and that damned Lancelot, would make this hard. For how did a man make love to a woman infatuated with someone else? How could he win her heart when she wanted to be in the arms of another?

The discovery that she wanted this, wanted him, was a weight of concern lifted from his mind and freed him to act, unguardedly, with all the passion he felt in the moment.

Suddenly he was aware of something more than Caelia's arousal at his fingertips, her curiosity near his waist.

He wanted to stop and watch her as she began to explore him, but if he did, she might stop and the touch of her hand on his shaft was tantalizingly tender. To encourage her exploration instead of hindering it, Liam used his finger to slowly circle her entrance and then dip the tip of his finger between her lips. He heard her gasp then felt the slow exhale of her breath. Her mouth was so close to his tip, if he moved much, they might connect. As much as he wanted that, to feel her lips wrapped around him, if he moved to far too fast it could scare her from continuing.

It took all his concentration to focus on his actions, gently playing her with his fingers, opening her as carefully as he could. Soon enough he would not have to be shy with his wife, she would soon not only accept their intimacy but crave it enough to initiate it herself.

With an aching slowness he began to kiss, to lick, to utterly devour Caelia. He wanted to drag it out so that she felt everything, every single sensation. There was only one chance to experience erotic pleasure for the first time and he wanted it to be perfect for her.

She must have enjoyed his touch because the hand that had been stroking him tightened its grip mid stroke.

"It is alright. Give in to it, Caelia. Just let go." He eased her from her side to her back and began to increase his pace. When she began to buck her hips against his mouth Liam paused. He moved to kneel between her legs and gripped her hips.

"Oh yes. Just like that." Caelia moaned, the hands that had been exploring his waist now gripped his hair tight. "Oh, Liam."

Hand and mouth worked together to bring her further, to bring her closer to the readiness for the final moment, for the true joining that would make the marriage unbreakable.

"You are so close to being ready, my sweet." He licked between the folds of her core with a hungry growl. She tasted like the sweet summer wine, sweetened with honeycomb, and he wanted to drown in her. "So very sweet."

The flick of his tongue against her bud of nerves caused her back to arch and her hands to grip the sheets as cried out. He licked again, grazed it with his teeth and sucked on it as though his life depended on her pleasure.

When her hands flailed again, he grabbed them, one at a time, to hold her slender wrists between his fingers.

"Shh. Hold on to that thought." He said, moving her arms with him as he inched back up her body, worshiping her body with his mouth. Her skin was delicious, she was delicious, and soon he had his shaft resting between her thighs with her hands pinned above her head.

The position was not only advantageous because it held her still, but also because it positioned her beautiful breasts right at the level of his lips. Like berries atop the frozen cream desserts that would be served that night, Caelia's nipples made his mouth water. When he took one in his mouth her cry had to be muffled with the hand that had remained playing in the dark hair covering her mound.

"No too loud, not now when everyone is awake in their rooms. You should feel free to make all the sound you like once we are not expected as guests of honor and a banquet thrown by the king." He said, chuckled at her enthusiasm while it sent a surge of fresh lust through him at the thought of her crying out passionately beneath him.

When he kissed her again, letting go of her wrists Liam thrilled when she wrapped her arms around his shoulders and held him close. He buried his face in her neck, kissing with a few bites to the lobe of her ear, but when Caelia raised her hips to grind against his erection he paused, lifting his head to stair down into her beautiful eyes.

"Caelia?" He asked, a rough husk to his voice.

"I am ready Liam, please? Please?" She begged, looking up at him with such tender affection that he could not help wanting to give her anything and everything she could ever ask of him.

"As you wish, Caelia." He said softly, kissing her gently. "It may hurt, though that is not my intention, there is little that I can do against that. I will be gentle for I would never want to hurt you."

"I know you would never, not on purpose." She whispered with just a trace of fear, he hoped for the last time.

His concentration was now focused solely on the woman beneath him. He could not make a mistake with this moment as it would set the tone of their bedding for the foreseeable future.

It had to go well.

Carefully, pausing to kiss her lips, her beautiful breasts, and the smooth white of her inner thighs as he moved Liam altered Caelia's position and his own to tease her entrance with his tip. He was propped above her, his hands firmly planted on the bed beside her shoulders, watching her face for signs of panic or the need for him to stop. The trust in her eyes was incredible and more than he could have hoped for.

He was slow and careful, as gentle as a man in lustful need for a woman, his woman, could be. When the moment came, when he had to claim her maidenhead, he lowered his head to capture the whimper of discomfort from her lips. He stilled when tears sprung to her eyes, not withdrawing but waiting for her to grow used to him.

"Are you alright?" He murmured, catching her tears with his kiss. "I promise it gets better. Move with me, allow me to show you?" Instructing her as his body moved within hers.

"Slowly." She said beginning to raise her hips, moving her legs to accommodate the movement that was now theirs not just his. "Show me everything, Liam."

That was all he needed to hear from her to make him smile and do just as she asked.

Chapter 29

Caelia had never felt so amazing as she did laying naked in Liam's arms. He was right, as she was beginning to learn he usually was, it had become amazing even if there were some parts that were uncomfortable. His attention to her body, to her needs, had been more tender and erotic than she had ever allowed herself to dream.

He had made her feel like a goddess and now that they were laying in each other's arms Caelia felt less divine and more cherished. They would be happy for years to come and soon enough he would see her as a warrior as well as a wife. She felt safe and warm with the hair of his chest tickling her back with each breath and the softness of his beard on her neck and shoulder. Their legs were threaded together, and her arms were crossed over his arm around her waist. Even though it was the middle of the afternoon she could have slept for hours. The king and court would not wait, which meant that it was time to get dressed again.

"Do you think anyone would miss us if we stayed in bed all day?" She asked, looking over her shoulder at him with a smile.

"As the guests of honor tonight I think it would be a little conspicuous if we did not make an appearance." Liam chuckled, the vibration flowing through her before he rose, slowly, from the bed.

"How late do we need to stay at the ball tonight?" She asked, picking up her dress from the floor and stepping back into it. "Can you help with the laces or should I call for Lynn?"

"I can still remember how to lace up a dress." He chuckled, walking towards her in all his naked glory.

Caelia was mesmerized by the way he moved, with the ease of a hunting hound returning from a winning chase. Though he was not as bulky as Gerard or tall as Lancelot every inch of him practically hummed with power that had nothing to do with a crown or title.

"And how to bathe quickly?" She could not help but to tease when he kissed her shoulder.

"To answer your question about tonight; we will stay until we are excused by the King. We will eat. We will enjoy, or try to enjoy, the company of the courtiers and then we will dance. You will not be short of partners throughout the night. That does not mean that you must accept every invitation to the floor though." He said, climbing into the tub with a slight shiver.

"Is the water cold? Or does the thought of a night of dancing send shivers down your spine."

"Perhaps a little of both?"

"Perhaps." He laughed, beginning to wash, while Caelia sat to touch up her hair so that it was less obvious what they had been doing.

She smiled at his reflection in the mirror, happy in the moment of domesticity. Soon, times like this would be their everyday life. They would build so much together, a family and more, together.

"Do you see my shirt?" Liam asked her, looking around from where he had sat on the bed after drying off. "I do not think Arthur would appreciate my coming to dinner without it."

"Well, I would not mind that." Caelia said, getting up to retrieve his silken shirt from the floor at the foot of the bed just out of his side. "Though I cannot say I feel like fighting off every woman in Camelot if they saw how attractive my husband is without his clothes."

When she handed him the shirt, he caught her wrist and, to her surprise, pressed a kiss to her pulse.

"As much as I would enjoy that sight, you with a sword against the women of court, I would rather keep such skills a secret for myself. I have no intention of letting those vapid cats indulge any fantasies with or without my clothing."

He stared at her with such honesty and his voice was so certain that Caelia could not find an ounce of doubt that he meant his words.

"Unless you intend to take me back into that bed this instant we should go." She said, pulling him to his feet and handing him the formal jacket that he had worn for the ceremony. "I want to dance with my husband at the ball before we dance in bed again."

"I promise that I will dance with you until your head spins." Liam told her, spinning her towards the door and making Caelia feel as though they were already on the dancefloor.

"For that to happen all I have to do is look into your eyes."

Caelia took his arm and they headed down to the grand dining hall where it seemed that everyone was waiting for them to arrive. Men and women of all ages approached to greet Liam, Caelia's head was swimming when she tried to keep track of all the names. There was no way she could remember them after one meeting.

"You are well liked here." She said in Liam's ear while they walked towards the table where Arthur and Guinevere were waiting for them. "We are sitting with them? I thought we would be with the others from Redbourne. I would feel more comfortable."

"Nothing to worry about. Lionel and Ger are with us." He pointed to where the steward sat at the table with a young couple between him and the surly Gerard. "The others are likely with their friends they have not seen in some time and will save us seats for when the dancing begins. The dais will be crowded with those seeking words with the King or the Queen."

The presence of Gerard was not the comfort for her that Liam was assuming, but Lionel was friendly and warm towards her so that would be a little easier. The couple between the knights turned their heads in unison to stare at her after Gerard whispered in the man's ear and Caelia shivered.

"Who is that, with Lionel and Gerard?" She asked, climbing the steps behind her husband.

"Those two? Oh, they are the royal twins of Gore. Prince Banning and his sister Elin." Liam said, bowing to the King and Queen while Caelia curtsied. "Let me introduce you."

Sitting between Lionel and Liam Caelia smiled at the twins and Ger, who surprised her with a smile and a raised glass. Elin, as tall as the men around her was every inch a princess in her fine gown of dark red, had deep brown eyes and sunny blonde hair that was braided and twisted in an intricate pattern around her head. Her brother had slightly darker hair and flashing green eyes. He was dressed in a black shirt that did nothing to hide the broadness of his shoulders or the muscles of his arms. He would have been hard to beat on the tourney field, she thought, if he had built that form wielding a sword.

"Here she is. The little woman who is to help our Liam settle down and become a respectable man. A farmer instead of a fighter. A husband instead of a hero."

"Sir Gerard that is simply untrue." Caelia started before the Princess took over the rebuttal.

"Of course, it is untrue. Liam will always be a fighter and a hero to all the kingdom. I think if any of you have earned some peace it would be our silver haired knight." She flashed a smile at Liam and then Caelia. "Just do not make it too peaceful for him. He likes a challenge."

"Peace comes with its own challenges, as every woman knows." Caelia said, uncertain if the other woman was being friendly to her or flirting with her husband. "I am sure that we will find ways to keep each other quite occupied."

"Indeed, Redbourne is in need of many of the softer workings of a woman's touch." Lionel said, reaching behind Caelia to tap Liam's shoulder and get his attention from the story Arthur was telling.

"What's that? Redbourne? Yes, I think even the most basic improvements that Caelia and I have in mind will keep us busy. Of course, there is the knightly training of some younger royals that the king was just mentioning to me that will be quite occupying as well. Perhaps you will come and join us there, Banning?"

"Oh, that sounds delightful." Elin said, turning from Caelia to her brother. "You should. Your sword skills need touching up. If I can defeat you then it is certain that a French knight would be able to do the same. I should join you there and keep young Caelia from going mad in the company of all you men."

Her words sent a small thrill through Caelia.

"You are accustomed to sword training?" She asked, unable to hide the eagerness in her voice despite Gerard's frown. "More than the relief from the men I could use someone to train against and to help me convince Sir Gerard to make me a properly balanced sword."

"Elin was the only one her brother could train with for years." Liam said, putting a hand on Caelia's shoulder with a slight squeeze that she hoped was one of support and not trying to quiet her. "His older brother, the Crown Prince Eric, is ten years their senior and thus much too dangerous while they were children."

"While that is true, Sir Liam." The prince said, speaking for the first time with a deeper voice than Caelia had expected. "Now she trains with me and the others simply to annoy my father and push her agenda that all women should wield a blade with some skill."

"It is only logical." Both women said at once, causing the four men, even Gerard to laugh.

Elin looked at Caelia and reached across Lionel's lap to take her hand.

"I adore my training though few or none of the women here at court find it appropriate. I would enjoy testing your skills against my own when chance allows."

"It would be my honor Princess." Caelia gave a small bow. "Though I fear I am a touch rusty. Other than a brief skirmish in our training yard at Redbourne against Liam only a few days ago I have not had the chance to pick up a blade in months."

"You crossed swords with Liam?" Banning asked with a grin, leaning back towards Gerard. "You did not mention that when describing her decent upon the estate. Worried you will lose your sparring partner Ger?"

The twins, Lionel and Liam all laughed but Caelia noticed that Gerard's eyes were on her and there was no laughter in them.

Moments later the food was brought. As everyone began to eat Caelia looked at Liam and touched her head to his shoulder to bring his attention to her.

"What can I do for you, little wife?" He asked, picking a piece of carrot from their plate to place in her mouth before she could answer the question. "More wine?"

"Yes, please." She said after savoring the vegetable that had never been a favorite but suddenly tasted much better coming from Liam. "Tell me about the twins and Gerard? I have not seen him so friendly and happy since we arrived as he is in their company."

"Banning trained with us, though in the younger class, so Ger and I have known him for years. Elin, we met, I think, the day before we were knighted. Banning had not said a word about her the entire time."

"Of course not. I did not need the entire barracks acting like fools and trying to marry my sister." Banning called over from his seat. "I could barely stand the lot of you during training. I had no desire to see you at my home with her."

"Maybe not then but I have a feeling, now that I am married, perhaps Ger will finally act on whatever he has been putting into those letters to her for the past ten years." Liam said, raising his cup to the princess and the other knight. "About time too."

"I suppose, perhaps it is. What do you say Banning?" Gerard asked.

Caelia watched him stare down the Prince who had been his friend for years, marveling at his boldness and wondering why he did not just ask the Princess herself, who sat blushing with her eyes in her lap.

"I say, do what makes you happy Ger." Banning replied with a shake of his head, that brought his green eyes to meet Caelia's with a quick flash of joy. "If Liam is happy then it is time that we all were."

Chapter 30

The meal was long, and the food was rich. Caelia could not remember the last time she had eaten food so rich accompanied with amazing wine, more laughter, and stories about the knights that she had never heard before.

Banning and Elin were great company and, with their influence she was beginning to see why Liam and the others cared so much about Gerard. The trio that had trained together, Liam, Gerard and Banning were constantly telling stories, teasing the others, and bringing laughter to the entire table. The King and Queen even joined in the fun until the musicians began to tune their instruments.

"Seems like the dancing is about to begin." King Arthur said, rising to his feet and offering his hand to the Queen. "You newlyweds shall join us on the floor to open the dancing before the rest of the court is invited. I hope you have not forgotten how to dance Liam?"

"I think you will find me as smooth on my feet as I have always been. I will do my absolute best to not show you up in front of the court." Liam laughed and helped Caelia to her feet.

"I can dance too." She whispered, keeping a serenely excited smile on her face while they followed the others to the dance floor. "It is like a duel, without the weapons."

"Caelia." Liam said, taking the proper position. "You have weapons you do not even realize."

"Do I really? I could swear I stand defenceless before you." She replied, stilling when his hands took hold of her. "Utterly powerless."

The music began, and Caelia was swept away by Liam into a night she could never forget. They were floating, alone in the room, no one else existed as they moved around the dance floor. She became vaguely aware that the king and Queen were talking, it was not to Liam so there must be others dancing now. It did not matter. All her concentration was on the man holding her in his arms.

The day they had met, when he had come to bring her to Redbourne, she had though him to be too serious and too old for her to ever fall in love with. Her only hope had been to find some level of mutual respect. That was out of the question now. She was falling deeply in love with her husband and wanted him to fall in love with her right back.

Before she could believe it, the song was over, and it was King Arthur himself that tapped Liam on the shoulder.

"Allow me this dance? Before your wife is crowded with offers from men who cannot dance as well as we can." He said with a smile Caelia though was supposed to charm her but paled in comparison to Liam's laughter in response.

"My wife is still her own woman, majesty. You will have to ask the lady Caelia herself. I did promise that I would dance her off her feet, but I will let you have a chance to impress her before I do that." Liam said, nodding his head to Caelia.

She was surprised and impressed that he gave her the choice. When the king had requested her to dance, she had been certain that he would have at least encouraged her to give in to the request.

Arthur looked at her, seeming to be puzzled that she had not immediately accepted his invitation.

"Lady Caelia? Would you join your king in a dance?"

"I would be honored, your majesty." She curtsied before dropping a kiss to Liam's cheek and whispering. "Do not go too far, husband, I would have another dance with you."

"As Lancelot engages the Queen, I will wait here for you, little wife." Liam said, with a bow to the king as the music began once more and she was swept away in Arthur's arms.

"You two will be good for each other. You will give him some youthful energy and the children he so longs for. Of course, I am sure that my old friend will do all that he can to bring you such happiness as he is able."

"You make it sound as though he did not seek this marriage but is being forced into such arrangement against his will when it is, in fact, the exact opposite." Caelia said, as he spun her around the floor.

"You did not want a marriage to a knight?" He asked with a raise brow that Caelia noticed, now that they were close, had just as much or more, grey to it than Liam's. His smile and quick laugh had distracted her from the fact before, but he was not the boyish king of the great legends, and he was not as handsome as her husband.

"I wanted to marry the man of my choice, Majesty." She replied, hoping that the answer did not reflect badly on Liam. "My father chose Liam. The entire arrangement was made before my opinion was even asked for. I am fortunate that the man chosen for me is one that I can love. Many other girls are not so fortunate as that."

"Is that so? I thought all you lovely country girls got to marry for love without all the formality of court." He said, giving her a look that she thought carried genuine interest. "As glad as I am to see you with my friend, and I wish you both happiness, it never occurred to me that you would not have wanted this."

"My father was doing what he thought best for me. Many girls are married off to the first man that asks and, even if he were cruel to them, their fathers would turn a blind eye as long as they deemed the match to be beneficial for themselves."

"I will speak to Liam and the others about this. There is no need for such things, surely." Arthur said to her, glancing around the room at the men she knew to be his most senior knights.

Had she just done exactly what she had hoped not to do? She could not have Liam be ashamed of her before the sun had set on their wedding day.

"It is not a thing done with malice or ill thought on either part, majesty. Liam and my father did not think that they did wrong in arranging this. It is the custom that is wrong, not those that follow it." She said, passionately trying to keep her new husband and her father from earning the anger of the king.

"Then what would you suggest?" He asked as the music began to slow.

"Change the law to protect a woman's right to refuse a marriage. It will not solve everything, but it could help so many girls."

"I will look into that possibility, as a wedding gift." The King said, bowing at the end of the song then walking her to Liam.

"I return your wife for a second dance, Liam. When it is over I would have you join me and a few others for a round of ale and a deep discussion that must be held urgently."

"Yes. Of course, my King." Liam bowed his head.

Once the king was off the dance floor the rest of the court swarmed it as though a dam had broken. Couples spun and swung without the formality of the first two songs of the night.

"What did you and the king have to talk about Caelia? He looked quite serious and so did you."

She paused and then looked at him with a nervous smile.

"Well, I told him how we came to be engaged and how many girls are not as lucky in their arranged husbands as I am."

The tension melted from his face and the warm glow to his eyes returned.

"I am glad that you consider yourself lucky to be with me, though I am the luckier one by far. What did he say about your revelation?"

She could not decide if Liam was curious about the conversation or concerned that she had broken some rule of etiquette, but she was not going to let that moment of his interest go without an answer.

"He blamed the men who follow the custom that takes a woman's right of refusal. I blamed the custom and not the men, or the women who allow themselves to be used in such a way." She smiled up at his, reaching up to brush her fingers through his hair. "He agreed that, perhaps, the laws and customs need to be revisited and updated. He wants to speak to you after our dance. I would hazard a guess that is the reason."

"Well, I am impressed. We are in Camelot a day and you are already bringing about change. Heading right for the top too." He smiled at her and dropped a kiss to her cheek. "I look forward to talking to Arthur and the others about this. Changing the law on a suggestion from my own wife, I never thought I would see that day."

Caelia lay her head on his chest, not caring that it might be frowned upon. She was so happy that the man she married was proud of her instead of trying to supress her. There was so much they could accomplish together, so much he could teach her and the things they could explore together might change the lives of so many at Redbourne.

"Do you think that the talk will take the rest of the night?" She asked when the music came to an end and they walked from the dance floor to the table where the other men from Redbourne and Prince Banning sat laughing.

"If it involved Arthur and the others of his private council then I can promise it will last at least an hour longer than any of them will promise their wives." Lionel said with a laugh. "Do not worry Caelia. We lesser knights will make sure that you dance as much as you like."

An older knight that she had not met yet, with sandy blonde hair and dark brown eyes, stood and shook Liam's hand.

"It is good to see you again my friend."

"And to see you instead of reading letter, Hector." Liam replied. "This is my wife, Caelia. She is the new Lady of Redbourne. Caelia, my dear, Hector is the man who has stayed in Camelot and kept me apprised of all that has been going on while we have been away. A good friend though a lousy dancer."

The men around them laughed and Caelia could not help joining them.

"It is wonderful to meet you, Sir Hector. Are you truly that bad of a dancer or does my husband seek to downplay your skill?"

"She has spirit Liam, that bodes well. Go have words with the king as you used to. We will see that the Lady of Redbourne is well looked after." Hector said to Liam, dismissing him like a young boy instead of a renowned knight. "My lady, my skills on the dance floor are not to be missed. Shall we? After you have taken your refreshment?"

She wanted to protest. More than that she wanted to go with Liam to talk to the King, but she had not been invited.

"I would be honored, Sir." Caelia said, giving Liam a kiss to his cheek and a smile then watching him rejoin the men at the head table to begin talking about the suggestion she had made.

"Then let us see how well we fare." Hector led her to the floor as the music begun.

As much as she tried to concentrate on Sir Hector and his charming conversation, very courtly and well practiced, all Caelia wanted was to watch the head table and see what might happen there.

"He is good at what he does, and I am sure that the king will not keep him from you too long on your wedding night." Hector said with a knowing smile. "I have not seen him this happy in many years. I am glad for you both."

"As am I, Hector. May I cut in?" The man that had been watching her at the tournament said, interrupting their dance. "I am eager to meet the lady who brings such joy and change to our Liam."

"Though I was enjoying myself and the company I shall give way to better manners than you have."

He bowed and left her with the interloper before Caelia could protest.

"I do not know your name, good sir." She said with a curtsey, mentally cursing Hector's manners.

"Really? They have not told you about me? To stay away from me?" He smiled and Caelia felt a shiver. "Then I shall enjoy my advantage all the more. I know your name, Caelia of Redbourne" He said, pulling her closer than he should have when the music started. "I am Bedver of Devonshire."

Chapter 31

"Sir Bedver. I did not expect you as a dance partner." She said, trying not to let her unease around the man show too easily.

"Why would I not want to dance with the most beautiful woman in the room?" He asked with a smooth smile.

"Because I do not think you are a friend to my husband." Caelia said as they moved further away from the table where the men from Redbourne were sitting.

"I have known Liam since before he was married, the first time." He replied, gliding her around the dancefloor. "I doubt that anyone would consider us friends despite knowing each other all that time. Rivals might be a better description, but good natured of course."

She looked at him, suspicious of his intent when he tightened his hold around her.

"It may be good natured, but I would not be a part of it or let you use me against him." She tried to step out of the dance, his grip on her made it impossible. "Let me go or I will make a scene."

"You will do nothing that will risk your new husband's honor. His standing is fragile enough, whereas mine is solid and in good standing. No rumors or banishments are tied to me."

There was a threat in his voice that shook her confidence.

"What do you think is going to happen if I scream?" Caelia tried to catch the eye of Liam or Lionel but both were deep in conversation. Rion and Saffir were dancing which left

Gerard as her only hope and he was not likely to come to her aid, but Bedver could not know that.

"You are not going to scream. No one is hurting you and you will look foolish." He whispered in her ear. "Liam hates to look foolish and I think it would be a pity to anger him on your wedding night, agreed?"

He was enjoying the idea of making her afraid of Liam too much. Caelia wanted to wipe the smugness off his face or beat him with the flat of a blade. If only it was not against all the laws of Camelot to draw a blade in the presence of the king or she would have done it with his own dagger.

"I agree that you should not anger my husband, especially if he already thinks that you are scum who does not belong in Camelot."

"I am not the one who does not belong." Bedver growled, his grip on her hand tightening painfully. "What would a milkmaid who married an accused rapist know of belonging?"

"Rape? What are you talking about?" She asked, shock and dread flooding her.

The devious smile that spread across his lips told her that this had been his plan. Even with that information she had to know what he meant. Liam? Accused of rape? When? Who dared to lie about such a thing? It was a lie. It had to be.

"He did not tell you? Of course not. If he told you then you would not have married him." Bedver chuckled. "It is not too late though. You have not consummated the marriage. You have not been ruined. I am sure that the King could be persuaded to annul the ceremony and you can go back to your cows and country life."

"I do not believe you." Caelia said, hating herself for the doubt she could hear in her voice. "He is a good man. A great knight who would never do such a thing. The king would never have welcomed him back if that were true."

Bedver laughed, the sound finally getting the attention of Gerard where he sat with the royal twins.

"The king allows another man to sleep with his wife. Why would he turn his back on an old friend for satisfying his lust with a serving girl? Actually, she looked a lot like you. Perhaps that is why he finds you so appealing. He will get to relive the delight of prying open your slender thighs and plowing you like an old horse plows fresh soil."

Caelia was about to reply when a fist smashed across Bedver's face.

"Still your tongue before I rip it out with my bare hands." Gerard growled, delivering several more blows while Lionel guided Caelia back from the fight. "Stay away from her or it will be more than my fist you have to deal with you swine."

"Jealous that the old man finally found a wife when no woman in the land wants anything to do with your second rate, pathetic, follower ass?" Bedver snarled, swinging back at Gerard as the dance floor cleared around them.

"This is going to get ugly Caelia. You should get back to the table." Lionel said as the knights squared off. "What did he say to you? Bedver cannot be trusted."

"He said that Liam had been banished from Camelot because he had been accused of rape. That is not true. I know that, but it is upsetting and then he said..." She shuddered. "I could not even repeat it. That was when Gerard hit him."

She watched the blacksmith beat the other man to the ground until the king's guards took him by the arms and removed him from the dancefloor.

"Well, it is true that he did not do it. We all know that he would never do such a thing, no matter how drunk he was that night."

"Drunk? You mean it is true?" Caelia stared at him, her jaw slack in surprise before her head whipped around to search for Liam.

When their eyes met, she saw a flash of realization in his eyes before his shoulders slumped slightly. Most people would not have noticed, but she saw the shift from pride and joy to defeated resignation.

"He did not want me to know? Did he think he could hide this from me forever?" She said, half to herself and half to Lionel.

"I do not know what his plan was. He did not tell me anything except that we were to keep Bedver and his friends away from you. I am sure that he will have words for us regarding the failure to do that."

"He should never had hidden this from me, Lionel. If Liam will not tell me then perhaps Gerard will. Come, help me find him to ask." She raced along the wall of the dance hall with the young knight close behind. Heading towards the door that she had seen Gerard and the twins exit though. "I am sure that he will tell me what is going on and why I am being kept in the dark about my own husband."

Despite her words Caelia was not entirely sure. Would Gerard confirm that Liam had been accused of rape? It must have been a convincing situation for Arthur, who was so happy to see Liam now, to have banished a knight on the word of a serving girl.

They must have been together in bed. The thought suddenly made her feel ill. Liam in the arms of another woman, making her feel like he had made her feel. This was not his long dead wife that he had certainly loved with a devoted faithfulness but a living woman who could still be at court, ready to cause problems or seek revenge.

"Caelia." Lionel called behind her, trying to keep up in the press of the crowd. "Gerard is not going to tell you anything that will make you feel any better about this. None of us can do that. I am sorry. You should not have found out like that."

"No. I do not believe it. You are not much older than I am. How could you know what really happened? Gerard will tell me the truth. He does not like me enough to lie."

"Dammit Caelia. Stop. Please."

They were moving down the stair, the noise of the party masking the sound of their feet on the stairs, but she could still hear Gerard shouting to the Princess about how he hated Bedver.

"He had no business talking about Liam like that and especially not to his bride on his wedding day." His voice boomed up the stairs. "I may not like the girl, but she did not deserve that. I could kill the bastard myself."

Whoever he was talking to as definitely trying to talk him out of another round of fisticuffs with the other knight without much success. As much as Caelia would have like to see Bedver get his just desserts she had to agree with the other person he was talking to. There was no good that could come of another fight and it might make things worse for Liam.

Gerard raised his voice again, bringing her attention back to him and the reason she was following the thunderous man in the first place. She was just about to call his name and announce her presence when his next words caught her completely off guard.

"I know I have to be careful. We do not need him following me around and discovering us. It is bad enough that he was vile and disgusting about Liam, if he started talking about us, I would have to kill him."

Caelia turned to look at Lionel and whisper "And you thought there was nothing but friendship between them."

She stepped around the corner, expecting to see Princess Elin calming Gerard from his murderous rage but instead he had his arms wrapped tightly around Prince Banning's broad shoulders while they were locked in a carnal kiss that had the royal pinning the knight to the wall with his hips. The passion of the kiss intensified as she watched, the two men embrace. Dumbfounded by what she was seeing it was only when Ger started to reach for the strings of Banning's breeches that she found her voice.

"Gerard? Your highness?" Her voice sounded like a squeak, but it was loud enough to make both men turn their heads.

"What the devil are you doing here?" Gerard asked, straightening himself and glaring daggers at her that matched the same look he had given Bedver. "Lionel? You look like you are going to choke. Breathe or say something."

"I...I just wanted to ask if it was true." Caelia said, staring at the pair, Gerard looked terrified and Banning was flushed, his eyes darting from her face to the man beside her. "Bedver said Liam was accused of...that he had been banished after a serving girl said that he raped her. Is it true?"

"That was the lie and no he did not do it. He still had his breeches on when Bedver led us to the room." Gerard said, rubbing his forehead. "Caelia, I need you to not talk about what you saw. Not yet. Not even to Liam. Banning's father would not understand, it would be dangerous."

"It is against the laws of the new church that Arthur has made official. Ger you are mad to do such a thing. They will kill you." Lionel said, taking a step backwards. "You are a knight and he is a prince. It is not done like that. He is royalty."

"Lionel?" Gerard said with so much pain in his voice that it made Caelia want to cry. "Brother? The church of Rome does not command my heart, nor his." He pointed to Banning. "Love is love, no matter who bears it. There is no sin here. I am still the man you have always known. Nothing has changed."

"Arthur and Liam, when they find out..." Lionel took a step back up the stairs. "There are laws, and rules Ger. Liam will..."

Gerard waved a hand, trying to calm the situation while Banning gave Caelia a look that pleaded for understanding.

"Liam knows, Lionel, and Arthur will not judge me. Will you?" Ger asked.

The words seemed to choke in the powerful man's throat and Caelia thought she had never seen a man so vulnerable in her life. When Banning put his hand on Gerard's shoulder Lionel turned and stormed up the stairs.

"He will keep the secret, at least for tonight." Gerard said with a sigh. "I know him well enough for that."

The pair turned to Caelia, one with hope in his eyes and the other unable to meet her eyes.

"What about you?" Banning asked, the trace of a smile on his lips. "Can you hold back your judgment as your husband does?"

"As my husband does." Caelia repeated just as a wave of realization hit her. "Liam knows? Gerard? Liam knows? How well does he know your secret?"

Chapter 32

"I will rip his arms off." Liam growled, shoving back from the table, his eyes on Caelia as she fled the room after the guards broke up the fight between Ger and Bedver. "What the devil did he say to her?"

"You are not going to rip his arms off, and it does not matter what he said because it is merely words and you are not doing violence to another knight on your wedding day." Arthur said at his side. "You should find out what he said to her first, then you should thank Gerard for stepping in. I would suggest taking your wife to your rooms too. Get everything settled between you. Seal the marriage if you get my meaning."

Liam looked at him with an arched brow. "Arthur, I am not in my twenties now. I know what you mean and, not that it is your business, but that is already done." He brushed past him and headed out into the crowd to find Caelia, Gerard and Lionel. He had to find out how much damage Bedver had done and figure out how to fix it with Caelia.

His eyes found the jackass from across the room and answered the smirk with a murderous glare.

"I swear my blade will find your throat the next chance I get." Liam muttered under his breath.

He was so distracted by Bedver that he ran into Lionel at the top of the stairs, almost sending him crashing down.

"Lionel? Where is she? Where is Caelia and what happened? What did that bastard say to make her rum?"

The younger man looked as though he had just been sick. He was sweaty, flustered and Liam thought he saw his hands shaking.

"Answer me. Where is my wife and what is wrong with you?" He gripped by the arms and gave his steward a hard shake. "Is she alright? Is she hurt?"

"She is unharmed though I cannot say that she is alright. Ger heard more of it than I did, but I gather Bedver was quite crude with her, after telling her his version of why you were banished." Lionel shook his head. "We all told you that you should have told her about all that before we got here, and you did not listen. Now she has his version in her head. He advised her to walk away before the marriage is consummated, to avoid the scandal of your reputation. She might listen to him Liam."

"There is no going back and even if it were possible, I would not let it happen. She is my wife and I will keep her as such." Liam looked down the stairs. "Is she down there still? With Ger?"

"Ger and Banning. That is something else. Liam, we found Ger and Banning…we always thought it was Elin that he was courting. We were wrong, this is wrong. What are we going to do?"

Liam stopped on the first stair and made sure that Lionel was looking at him, meeting his eyes without a blink.

"We do nothing, no matter what. Say nothing about what you saw. Keep it to yourself and tell no one, and I do mean no one."

Lionel nodded, a troubled expression on his face.

"If that is your order Liam. I do not think it is a good idea. Banning may not be the crown price but he is a prince and his father will not accept this. Even if you do." Lionel frowned and looked back into the crowded dance hall. "His father will be sure to have an arranged marriage in mind. He wants heirs, as many as he can force his children to have. Banning and Ger are not likely to conceive any."

Liam laughed. His concern was real but even so Lionel was able to make a joke. "I have heard that Elin refuses to marry anyone. I thought it was because she wanted to marry Ger, but perhaps she does not want children? Or simply wants to irritate her father."

Rubbing the bridge of his nose Liam shook his head. "Royal weddings are not what I am worried about tonight. Where is my wife and where is my best friend?"

Lionel pointed down the stairs and stepped into the ballroom, heading towards the table where the rest of the company from Redbourne were sitting in deep conversation.

"Now to see what damage is done." Liam muttered, thundering down the stairs to meet with Caelia, Ger and, apparently, Banning.

Ger should have kept her safe. He had been tasked with that exact thing, and yet he had let that troll of a man dance with Caelia. Of course, Bedver would have taken the opportunity to poison her mind with lies.

Dammit why did Ger have to choose tonight to be romantic and why was he so foolish as to pursue Banning like that? He could not think that he could be with him, not really. A prince had even more responsibility than a knight and had an even greater expectation on him. They had no chance.

Liam sighed, neither did Ger and himself. That had to be over, immediately.

"Liam? We were just coming to return your little lost lamb of a wife." Banning called from the foot of the stairs. "Then we discovered she is more of a terrier. Small, cute and viciously loyal." The prince chuckled.

"Caelia?" He looked at her but her back was to him, her slender shoulders squared resolutely. "Sweetheart? I am sorry about Bedver. I should have warned you."

"You should have told me, Liam." She said, turning to face him. Her dark blue eyes were flashing with anger. "You should have trusted me. Now the coward thinks he has divided us."

"Us?" Liam's voice held a note of hope as he glanced at Ger.

"I told her what happened. I also said that we all told you that you should tell her, but you were afraid that she would not believe you." He shrugged his broad shoulders and smirked. "Apparently you have on honest face, or something like that."

"If you were the man that Bedver tried to say that you were then the night at the inn, when we shared the bed, would have gone very differently." Caelia said, watching Ger and Banning until Liam turned her head to face only him.

He was trying not to smile. This was a serious situation and what he had been accused of was a serious crime, but she had faith in him. That was all he needed.

"I suspect that if I was that kind of man, I would be lying dead on that mattress from a knife wound." He offered her his arm, unsure if she would take it or ignore him. The other two men seemed to share his trepidation because they both offered him smiles of encouragement that also looked slightly nervous. "May I beg that my wife join me on the dancefloor at least once more before we retire for the night?"

"Definitely not." Caelia shook her head.

The expression on her beautiful face was grim and determined. With a deep sigh he shook his head. She was still angry, and she had that right. Liam was not sure what he could do to make things right with her, but he would not give up.

"Caelia, I will…"

"You will dance with me at least twice and we will talk about the rest of this when we are alone."

He noticed that she shot Ger and Banning a look that made both men look away. Now was not the time to ask exactly what happened. Later, after he had said and done everything that he could think of to put the smile back on Caelia's face and the trust back in her eyes he would find out.

"Highness." He bowed his head to Banning, briefly, then tucked Caelia's hand into his arm.

"As you wish, little wife, two dances at least." He said, leading her up the stairs. "Do not linger, Ger. You and I have a few things to talk about as well."

"As you wish, Liam." Ger said with a frown, falling in behind them.

The way he copied Liam's address to Caelia was not lost on Liam. He knew exactly what the words meant, even if the others did not.

As soon as they reached the top of the stairs Liam swept his wife out onto the floor. He was trying to his best to ignore the whispers and long looks that more than a few courtiers kept giving them.

What would the gossip be this time? That he was too old for her and that she would soon find a lover among his knights? That they would never find love because of his age and her brashness? Or would it be the same as it had been for years? Did they all still think he was the monster that Bedver had tried to create in their minds.

"Liam? Do not worry about them." Caelia said softly. "Focus on me."

"You are not angry anymore?" He asked with a hopeful smile. She was young, it was possible that a few dances were enough to get back to her good graces.

"I am furious actually." She said sweetly. "But there is no one here in this room that needs to know that except you. Never fight in public if it is something you want to stay private. I learned that from my parents. They disagreed about a lot of things, but no one knew it unless they lived in our house. Even my brothers do not know how often they argued."

"They were wise to do that. The members of court will pick up on the smallest things and make them seem bigger than they are." He said, spinning her around the floor.

"I am not surprised. I would rather not give them anything more to gossip about tonight though." She replied. "We made a commitment. A binding agreement and we can make each other happy for the rest of our lives together or we can make each other miserable. So, I hope that you are prepared to be honest with me tonight."

"I do not think you could find a more honest man than our silver haired knight." Lancelot said, interrupting Liam before he could answer her. "I think it is my turn to dance with the bride Liam. Why no go and see why our Gerard is sulking in the corner. Bedver has been told to stay away from him so there should be no more problems tonight."

He wanted to smash the man's smug face into the floor for breaking in. He was trying hard to fix things with Caelia and of course the smuggest 'hero' of the country had to choose that moment to cut in.

"Lancelot, if you keep interrupting me with my wife, I am going to have to start thinking you are up to something." Liam had to force himself not to growl. "If Caelia wants to dance with you I will not object but please bring her back to me. I would not want anyone to cause her any more grief tonight."

"A man possessive of his wife. That is something new in this court." Lancelot said with a grin. "Shall we dance, young lady?"

Caelia nodded with a quick glance to Liam and once they were out among the courtiers Liam turned to level his gaze at his best friend.

"Liam, I know what you are going to say, but she was with Hector and I did not think Bedver would be so stupid as to do what he did." Ger said, not even getting to his feet even though he was being addressed by his leader.

Banning was on one side of him and Elin had reappeared to sit on the other side. Liam was not sure if it was simply a show of support for Ger or if they were creating a united front against him.

"I gave you a single task tonight and I know that you have not seen the royal twins in some time, but this was important. Now I have a bride of less than a day that does not trust me."

"Liam, had you not told the girl anything about why you were made to leave Camelot?" Elin asked, standing to stare him in the eyes. He had always been unnerved by her, impressed by the way she was stood up for her brother and for the things she thought needed to be done. Even Arthur was known to listen to her suggestions when she came to council meetings.

"I was going to tell her tomorrow. I wanted one more day where she looked at me with that innocent adoration. Now everything is different."

"That is no one's fault but your own, old friend." Banning said, taking a drink. "Blame Ger for not following orders if you must, but it is because of you that she found out about that night from someone other than you."

Chapter 33

Caelia watched Liam talk with Gerard and the twins with curiosity. What was he saying to them? How angry was he with his friend? With her for causing a scene?

Her heart had been racing when she had told him that she was furious with him. His standing at court and the fact that he was closer to her father's age than he was to hers and, of course, being a man, gave him all the rights he needed to be absolutely furious with her and to punish her accordingly.

"You seem distracted, Lady Caelia." Lancelot whispered in her ear. "Am I not interesting company this evening?"

A few months ago, she would have thought she was the luckiest girl in the world to have the attention of the famous knight, but tonight there was no thrill. The golden hair seemed average and his blue eyes seemed dull, almost lifeless when she thought of the way that Liam's eyes sparked, especially when he was about to laugh.

"My apologies, Sir Lancelot. I just cannot seem to focus on anything or anyone but my husband tonight. I am sure that you understand?" She patted his shoulder and walked away towards Liam, her Liam. There were a few gasps of disbelief from the ladies nearest to her, but Caelia had her eyes on her husband. No one else could compare to him. Even the king did not have the drawing power of Liam.

"Husband? I would retire for the night, before the wine goes to my head." She said, putting her hand on his arm. "Can we go, now?"

"Yes, of course Caelia." Liam replied in a voice that she thought sounded tired, defeated, not at all like the passionate man that had come to find her not long ago.

Maybe she should wait for another night to have the conversation about what he was hiding from her. No, it had to be tonight. Another lesson she had learned from her mother was to never go to bed angry.

The farewell to the other knights and the royal twins was brief and polite. The king was jovial and teasing when he embraced first Liam and then herself.

"It makes me happy to see you two together. I hope you will make each other just as happy. There might be fights but remember that making up from those fights can be quite a fun time. If you let it." He winked at her, the delight in his big brown eyes making her smile back at him.

"I will keep that in mind, majesty." Caelia nodded. "Tonight, and all other nights where my husband vexes me, as I am sure that he will."

"I can promise you that he certainly will, as you will irritate him. Just be patient with each other and things will work out better than you think."

"Yes, sire." She bowed her head and turned to the Queen who kissed her cheek and whispered in her ear.

"Relax. Sip the wine I had sent to your room slowly and try to enjoy yourself. It will get better every time you are together."

"I am sure that I will teach her everything that she needs, as she will show me what I need to know. Thank you, your highness." Liam said, taking Caelia by the arm. "Shall we go, little wife?"

"Lead the way." She said with a smile that was more for the court than it was for Liam.

He had to know that she was furious at being kept in the dark regarding such a secret. Did he think she would believe that kind of gossip? There was more to him than this place. He had shown her that when they were together at Redbourne. When they were there, home, she had felt an understanding from him and here there was so little of that. It was like being in Camelot made him so nervous about doing and saying exactly the right thing that he forgot how to have fun, how to relax. He was tense and nervous, except when they were away from the courtiers. Alone with her, Liam smiled and laughed the same way he did in the training yard at Redbourne. As much as he said he wanted to be here, he was not as happy as he wanted others to believe.

He was quiet the entire walk to their rooms and even once the door closed behind them, he said nothing except to ask her if she would like some wine.

"I would enjoy a glass, after you help me undo the back of this dress. I would hate for anything to happen to it."

"What would happen to you dress? I do not anticipate a sword fight or anything of that nature tonight." He chuckled, obviously amused with himself as he unthreaded the back of the gown.

"Nor do I but I cannot promise that I will not be tempted to pour the same cup over your head for being a damned fool."

"A fool? Not many would use those words to describe me." His eyes narrowed to a sharp glare. "What, pray tell, makes me a fool to my young wife, exactly?"

She paused, watching his face and body for warnings of violence. He was a warrior and despite the age difference there was no doubt in her mind that her husband was a deadly man. Not towards her though, his hands remained unclenched and his shoulders did not tense up. He was not going to raise a hand, perhaps his voice, but she was safe even if he was angry.

"The lack of trust and faith you have in me while expecting me to have blind faith in you." She said, putting the dress on a chair and turning to face him. "You thought I could believe that worm Bedver, so you did not tell me the truth? Liam, I married you, even before that I would have believed you because you are a good man, trustworthy and honorable. You are as likely to rape a woman as you are to strike me right now."

"Strike you? Where on earth would you get such an idea?" Liam barked, pulling his shirt over his head, and tossing it across the room. "I have never raised a hand to a woman, not even the one Bedver paid to entrap me."

Caelia stared at his bare chest, the candlelight giving him a bronze glow that reminded her of the tales of ancient gods. It was mesmerizing and distracting. She wanted to touch him, even though she was livid, she wanted to run her fingers across his chest and through his hair.

"Never?" She asked, forcing herself to take her eyes off his form and meet his angry gaze. "I have never known a man who can claim that with complete honesty. Is this another lie to withhold a truth you do not think I can handle?"

"I doubt you could handle most of what I think, Caelia."

His voice was dark and held just a hint of danger. Enough to stir her desire but not enough to make her afraid of him.

Stepping up to Liam, close enough that he could grab hold of her, Caelia silently dared him to prove her right. All men were capable of darkness. She had enough married friends to know that. Was he telling the truth or simply trying to convince her that he was the storybook hero he thought she wanted?

"I am not a child Liam, as you should well know from this afternoon." She hissed.

Her fists rested on her hips, she knew it likely seemed shrewish, but she had to make her point, stand her ground. There would be no lies between them, not now or ever. Not if this was going to work.

"A child? No. You are not a child though if you continue to push me with such tactics, I may be tempted to treat you like one." He smirked and used the tip of his finger to brush the strap of her bodice down her arm. "Believe me or not, Caelia, I am not worried. I have a lifetime to show you how a man, a real man, treats his woman."

She shivered, everything about him, his stance, his words, and the way he touched her, hummed with pure masculine power. The desire to give in, to submit, was strong, almost as strong as her desire to prove herself to him. She craved his respect and with it, his honesty.

"Tell me the truth, about that night and about Gerard, did you know he and Prince Banning are lovers?"

She wanted him to be shocked at her words and what they meant. Staring into his eyes she waited for the surprise to register. Instead he merely blinked, nodded and stepped away.

"You caught them together? Doing what?" He asked, sitting down to tug off his boots and leaving her standing breathless with the lingering scent of him.

"Lionel and I found them kissing at the bottom of the stairs."

She watched Liam down an entire cup of wine, but he did not look up at her before pouring himself another. Had he known about this? Had he known that Gerard loved men? He had to have known. They had been friends for their entire lives and Liam was not stupid. What if...oh gods in heaven were they? Had they?

"Liam, you are not surprised by this. You knew this about him? Tell me the truth."

"I knew. No one else needed to and no one else needs to know now. Do you understand this? It would be dangerous for both of them, perhaps for all of us."

"Your best friend, and you did not trust me with that knowledge either? When it is, as you say, a danger to all of us. Did you have another reason that you did not want me to know Liam?"

He stood, his back was still towards her and his hands unfastening the belt of his breeches, completely silent in response to her question.

"Liam? I need to know. Is our marriage a sham to cover up your love affair with Gerard?"

"What?" He roared, spinning around, and stalking towards her. He was nearly naked, a state that would make most men uncomfortable, but not Liam. The emotion in his face was not rage and it was not surprise but somewhere in the between the two.

"You think that I am not as committed to this as I said? Do you think I am nothing more than a liar Caelia?" He growled, taking hold of her arms, a firm grip but not crushing. "Trust me, I did not need a marriage that badly that I would wed a girl half my age to cover up a love affair with a man less than five people could possibly know about."

"How can I trust you when your actions and words are not the same?" She cried, struggling in his hold, which only served to demonstrate his strength and loosen her underdress so that it slid down her arms and the neckline revealed the pink of her nipples. "Tell me how I am to believe you Liam."

"Words be damned, and I will be damned with them. I will show you what this marriage means, woman."

He crushed her to his chest, the hair she had wanted to touch now rubbing against her skin and teasing nerves to arousal.

Looking up into his eyes Caelia pushed back against him, fighting his hold. Her fear of the passionate anger in his eyes battled with her wish for him to desire only her, for her fears about Gerard to be baseless, and for him to love her. She had to know for certain what she meant to him.

"Show me the truth then, if you cannot say it." She whispered.

Her words seemed to push him over the edge of his control. Liam's mouth crashed down on hers, hard and unforgiving. His tongue forced her lips apart and thrust deep inside. This was not a courtly kiss or even frantic passion. This was desperate possession and she was helpless to fight it. Without breaking the kiss, Liam bent and caught her behind her knees, sweeping her from her feet and into his embrace before he carried her to their bed.

"I will show you everything. Remember the day we met? When I told you there was everything to fear?"

He barely waited for her to nod.

"Now is the time you should be afraid." He lowered his head to take her lips in a crushing kiss that was full of a promise she could not understand, not yet.

Chapter 34

Liam was enraged and impassioned by the woman on the bed. No woman had ever gotten under his skin like Caelia. He could usually ignore a few taunts and jibes. The way women teased usually amused him or, if it annoyed him, he could crush them with only a few words.

Caelia was neither amusing nor annoying. She was intelligent, articulate and her boldness fascinated him like no other. She was also infuriating. Why did she have to ask these kinds of questions? Was it too much to ask that she ignore this, the question of he and Ger? Did what they had shared change things? Did it change everything?

No. He had made his choice and damn it all, he did not look backwards.

If she thought that he was going to be cowed by her accusations, then he was going to show her exactly the kind of man she married. Not the quiet man or the courtesan of the king. He was going to show her the warrior that had fought at the side of the king and defeated Saxons and French alike.

"You think I want a man in my bed tonight Caelia? You think that when I look at you that I do not see a beautiful, desirable woman. A woman who needs to be shown the difference between other men and the one she married."

He shucked off his breeches and reached for the loose material of her linen shift. When she scrambled backwards across the bed, he could not help the devious smile that spread across his face.

"Not so bold of word now, wife?" He asked, grabbing hold of her ankle, and dragging her back across the bed until her legs straddled his hips where he stood at the bedside. Her yelp of surprise brought a laugh rumbling from his chest. "Nothing to say?"

"What do you mean other men? Liam you would not...you are not going to hurt me."

"No. I am going to make you scream though. Like you have never done in your life."

He moved quickly, too quickly for her to react to, and pulled the white fabric up over her head, loosing a few of the curls that had been pinned up. They fell across her bare shoulders and down her chest, one even seemed to curl around the bud of her breast before she raised her hands to cover them.

"That will not be allowed. I want to see my wife, all of her. You will obey me in this, or I shall have to punish you."

His voice was thick with desire, the excitement he felt was almost uncontainable. He wanted, so badly, to exercise his rights as a husband. More than that, he wanted to make her beg for him. To make her want him, need him, and seek her satisfaction with him alone. To make her his woman and send her to sleep with the knowledge that he was a man of his word, her man who would not falter in his promises.

Caelia stared at him, her eyes wide while she lowered her hands and rested them on the bed.

"Yes, husband." She said softly, not breaking eye contact. Her spirit shone back at him, timid in the moment but unbroken.

She had looked beautiful in her wedding dress, but naked before him, sitting demurely on the edge of the bed with a knee pressed at either side of his hips, she was a divine goddess brought to life for him alone.

"Good girl, Caelia." He said with a smile. Brushing his fingers from her cheek to her collarbone, Liam was rewarded with a slight shiver from his bride. "I think you might enjoy this more than you expect."

"You think I will enjoy my husband behaving as a brute? Treating me as though the only reason I exist is for his physical pleasure?"

Her voice was angry, and her eyes had narrowed slightly. Liam knew that she was strong and stubborn. She was used to having to yell to be heard, to be as strong and fast as a man to be taken seriously. He doubted that anyone in her life had ever celebrated her as a woman. Had anyone let her be a girl and know that was more than good enough to be loved. Just as she was.

"Yes. I think you will."

The look in her eyes changed from anger to surprise when he leaned down to kiss her firmly on the lips.

"I am going to treat you like the sensual, desirable, strong woman that you are." He whispered in her ear while a hand caressed down her side and across the top of her thigh to dip between her legs. The heated moisture there confirmed his suspicion and he began to play between the lips of her core, enjoying her reaction to his attention. "You are going to enjoy being treated like the sole object of my desire, giving up control, surrendering to me."

"Liam, I have no idea, I do not know how…how to do what you want me to do."

She sounded unsure of herself for the first time since he had met her, making him pause. Could she handle what he wanted to teach her? When her body tightened around his intrusion in a precursor to her ultimate pleasure, he knew she capable of more than she knew and made the choice to prove it to her.

"You will learn, Caelia. You will learn so much under me, under my attentive tutelage." He eased one finger inside her, when she gasped, he licked his lips and added a second. "The passion you have for equality and all your other causes can be between us as well. Explored and ignited into more. All you have to do, when we are alone together, is give in to it."

Her body was responding even if she had not made up her mind to follow it.

"How can I when I am not even sure that it is me you want?"

He heard the sadness in her voice and that angered him more than the questions she had asked about Ger. She should never, ever, doubt her worth because of things he had done, or said. Words were not going to be enough.

"Let me show you." He dropped to the floor and rested a hand on each of her knees, guiding them a little farther apart so that he could reach her with his mouth. The first sweep of his tongue made her shudder, the second and third had her hands on his shoulders, by the time he had given her a dozen stroked her body was trembling and her hands were in his hair, threading deeper and tugging when he speared her core with his tongue.

"Liam..." She moaned, leaning back before he caught her wrists with one hand.

"Do not lay back. I want you to stay connected, your attention here with me." He growled, using his hold on her wrists to keep her where he wanted while gripping her hip with his other hand. "I am not finished with you yet."

She whimpered with pleasure and he grinned against the smoothness of her inner thigh, rubbing his beard against her skin until she squirmed, bucking her hips towards him.

"Well we can safely say you like that, hmm?" Liam said, looking up at her.

She nodded, pressing her lips together. Her skin was flushed, and she was pulling against his hold, her need for things she could not express written on her face.

"I wonder what else you might like? To touch? To taste?" He asked rising to his feet. Her eyes followed him, flicking briefly to his waist, and he smiled. "Anything you want to try Caelia? I will not command anything, but I am curious about what you want."

"May I? I want to touch you? The ladies told me about something that men like. I want to see if they told the truth."

"The truth is important to my wife?" He asked her, stroking her cheek, and watching while her hand cautiously reached out to touch him. When she nodded, he mirrored it back to her. "Then do anything you wish."

Liam marveled at the innocence of her curiosity when she took him in her hand. She had almost done it the last time they were in the bed together, but he had decided to make that time all about her pleasure. This time he wanted her to want him, to want more of him, to want him to feel pleasure like he gave to her.

The first stroke of her hand was tentative, and he held his breath as she continued. Soon she was working him with a smooth strength in her hand that surprised him, given her slight frame.

"Caelia, you are amazing. That feels…better than I thought you could be when you are so new to this intimacy."

"Elin told me to use the same strength and technique that I use when I am holding a sword, only gentler."

"She was right." He swallowed hard, his eyes open wide as she lowered her mouth to lathe her tongue across the head of his shaft, licking up the bead of moisture that had collected there. Dear heavens, she was going to bring him to his knees when she grew more confident. He would be even more powerless against the flash of her smile knowing what those beautiful lips were capable of.

"What about this?" She asked, dragging her tongue down the length while staring up at him.

"That is…" Liam did not get to finish the sentence before she closed her entire mouth around him and took him deep into her throat. "The most amazing feeling. You need to stop now." He eased her back with all the restraint he could muster. Coaxing her husband to release with her mouth was not the lesson he had in mind that night.

She pouted up at him in a way that reminded Liam of Lancelot when he used to be excluded from things between he and Ger. Though she could not have known what that look did to him it killed every romantic thought for that night. Her doubts and the question of Ger came back to him, as did the sense of ruthless, passionate need to teach her how a husband took his beautiful wife on their wedding night.

He would never hurt her, but he would show her that she should never question his desire. She should never doubt him or the passion growing between them.

"Liam? What are you doing?" She asked as he eased her to her back and firmly guided her knees to her chest.

"Bedding my wife. I am going to exhaust you, tenderly ravage you and show you how to let go. You will give in to me. Trusting me with your body so that you can learn to trust me with your heart."

Leaning over her legs, letting them press into his chest, Liam guided his shaft to her entrance, wet again though he had not kept up with his dexterous attentions. Her mouth had hardened him and thinking about it had kept him in a state of such arousal that with two strokes he was buried to the hilt in her core.

Caelia cried out, her head rolling back while she arched her back, pushing upwards with her hips. As he had hoped, she enjoyed the brutish behavior more than the tenderness of earlier, which spurred him on, each thrust harder, deeper inside her welcoming heat.

Liam slowed his thrusts, making each one a deliberate act. He was not going to let his wife leave their bed without feeling as though she had been thoroughly, physically, claimed, body and soul, by her husband.

As soon as her cries reached a note of desperation Liam stopped; he was not going to let things end so quickly. Moving her legs from their press against his chest he eased her to her side, keeping a grip at the top of her thigh to leverage his body into hers at this new angle.

His eyes closed, reveling in the pleasure of their joining, when suddenly her hand gripped the top of his and she hoarsely whispered his name.

"Liam? There is such pressure. It feels so good, tight like the string of a bow. Unlike anything I have felt before."

He grinned and helped her roll to her back.

"Wrap those beautiful legs around me, Caelia. I will take you over that edge if you will let me." He said, a deep growl when he sank home once more. "Let me show you more."

Chapter 35

He showed her pleasure she could barely believe and a blissful release that Caelia had never imagined was possible. All she had to do was surrender, to submit, to trust him.

The way Liam had exercised his passion for her, taking her body in that slow and powerful way, left no room for doubting the way he desired her. It was an incredible feeling. She had expected to feel sad, used or enslaved but, as she looked at the man sleeping beside her, with his arm across her chest, she felt a sense of freedom and deep joy. There was so much they could and would do together as a team. The conversation he had with the King that night was proof of the power they could exercise together, of the change they could help guide into policy that would protect women across the nation.

Caelia had been afraid, when he had been so angry with her question, that he would hurt her. It would have been easy for him to use her physical inexperience as the excuse for pain. There would have been no one, not even the Queen, who would have taken her words as anything more than a virgin's inexperience. Her fear was unnecessary though. The ferocity of his passion and how he exercised command had amazed her and awoken a desire she had never acknowledged. The desire to submit to her husband, in bed that is.

"Liam?" She whispered, stroking her hand across his cheek to see if he was awake. The hair of his beard was soft, smooth to the touch unless it was being rubbed against her thighs. The memory of that sensation was enough to send heat flooding to that area, arousing her all over again. "Are you awake?"

"Mmhmm." He murmured, opening one eye, and turning his head to kiss her wrist. "Good morning. Have they knocked on the door yet?"

"No, it is still early, I think." She said, rolling to her side.

"Did you sleep well?" He asked, moving a strand of hair from her cheek. "Not too sore this morning? I hope I was not too rough."

"I slept wonderfully. You, you held me all night." She said, cuddling closer to him, feeling safe enough to ask another question.

"How did you sleep? I thought, perhaps, you had a fight with Gerard?"

"Oh? Why would you think that? I am not pleased with him after he neglected to keep you away from Bedver." He said, the smile that had been on his face slipped slightly.

"You said his name several times in your sleep last night and you were restless. I thought you were dreaming of a struggle. Why was he supposed to keep us apart?"

"No, it was not a fight or a struggle. Perhaps I was dreaming of being the one who got to punch out that fool for being so rude to you and twisting what happened before I could find the best way to tell you. I wish that it had been me to tell you and I regret that I did not do so earlier. Can you forgive me?"

"Of course. I wish you had told me too. He is despicable and revelled in trying to destroy what we have been building." She sat up and swung her feet over the side of the bed. "He must truly despise you. Why? Did you beat him in a tournament, or a woman chose you over him?"

"Quite the opposite actually. He and his sister want Redbourne and me. She threw herself at me and he encouraged the match, but I had no interest. I never liked him, and she is just as crude as he is." She watched him cross the room to get his clothes. "I rejected her, of course, and they knew that they would never get me or the property. It is a wealthy estate and there have been many families over the years that have tried to marry me to their daughters so they could get their hands on it but none of them were...interesting or compatible with me or the rest of the men."

"You took the men into consideration for your own marriage?" She asked, standing, and beginning to make the bed after she put on her linen shift. "I did not meet any of them before you agreed to marry me. What was the difference?"

"Your father did not ask for part of Redbourne and he was more concerned for your wellbeing than anything else." Liam tugged on his breeches and smiled "I find myself with similar feelings. I want to make sure that you are taken care of should anything happen to me."

His smile made her blush and when he wrapped his arms around her waist, kissing her shoulder, she leaned back into him.

"I am already safer than ever with you at my side. I will be even safer with a sword of my own." She could not help dropping the suggestion, eventually he would have to listen and help convince Gerard to make one for her.

"I do not know if Gerard is ready to make you one, he is set against the idea of women and swordplay." He touched her cheek. "I will try and convince him. After I go get us breakfast."

"You are going to bring our breakfast here? We are not going to eat with the others?"

Turning to face him, Caelia wrapped her arms around Liam's neck and gave him a quick kiss.

"I think I would enjoy a private breakfast with my wonderful husband."

"I am a wonderful husband now, am I?" Liam chuckled. "Wait until we are home, and I do not need to worry about king or court during our day. There is so much more I can show you, do for you and with you. There was barely time to show you around the house and there is so much more to Redbourne than just the house."

He sounded so proud of his home, of their home, if she had not been falling completely in love with him before then the way he spoke about Redbourne would have had her heart swooning.

"I cannot wait to go home. I want to see every part of it and get to know the whole place as well as you do. That way, when children do what they do and hide I want to be able to find them because I will know all the best spots to hide."

"And who will you be hiding from, hmm?" He asked her while he put on his shirt. "Not me I hope."

"I might be hiding with you. From the others." She teased with a wink. "Why not get the breakfast and I will get dressed, then we can go find a few hiding places here in the city."

"I think that sounds like a wonderful idea. I will do my best not to get pulled into a council meeting with Arthur." He stepped backwards towards the door, reluctant to take his eyes off her before he had to.

"I will be here when you get back." Caelia smiled and waved at him to go.

Once the door closed behind him, she returned her attention to the bed. Even though there would likely be palace staff that would come to tidy the room she had spent too many years taking care of a house to simply leave it unmade.

Tucking the sheet under Liam's pillow her fingers touched something metal and she pulled a silver medallion out from under the pillow. It had some kind of symbol in the middle and was adorned by light blue stones that sparkled in the morning light. She stared at it, spinning on its chain while it dangled from her fingers.

"What...who do you belong to? This cannot be Liam's" She said to herself, setting it down on the table beside the bed. While she dressed in what seemed to be another ballgown but was likely barely acceptable by the court standards and definitely not fashionable to the taste of the other ladies, Caelia tried to think of where she had seen it before.

"Perhaps Lionel will know. There is little sense in bothering Liam, if it is his then he is sure to miss it soon and he would be delighted if I surprised him with it at just the right moment."

Caelia was dressed and waiting by the time Liam came back, without the food he'd gone to get.

"I'm sorry Caelia. Arthur has invited us to his private breakfast. I know we wanted privacy, but I think he wants to talk more about your conversation last night. Are you ready?"

"He wants to talk to me? Really?" This was more than she had hoped. The medallion in the pocket of her dress was forgotten about in the rush to quickly sweep her hair up to be ready for her meeting with the king.

"It's nothing formal." Liam said. "You could have left your hair down."

"Because it's informal or because you like my hair?" She replied with a teasing smile. Last night he had stroked her hair until she fell asleep.

"Perhaps a bit of both. I hope you'll wear it down at home, for me."

"I have gotten used to wearing it up, my brothers used to pull it horribly, so it was the only way to save my scalp."

"I'm sure I could pull it in a way that you would like. I may have to show you tonight."

The hinted intimacy in his voice had a blush on her cheeks when they arrived at the King's breakfast chamber. The table was set with a feast of breads and fruit and the smell coming from the steaming platters told her that they contained almost anything she could have asked for.

"Good morning, both of you." Arthur said, pointing to a pair of chairs. "Come and get something in your bellies. I am sure that you have strong appetites after your evening activities."

The casual way he referred to their wedding night, as though it was nothing more than a stroll thought the city or a ride in the forest put Caelia at ease as she sat down next to the Queen.

"A pleasant evening my dear?" She asked, handing her a plate of bread that was still warm from the oven.

"I could say it was a rough start, but I find a smile upon my face at the thought of it, my lady." She said, accepting a cup of small beer from her husband. "I hope the rest of the celebration was peaceful. Did you get to dance?"

"I did. My husband is not quite as skilled as yours but between he and Lancelot I thoroughly enjoyed my night, despite being denied two of my favorite dance partners."

"Two?" Caelia asked. "Who else was missing?"

A glance at the men for the answer did nothing but reveal that they were already deep into conversation about policy and how to try and bring about the change that Caelia had suggested.

"Yes." Guinevere said. "Your Liam and Gerard. He was removed from the dance after accusing Bedver of stealing something of his, a necklace of some sort, during their skirmish when you were on the dancefloor."

Caelia suddenly had a knot in her stomach thinking of what she had found beneath her husband's pillow.

"Did he say what it looked like?"

"Silver with blue stones and some sort of symbol in the center I think he said."

Her hand, beneath the table, reached into her pocket to touch the medallion.

"Was it important to him?"

"I have never seen him without it. It was a gift he received the day he was knighted." She said, taking another bite of food.

"From the Princess Elin?" Caelia asked, hopeful that the feeling in her gut was wrong.

"No. He got that necklace from me." Liam said, finally joining the conversation.

Chapter 36

Caelia's heart sank. Gerard's necklace had been under Liam's pillow. He slept with his arm under there. Had he ignored it or known it was there and hoped that she would not find it? What did it mean? How did something that the other man wore so often, that meant so much to him, end up under her husband's pillow in their marriage bed? She did not want to think about it and yet it was all that she could think about.

Conversation buzzed around her, she did not even hear it though she heard herself agreeing with both Arthur and Liam. All she could think of was that Liam had told her that he cared for her, wanted her, everything except that he loved her and had done all this with the token of another's affection beneath his pillow. A man's affection. What had she gotten herself into? How could she believe anything now? All around her the finery that had been so beautiful and awe inspiring now seemed tainted by secrets and lies.

"Caelia? Did you hear the king? Dear?" Liam put his hand on her arm. "I am going to join the king and a few others, knights and nobles, to see what we can do about getting this suggestion of yours into a proper law. Something that will give young women more safety and allow them to refuse a marriage without interference from a father or brother."

"That would be good, wonderful. I am glad you agree, your majesty." Caelia bowed her head slightly to the king.

"Thank you for the idea and the honesty behind it." Arthur said with a brief nod and that smile that was impossible not to reflect back at him. He was so charming and handsome when he was happy like this that she could not help but blush.

"Lucas or Lionel will take you anywhere in the city you want to go." Liam said, walking to the door with her and Arthur while the Queen joined her ladies in the salon. "I hope you will buy a few things for yourself. Enjoy the market. Bring me back a pear?" He added with a smile when he kissed her cheek.

"Oh. That sounds good. Bring one for me too?" The king said, tugging Liam away and down the hall where a few other men had gathered outside the chamber door.

How could they act as though everything was simply a happy fairy tale? Arthur might or might not know how Liam lied to her, about he and Gerard but Liam did and was pretending that there was nothing in the way of their potential happiness.

How could he do this? For him to like this after everything they had shared yesterday and last night felt worse than a physical blow. Her heart ached and her stomach felt unsettled, nauseous, and clenched tight as though it was trying to hold on to what she had eaten.

Heading back towards the room Caelia was torn between what she felt for Liam, what she was becoming certain was love, the commitment they had made to each other and the feeling of betrayal that she felt with every step feeling the weight of the medallion in her pocket. What was she to do? What choices did she have now that the marriage was consummated? Even though her suggestion might save many other girls from marrying strangers or monsters it was too late to save her and her heart.

She had to leave, and she had to do it as soon as possible.

"Caelia?" Lionel called from outside the bedroom door as she rounded the corner. "Liam said that you might wish to go down to the market. May I escort you? It is easy to get lost down there."

"Oh, Lionel." She blinked back the moisture that had come to her eyes with the realization of what she needed to do. "I think I would rather go for a ride. Do you think you could saddle Aldon? I am feeling a little confined."

"Certainly. Lucas will be jealous. He is a little in love with that charger of yours, not that I blame him. He would be a wonderful battle horse."

"Aldon? You think so? I thought he would be too high spirited for that. He does not like a lot of noise. I doubt he is enjoying the stables here."

"We will give him a good exercise in the quiet outside the city then. If you will change into your riding attire, then by the time you get downstairs he will be ready for you."

"Thank you. I will be as swift as I can."

She closed the door behind him and rushed to the closet to get her riding clothes and pack a few extra pieces of clothing along with the coin purse that Liam had left for her. Hopefully, there would be enough in there to pay for the inn on the way home, if not she would have to ask Lionel for help.

He would do it, of course. As a knight and a friend, he would never let her get into a situation that would see her hurt and he would, without a doubt, see her home. He might even understand why she had to this and why she had to do it now.

Pulling the medallion out of her pocket she stared at the evidence of her husband's betrayal and then at her wedding ring on that same hand.

"I cannot back down from this, not until he answers for this with the truth."

Swinging her riding cloak around her shoulders Caelia quietly closed the bedroom door behind herself and nearly bumped right into Gerard.

"Whoa there. Where are you off to in such a hurry young Caelia?" He asked with a distracted looking half smile. His strong hands gripped her arms tight to keep her from falling over.

She wondered if he had been coming to look in her marriage bed for his lost trinket and the thought hurt her more than she could stand.

"I am going where I belong. Out of your way, and his."

"Wait. What does that mean? Caelia?"

She detangled herself from his grip and rushed away. A single pause to look backwards gave her a glimpse of the blacksmith watching her go before running down the hall to meet with the others. They would have to hurry if her intention to be gone before anyone could stop her was to be accomplished.

"I am sorry Liam. I hope you will understand, eventually."

She flicked her hood up and raced for the courtyard to ride out with Lionel before anyone knew what was going on. In her hurry she did not see Sir Bedver in the shadows or the smile of complete satisfaction on his face.

"Go my dear, it will not be long now, no matter what road you take my men will be ready for you and the bookkeeper."

***

"You are not in the way…damnit girl."

Ger was confused by Caelia's words. He could not recall there being a special event that morning that she would be going to or that she could consider herself in the way of. Maybe she had been told that she was not allowed in the king's council chambers even though they were discussing her idea to change the laws regarding marriage? It was a ridiculous rule. Elin and Banning had been talking about their own excitement for the possible change in law all night and again this morning while he had been scouring the dance hall looking for his medallion. He agreed with them and if he had been in a better mood, he would have been a happy part of the morning's debate. Instead, he was going to tell them his vote was for giving girls the right to choose or refuse any man then go for a ride with Banning and try to clear his head.

"There is the last piece of our little group." Arthur said when Ger opened the door to step into the council chamber.

It was not the round table. This was not a matter for the knights but for the lords and politicians. He was only invited because of his friendship with Arthur and the fact that, years ago, Liam had made it clear that he considered Ger to be the equal to any of the peers of the realm and that any man who protested his common birth needed to hear the voice of the common man more than the rest.

"I am not here to stay, not this time." Ger said, giving Liam a nod but a wide berth. He was not going to get close to him and risk smelling Caelia on him. He had made his choice, they both had. There was no going back now.

"Not staying? What pulls you away and what have you to say about this matter then?" The King of Gore asked with a narrowed gaze that made Ger wonder if he suspected the relationship between his children and the lowborn knight was not what most suspected.

"Well, I stand with Liam and his wife, of course." Ger said with a smirk, nodding respectfully to the lesser king that he hated with every fiber of his being.

"I thank you and so does Caelia." Liam said with a smile that was not the one they used to share.

"Why not stay and help me convince the doubters that it's the right choice?"

"I have other commitments this morning that cannot wait. I am going to..."

At that moment there was a knock at the door and Lucas stepped inside.

"My apologies, Majesty, I am looking for Caelia, I mean Lady Caelia. I was hoping to have her charger tested for battle training, but he is not in the stable."

"What do you mean Aldon is gone?" Liam said. "No one but the two of you can ride him, he is only half broken."

"He is not in the stable and his saddle is gone too. Caelia did not tell you where she was going?"

"No. She was supposed to be going to the market, with Lionel." Liam said, pushing his chair back from the table.

Ger's gut tightened. He had seen her not that long ago, dressed for riding. Where in the hells of the underworld could that girl have gone?

"I saw her a few moments ago. Liam, I am sure nothing is wrong. I will go to find her myself." When his friend began to protest Ger held up a single hand. "You should stay here and get her law written. That is what is important."

Liam looked worried and Ger was concerned as well, but they both knew that if he left that room then there was no chance that they would make the changes. Liam was the force behind this change as much as Caelia was the thought. If it was going to happen then Liam had to stay.

"Alright. Bring her back to celebrate. I will talk to her about the rest of it later."

"As you wish." Ger nodded to Lucas. "Follow me Lucas. We have work to do."

Liam sat back down even though Ger could see the worry in his eyes. Damn, he loved the girl, even if he was not aware of it yet. This was about more than an heir and impressing Arthur. This girl, Caelia, was the one for Liam. He had to admit that he had done everything he could, short of physical harm and telling her about the two of them, to drive her away. It was time to fix that.

As soon as the door closed behind them Ger turned to the younger knight.

"I am going to ride out after them. Someone at the gate will have remembered that horse. You are going to search her room and talk to Lynn and see if she has any idea about what happened. Something is not right, and I have a feeling our lady of the manor is in over her pretty little head."

"You think Bedver is involved?" Lucas asked, glancing up and down the hall.

Any of the servants could be a spy, which could work for or against their search.

"I think if he is not yet then he will be soon. He was not in the chamber with the other lawmakers. Why would he miss that chance? To destroy an idea given by a woman, the woman he failed to dissuade last night? He is up to something and I think Caelia is in trouble. Even if Lionel is with her, they are no match for that snake.

Chapter 37

"Are you sure you know what you are doing? Leaving like this?" Lionel asked Caelia. "What do you hope to accomplish that you could not do by staying?"

Caelia could barely believe what she was doing. Running from Camelot, which held the man she was in love with and going back to Redbourne because Liam was Gerard's lover or had been or wanted to be. She was not entirely sure of anything anymore. She had been trying not to cry when she told this to Lionel, or tried to tell him, why she was sneaking out of the city. He had mumbled, uncomfortable with her tears, when he attempted to tell her that, even if they could not see her face there was not a man alive that would not remember that giant black horse with such a tiny rider.

"I am sure." Caelia said with a sniff, nudging Aldon faster along the road so she could try to outrun her lies. "I could not stay there and sleep in that bed one more night. There is no reason for me to stay. My husband can stay there with his lover and I will stay at Redbourne where I will not have to pretend not to see it."

"Lover?" Lionel could not believe what he was hearing. "Liam has no lover Caelia. Only you. You cannot let Bedver make you think otherwise. If Liam did not want you, care for you, he would never have married you."

"I do not want to be second to someone else. I know he might not love me yet, he may never, but I am not able to turn a blind eye to the man I... married having someone else in our wedding bed. Someday I might be able to but not the day after our wedding."

"The man you…? You love him?" He pulled his horse to a stop in the middle of the road and turned to face her. "Caelia if you love him you cannot do this to him. This is going to ruin things that you cannot mend."

"What do you mean? What does it matter if I love him when he does not feel the same?"

"He might take his time and wait too long to say it, but I have seen him looking at you. You are the only one on his mind and the only one he has eyes for. The man may or may not have fallen yet, that is not for me to say. What I can say is that he is falling for you, hard, and if you want him and any others who doubt your age difference to take you, the two of you, seriously then you cannon run away and act like a child. Go back, as his wife, and tell him your suspicions about the other woman."

"You mean other man." Caelia said, urging Aldon past the knight. She pulled the medallion out of her pocket and tossed it to Lionel. "That was under Liam's pillow. I am sure you can tell me who it belongs to."

He did not get the chance to answer her. The sound of thundering hooves coming down the road behind them stopped whatever he was going to say.

"It looks like my husband is coming to claim his property." She sighed, not sure if that meant he was enraged or genuinely worried about her safety.

"That is not Liam or the knights of Camelot." Lionel said, drawing his sword and tossing the dagger in his boot to her, nodding when she caught it. "Get out of here. Go hard and fast. Do not stop and do not look back, no matter what you hear. Go! NOW!"

Aldon understood before she did and took off down the road. Flying through the forest so fast Caelia was struggling to understand what had just happened.

They had been attacked on the road, she did not know by whom, but Lionel was willing to risk his life to give her the chance to escape. He was fighting at least four men for her sake and she had not been willing to stand and face the truth, to fight for her marriage. If she loved Liam why was she running away from proving it? She could fight for marriage rights but not her marriage? That was not who she was. Things might not be what she had hoped but that did not mean she could not be happy, that she could not be loved. She had to get back and save Lionel too.

She was slowing Aldon so that they could turn safely, near the roadside clearing the company had stopped at when they approached Camelot. Suddenly, there was a hard pain across her chest, a sensation of flying and then, darkness.

***

Ger was trying to keep calm and for the first time Banning's hand on his shoulder did not help. He could not fail to bring the girl back. Caelia. He also had to stop thinking of her as just a girl, she was family now. Whether he liked it or not.

"Take a breath my love. You will never find her if you are not thinking clearly. Where would she go with Lionel? Where would he take her?"

"Sir 'rules and honor' Lionel? He would take her anywhere she asked to go. Hopefully, her home or Redbourne. Which is more likely though?" He said, embracing his prince and trying to find some comfort in his touch. When the door began to open they both jumped back to avoid discovery.

"It is only me. No need for any of that." Elin said stepping inside. "What is wrong?' Her voice grew serious when she saw their faces. "Is it father? Does he know?"

Ger added a third dagger to his belt as his lover took Elin's hand. "Not that."

"Not yet " Ger countered. "He begins to suspect, I fear. Today we must find Liam's wife. She and Lionel took horses and left no word. Bedver is unaccounted for too, as well as several of his men."

"Caelia? Why on earth would she leave? They seemed to be happy and even, dare I say, falling in love at the dance last night." Elin said, looking out the window as if she might catch a glimpse of the girl. "Banning said that you convinced her that what Bedver had said was a lie. Did something else happen?"

"Something must have happened after they left or this morning. Liam is not known for saying the right thing, politely, especially to a woman." Banning said, looking at Ger for the answer.

"He did not say anything to me. She did though." Taking a deep breath, he looked at them both. "She said she wanted to get out of my way and out of his."

He waited for Elin's reaction. Banning knew how he felt about Liam, had always felt about him, but neither of them had ever told the Princess. She was protective of her brother and would not understand that the night he had shared with Liam here was the culmination of years of stolen moments, touches and more long glances than Ger could count even if he wanted to try.

"What Ger did not tell you, Elin, was that when we spoke to Caelia it was after she caught us kissing at the bottom of the stairs." Banning said.

When his arm slid across Ger's shoulders, the knight could not help but lean into him. Moments like this were so rare. Moments where they could be affectionate around others and not worry about their safety.

"Does that matter to her? You and Banning? Are you in danger? I will talk to her if you need me to. I can convince her to try and understand." Elin said. "Once you bring her back that is."

"I may take you up on that." He put a finger on Banning's lips. "Do not argue. Stay here, see if you can get that law of hers made. Help Liam if you can."

"Elin is better at that than I am. You know how I get when my father argues with me." Banning said with a frown.

"Liam was counting on me to be there to help and I have to do this now. Please, Banning?"

"Go get his wife and I will see what I can do to help him here."

They shared a brief kiss, Ger gripped the back of his Prince's neck to hold their forehead's together.

"You be careful in there. They are monsters when they do not get their way." Ger said.

"You be careful out there. Bedver is always a monster and will do whatever it takes to hurt Liam. Do not underestimate him or try to reason with him."

"There is no danger of that." Ger chuckled and left them behind.

It felt strange to ride into what was sure to be a fight without the medallion that he had worn since the day he received his knighthood. At least catching up to Bedver would give him the chance to search his body, dead or unconscious, to see if he were withholding the necklace.

"Tell Sir Liam, when he asks, that I took the road to Redbourne." He told the gatekeeper after enquiring about the direction the memorable horse had gone.

Kicking in his heels he road off down the road. Ger could only hope they had not gotten far or that Lionel was able to defend Caelia until he arrived to help. Who knew how many men Bedver had with him or what it was that he intended to do? If they had any luck he would simply be plotting to embarrass Liam by retrieving his runaway wife, but it was more likely that he meant to injure or kill the girl and find a way to blame Liam or one of the knights, possibly even Lionel since he was foolish enough to help the runaway.

"Where the devil are you, Lionel?" Ger grumbled, scanning the treeline and the road for signs that they had left the road. There were at least eight different track sets that were fresh enough to be from that day and likely meant a bigger danger than he and Lionel could deal with together.

The air suddenly seemed still, an unnatural stillness without the sound or movement of a bird. There was a flash of colour to his right and Ger turned to find Lionel's horse blinking nervously from the bushes.

"Damnation." He cursed softly. This was almost as bad as it could get.

"Steady there." He said to the horse, dismounting and carefully making his way over to the animal. "You know me. We are friends, are we not? Hmm?"

He managed to take hold of the reins, but the horse refused to step onto the road. Locking his knees, he tugged back on the reins. Since there was nothing on the road for him to be afraid of, Ger had to assume he was either stuck or was protecting Lionel.

"What are you hiding back here fella?" He asked, scratching the horse's cheek and behind the ear. "Lionel? Are you back here? Make a noise if you are and I will find you."

Ger paused, listening closely, feeling some relief when he heard the kick of a boot against one of the trees.

"I am coming. Keep kicking Lionel. I am going to find you." He thought for a second then added "Caelia? If you can hear me, it is Ger. I am here to help. Just make some sound so I know where to find you."

He kept hold of the reins so the horse did not bolt, in case Lionel was tied to him with the intention that he would be dragged. Thankfully, there was nothing tied to the horse and it took only a moment to find the savagely beaten and gagged body of Lionel hidden behind some branches.

"Good lords. They did their worst I see." He crouched and pulled down the gag from his friend's swollen and bloodied lip. "How bad are you?"

"Get me to the roadside and I will be fine. You can get me on the way back. They have Caelia. You need to save her. Bedver means to kill her and make it look as though Liam drove her to suicide. His tree, whatever that means. They are going to his tree. Do you know it?"

"Bastard." Ger cursed. "Yes, I know it. The old gods know what madness he has in mind. How long ago was he here?"

"Get me to the damned road and get going. You have no time Ger. Save her. Liam loves her."

"I am aware of that Lionel." He growled looping his arm around his shoulder and making their way towards the road. He would leave the man with his horse if he were not able to ride, either the next search party from Camelot would find him or Ger and Caelia could retrieve him on their return.

"Yes, but do you know that she loves him back? That was why she was leaving. She loves him too much to see him be with another and will not cause him the scandal of a divorce just so that he can be with his lover."

"That is what she meant." Ger shook his head and climbed aboard his own horse after resting his friend against the tree. "Tell Liam where they were going, nothing more. Send him to the tree. I will do my best to save her."

"Just go." Lionel leaned back to the tree and Ger bolted, running like a hound from hell was coming for him.

Chapter 38

When Caelia opened her eyes, she had to blink before she realized what she was seeing: the leafy canopy of the forest, not the ceiling of her bedroom.

Her back and ribs hurt when she took a breath. When she tried to sit up, she whimpered in pain and the memory of flying off Aldon's back came back to her, but not the landing or how she got to the grass from the road.

"Easy does it, my lady." A Vaguely familiar voice said from her left. "You may have a broken rib or two. Do not concern yourself though, the pain will not last long."

Her head followed the sound to see the man leaning against a tree, the very tree that Liam had shown her the secret entrance to only a few days ago. Sir Bedver. Of course, it was him. Who else would be responsible for the attack Lionel had tried to get her away from?

"What did you do to Lionel? Is he dead?" She asked, getting to her feet slowly. Her entire body ached from the fall, but she had to stay focused. If she slipped or let her guard down Bedver could become deadly instead of merely dangerous in the split of a second.

"My men have taken care of him and soon enough you will be taken care of too." Bedver said, walking towards her with a slow, menacing pace.

Her hand flew to her belt where she thought she might still have the dagger that Lionel had tossed to her before she rode off.

"Oh, do not worry about the dagger, young lady. I took care of that. We would not want you to lose the gift from your lover, Lionel, Would we?" Bedver said, spinning the dagger in his fingers before throwing it into the tree trunk near her feet.

"My what? Lionel? I have…he would…never. Why would you say such things?" Caelia pressed back against the tree, trying to inch a little closer to the dagger.

"Because my dear. It is his love for you that drove poor Lionel to kill the woman he could not have and his guilt for the act that will cause him to take his life by jumping from a cliff into the river." Bedver said with an evil smile. "Liam will not only be devastated by the loss of his second wife, but destroyed by the fact that his young wife of barely more than a day ran off with a man, a fellow knight, who stood beside him as a brother for years."

"Why do you hate him so much? Why do you wish destruction upon such an honorable man?" Caelia dared to ask when the side of her boot touched the blade of the dagger. "He has never done anything to you that would merit such hatred."

"You will never live to know all that bastard and his sodomite blacksmith have done to ruin my plans and my life. If it were not for them, I would be the head of the king's council instead of bowing and scraping to the like of Gerard, Lancelot and Banning. They will all get what they deserve. One by one I will see them fall. With each descent I will rise a little higher until the court is mine while the king plays the hero in foreign battlefields. Julius of Gore and I will unite the kingdoms and wipe those heathens from the court and the nation."

"You cannot be serious? You think you are going to be Arthur's right hand? He has no use for you. He does not even like you."

His hand flew across her face. Caelia cried out, cupping her cheek where his ring had cut deep enough to bleed.

"You think he likes you? That either of them has any use for you besides your ability to give Liam an heir?" Bedver snarled, pinning her to the tree by her throat. "I wonder if he will feel anything besides annoyance that he has to go through the entire process again."

"You do not know him. He will see through this plot just as they all saw through the first one. They're going to expose you to the king. He may even kill you for this."

"You will never know. Your corpse will be found hanging from this very tree by whomever is sent to look for you. I hope that I will be back in time to see Liam's show of false mourning. He is a good actor even if that is all he is good at, but then, you know that intimately of course."

"You deserve the ax." Caelia said softly, trying to jerk her head away when Bedver snapped a rope before her eyes.

"Perhaps, but no one will ever know that now. You will not live to tell them, not that they would care if you did. They are all too busy with private affairs behind closed doors to even notice that you are gone. It is sweet that you believed the act though."

Caelia's heart sank. How could she have been so blind not to see that everything Liam had ever said to her was nothing but a joke. Perhaps he was laughing about it now with Gerard and Banning. She was an annoying duty to him and nothing else, no matter what her heart had said when she woke in his arms. This was not the story she had hoped for but a nightmare.

***

Ger watched as whatever Bedver was saying utterly crushed Caelia. The man was cruel and more vengeful than any of them had ever considered. Her head bowed and he thought there might be tears on her cheeks. The fire in her that had irritated Ger and had attracted Liam was extinguished. Liam would be able to fix that, he hoped once they had her back in Camelot.

There was no sign of the other riders that must have been with Bedver to defeat Lionel the way that they had, at least not yet. If he was going to do this on his own, he had to do it fast, before they returned.

"Bedver." He called, strolling casually from the treed path that led from the road. "Once again you are completely and utterly wrong."

He had to hide a smirk when Caelia's head whipped up, a trace of hope in her eyes at the sight of him. This just might work. The drop of blood on her cheek had dried, but Ger's rage was just starting to burn.

"What are you doing here, accursed sodomite." Bedver growled, stepping between Ger and the girl.

"That is not very nice, for a man who wants the favor of the king and court." Ger said. Stepping closer he was careful not to move too suddenly. The gods only knew what kind of traps the man could have set or weapons he had hidden.

"Wants the favor of the king? Are you sure you do not speak of yourself and your sinful ways? You and Banning seek to corrupt the entire court and I will not allow it to happen."

"You have no idea what you are talking about." Ger shook his head. He tried not to look at Caelia when she crouched low to the ground.

"Your actions are what drove the girl from Camelot and into my plan. Who else might take offence to your actions? You are going to divide the court and the nation just enough for the new church to unify it and cast out infidels like you."

"You are forgetting a few things, Bedver." Ger said, his eyes narrowed with hatred. "Caelia and I both know your plan and at least one of us will be getting out of here alive."

He saw the glint of light off a blade in Caelia's hand, if they were both armed this was going to be easier than he thought. He met her eyes and gave a brief wink, hoping that she understood.

"What makes you think that?" Bedver chuckled, drawing his sword slowly.

"The fact that if you move an inch, I will see your spine severed so that all will know what a spineless little shit you are." Caelia said, moving the dagger to the other man's back and sending a wave of relief through Ger. She was a smart girl, more so than he had anticipated.

"You little wretch." Bedver snarled, turning to attack Caelia.

Ger had expected her to cower or run but to her credit she drove her little fist into the man's stomach while keeping a grip on the dagger.

The few seconds of distraction was all Ger needed to draw his own sword and smash the pommel into the back of Bedver's head. When he crumpled to the ground Ger grinned at Caelia.

"Well done, young...I mean Caelia. That was the perfect distraction." Ger rolled the other man to his back. "Liam and I could not have done it better ourselves."

He must have said something wrong, the smile of relief that had been on her face suddenly fell. She looked as sad and broken as she had when Bedver had been preparing the rope for her. He looked around for the rope and saw that it was a noose that he had prepared. He was going to hang her and blame Lionel? Bedver was an even crueler bastard than Ger had thought.

"I mean that as a compliment." He said, working to untie the knot. "He will be proud of you."

"Even prouder when I return home, I hope." She said, sheathing the dagger and walking towards her horse to untie the reins. "I told you that I would not stand in your way."

"Caelia? Did you, are you, leaving because of what you saw in the stairs?" He asked carefully. "Because of Banning and I? It will not hurt anyone. He is not the crown prince and his sister will step up and marry to create an heir to the throne if needed. Our love is no less than yours. I...I hope you can understand that."

"No Sir Gerard. Prince Banning has nothing to do with why I am leaving." Caelia shook her head.

She was stroking the nose of her great black horse, but whether it was to comfort him or herself Ger could not tell.

"Then why leave? Why now? When Liam is arguing to have your suggestion amended to the law right now?" He asked, taking hold of the horse who shifted uncomfortably under his touch.

Ger knew that he was missing something. He could not go back to Camelot without her and without understanding why she was trying to leave his best friend when she loved him.

"Because you and I love the same man, do we not?" She asked. The tone of her voice told him that she knew the answer, but how? When he did not answer she continued.

"After I saw you and Banning together at the bottom of the stairs. I spent the night with my husband in our wedding bed, in his bed." She watched his face but Ger gave no sign of the dread he was feeling about her next words.

"The morning after we made passionate love, after he made me feel things that I never knew were possible, after he made me feel loved, I found this under his pillow." She drew something from her pocket and threw it at his feet.

He looked down and sighed before crouching and picking up the medallion.

"Under his pillow." Ger put the pendant around his neck and tucked it into his shirt. "So, what will you do then?"

"I do not want to get in the way of love, any love, and I will not dishonor him by revealing the secret. I will go to Redbourne and try to find a way to be wife and mistress to the same man, at least until my duties of providing children are done. My daughters will marry for love, my sons will be able to follow their hearts and not the guiding hands of the court. That is what Liam will give me for turning a blind eye to what you share and for denying my own heart."

It would be so easy to let her go. To have both Liam and Banning. For the choice to be his for the first time in his life. There was no honor in that manipulation though, not if she was making her choice without knowing the truth.

"He chose you Caelia. He loves you enough to walk away from anything we might have had. I am his past and you are his future." Ger said, covering her hand on the saddle with his.

"Liam did that?" She could hardly breath. "He loves me?"

"He does. So, stay in Camelot." Ger said softly, trying to hide his pain. "Do not go back to Redbourne alone."

"Sorry, both of you, but that is against Sir Bedver's orders." Said a man in a dark brown hood, leading a squad of thugs. "You are both going to have to stay right here, permanently."

Chapter 39

Liam was buzzing with impatience. Arthur and the others were acting as though nothing in the world was wrong, as though Caelia had not left him the day after their wedding.

After they had shared every physical intimacy a man and woman could share with each other, laying their souls bare before the other, she had left him. There was not even a note to explain, though he knew that she was fully literate. What had happened?

He was going to find her. Now that the law had been debated and voted in Liam requested Lucas, Saffir and Emrys to mount up and join him. With Bedver missing it was likely that there would be trouble on the road. He had not counted on Arthur and Banning joining them. The two men were acting as though this was nothing more than an afternoon adventure instead of the rescue of the woman that he held dear to his heart.

"If you two are done reminiscing about the past can we focus on the now? I would like to find my wife before Bedver makes me a widower for the second time." Liam growled at the royals.

"Liam, you worry too much. We will find the girl. She is probably sitting under a tree talking to Lionel and Ger about whatever it is that caused her dramatic exit." Arthur said with a grin. "Women are like that, especially the younger ones. Did you forget that?"

"She is not like the flighty girls of court Arthur." Liam said, scanning the road and the treeline. He gestured for Saffir to ride ahead. "She is unlike anyone."

He noticed the look that passed between his old friends and when Banning scoffed he glared.

"You must know that you sound like a lovestruck squire." The prince teased.

"Do I? Then you tell me what other woman ever suggested the basis for a new law to benefit others but not herself, within days of coming to Camelot?" Liam said, challenging them all to suggest one woman who could compare to his wife.

"Elin has made suggestions all her life." Banning countered. "It is not her fault that no one, including those present, listened to her unless I gave voice to the cause."

The prince had a point and Liam could not deny it. The look that Arthur had on his face said that the king was guilty of the same prejudice. Did he even listen to his own wife?

"Perhaps now, with Caelia's boldness as an example, we will all be forced to listen a little closer to those we may have ignored before." Liam said with a hope he did not feel as deeply as he should.

A grim feeling settled over him when he saw Saffir riding back towards them as though he was in a race for his life.

"What is it? Did you find them?" Lucas asked, putting his hand on Saffir's horse to steady him.

"I found Lionel, bloodied and beaten by the roadside. His horse is with him." Saffir said, taking a drink of the water offered by Emrys. "He needs medical attention, and I do not think it can wait."

"Instead of talking about it here, lead the way Saffir." Arthur said, finally growing serious. "It is better to show than to tell."

The six knights rode hard down the road. The attitude of jokes and laughter was gone, this was no longer a game but a mission of life and death.

"Saffir, was there any sign of Caelia? Or her horse? Anything?" Liam asked, bringing his horse alongside the younger man.

"I looked Liam, there was no sign of her. When I was able to revive Lionel, he told me that Gerard had taken him from deeper in the bushes to the roadside so that we might find him. The men that attacked him likely went after her."

Liam barely held back a groan. Why had he so stubbornly refused to get her a sword of her own? Instead of having a chance at defending herself all Caelia had was the speed of her horse and the hope that she would find a friend or a place to hide along the road. Place to hide? Of course.

"I know where she will ride for. Lucas I need you with me in case Aldon is jumpy. He likes you. Emrys, you and Saffir get Lionel to safety and stay with him. He will know who attacked them and will need to be able to speak to the Sherriff and the court."

"Where are we going, Sir Liam." Prince Banning asked, drawing up on Liam's right while Arthur was on his left.

"Once we confirm Sir Lionel is in fact alive, I will confirm with him that he sent Caelia to our tree. The only other person who knows the secrets of that location is Gerard. It is the safest place she could be, if she got there before she was overtaken by the attackers."

"Let us hope that it was Ger that found her first then." Banning said, a note of worry in his deep voice that Liam was not used to. It told him more about how the man cared for Ger than he likely meant to reveal.

"Gerard will be fine. I have rarely known him to be otherwise, Highness." Liam said quietly.

"That is true. Perhaps more so than either of us have ever realized."

"If you two are done worrying about the very dangerous knight skinning his knee or something, perhaps we should ask Sir Lionel if he was even here?" Arthur said, gesturing to the horse tied to a tree and the man on the ground, propped against it.

"Lionel? Are you still with us?" Liam called from the saddle while Emrys and Saffir dismounted to help him to his feet.

"I may not feel like it, but I am, Sir Liam. Saffir has always told me that pain is the only way you can always tell that you are alive." Lionel said, his voice tight and words slurred from the swelling on his face.

"Well you certainly are not the prettiest I have ever seen you." Banning chuckled. "They worked you over well. I am glad you are with us though."

"And will be as long as you stop those renegades and bring them to justice." Lionel said, leaning on Emrys.

"What about Caelia?" Liam said, trying to sound sure of their ability to keep her safe. "Which direction did she go? Did they catch her?"

"She was riding hard for Redbourne when I saw her last but three were after her. Gerard has followed in pursuit."

Emrys and Saffir had helped him to his horse, the three of them were getting ready to head back towards Camelot.

"How long ago, Lionel? When did Gerard leave to get her?" Liam said, itching to go and get his wife and help his best friend.

"Not long. He said something about a tree. Do you know it?" Lionel asked.

"Very well. Get back to the city and get yourself looked after. I will come find you there so that we can discuss the rest of this."

He dug his heels into the horse's side and took off down the road with Lucas behind him. He was not worried if Banning or Arthur could keep up. The two would stay together and were capable enough knights that he did not have to worry for them.

Turning off the road and into the trees Liam made sure that there was a big enough mark in the ground that the others would be able to follow him from that point. It did not take long to confirm the truth in his wounded friend's words. The sound of a skirmish with blades cut through the silence of the forest.

"You must get to the horses, leave Ger and Caelia to me." Liam said quietly.

Dismounting once he was close enough to see the flash from the swords, Liam made his way through the bushes to see what was happening. Stepping into the clearing he could hardly believe what he was seeing.

Ger and Caelia fighting back to back against five thugs while two men lay on the ground, at least one of which was bleeding. Bedver must have had more men than Lionel thought or those that had beaten the knight joined them.

"This dagger is not working Ger." Caelia said, blocking a shot and reaching for one of Ger's back up swords. "I could really use a hand right about now."

"Yes, dear." Ger said with a playful sarcasm that Liam could hardly believe he was hearing.

He spun away from her, towards the attackers, loosened a blade and tossed it to Caelia before turning to find himself back to back with her again.

"Is that better?" He asked, reengaging the enemy.

"Better than it was, but do you think you can help with these invasive visitors?" Caelia said.

Liam was mesmerized for a moment, watching his wife battle the armed thugs with more skill than he saw in some squires, but the odds were not in their favor. His relief would have to wait.

"Would you two like a hand or is this a private matter?" He called, stepping towards the fray with his sword drawn.

"Liam?" Caelia said, her eyes widening when she saw him striding towards her, ready to fight, to kill, to keep her safe.

"Your one and only, little wife." He said, nodding to Ger and engaging the man nearest him.

"You are supposed to be in court for hours." The thug said, swinging a sword towards Liam's head.

"Your employer must have over-estimated how many men would be opposed to women having the right to refuse a man. Caelia's law will be announced tonight and messengers will go throughout the kingdoms tomorrow."

"Too bad she, and you, will not be alive to see that." The man said, thrusting his sword towards Liam's unprotected abdomen.

He twisted away and tried to bring his blade down to block the blow, but it was not fast enough. A moment before the blade struck home Liam's attacker grunted and fell to the ground, a familiar dagger sticking out of his back.

"Did you catch the blade?" Caelia asked, stepping over the man she wounded that lay bleeding at her feet.

"No. Your dagger struck just in time." He caught her hand when she reached to touch the cut in his shirt, the only damage done by the attacker's sword.

"As well timed as your arrival." Ger said, delivering a blow across the temple of the last attacker. "Come alone, did you?" He asked, wiping his blades on the grass.

"Of course not. We simply did not want to interrupt the show." Banning said, stepping into the clearing with Arthur and Lucas, who went right to the horses. "Well done. It seems we barely needed to worry about you at all."

Liam watched Ger's eyes light up at the sight of the Prince and knew that they had both made the right decision. He gave a short nod to his friend then turned to address the King who was walking around the bodies.

"Bedver is here? Involved in all of this is he?" Arthur said, turning the knight to his back. "Did he finally cross a line he cannot step back from?"

"His treachery is more than an attack in the wood, Highness." Caelia said, cleaning her borrowed blade. "He is planning, with others, to take over your court and make you a puppet until they can find a way to usurp you."

"Are you sure of that Caelia?" Liam asked, putting his hand on her shoulder. "It is a bold accusation to make and Bedver will deny it."

"He told me himself. As he prepared to hang me and blame Lionel for the act." Her eyes widened and she gripped his hand. "Lionel? Is he alive? It was supposed to look like a he murdered me, then took his own life."

"Saffir and Emrys have taken him back to Camelot. Where we return to right away." Arthur said. "Lucas, Gerard, see these men bound right away so that we may escort them back to the capital. We have a new law to celebrate."

Liam turned to look at Caelia, certain that she would be as pleased as he was, but the smile was gone from her eyes and her shoulders sagged.

"Caelia? Little wife? What is it? What is wrong?" Did he hurt you? Did he touch you darling?" The thought that the bastard might have assaulted her made Liam suddenly sick. "I thought you would be pleased that we passed your law, to give women the right to choose their husband and to refuse an arranged marriage. That has happened for girls across the land because of you."

"But too late for me." She stepped away from him. "This was a lot of work for a wife you are only bound to by the law and your sense of duty."

"Is that what Bedver told you? Or what your heart tells you, Caelia?" Liam said carefully. "When I touch you, talk to you, do you feel my sense of duty? Or the love that is growing between us?"

He stepped closer, laying his hand on her arm, and stroking her hair with the other.

"Does this feel like duty?" He raised her hand to his lips, noticing the tremble in her fingers when he kissed them firmly.

She shook her head, a slight motion but an encouraging one.

"Does this feel like the law?" He asked, taking a risk, and pulling her against his chest and lowering his mouth to cover hers.

She was stiff in his arms for just a moment and then she melted against him.

"Only the law of the heart, my Liam." She whispered in reply.

When her fingers rose to touch his beard, stroking his cheek before threading into his hair, Liam deepened the kiss with a sweep of his tongue. She returned the passionate play with a dart of her own and Liam smiled against her lips.

He was lost in the taste of her, the feel of her pressed against his hardening body, he wanted to take her to the private chamber within the tree and show her all over again the depth of his passion for her. The tap of a man's hand on his shoulder pulled him back to the present, the captives, and the company around them.

"Sorry as I am to break up such a show of passion, we should really return to Camelot." Arthur said with a smile. "We need to discuss your return to the round table, Liam."

"Of course, your majesty." He said, keeping Caelia's hand in his while he walked her to his horse.

"Ride with me?" He murmured in her ear, dipping his head to kiss her neck. "Hmm, little wife? Let Lucas ride Aldon and put Bedver upon his own horse."

"Yes, husband, as soon as I return the blade I borrowed." She kissed his cheek and walked to were Ger and the prince were standing.

Caelia held out the sword to Ger who shook his head.

"Keep it, until I have yours ready. It will be a late wedding gift but one I think you will use often, when we three train together at home."

Liam beamed at his friend, the message in his words was clear. His choice was accepted, Caelia was accepted, and if the way that Banning and Ger looked at each other was any indication, his friend had made a choice of his own; to be happy.

"I look forward to the rematch and a few more lessons, when we get home." Caelia laughed while Liam climbed up behind her and wrapped an arm around her waist.

"I think your lessons will continue tonight, my wife." He whispered.

"Teach me everything, my Silver Knight." She replied with a kiss.

Epilogue:

"Arthur you cannot ask this of me." Liam said, pacing before the window. "Each of them stood by me when no one else would. I will not leave them to return to the table. Not if they are still banished."

"Not banished Liam." Arthur said, shaking his head. "Simply not invited to the table yet. I intend to extend the invitation eventually."

"Why not now? They are good men, good knights. Look how they helped with Caelia and brought Bedver to the courts. It is not their fault that he escaped before the trial." Liam was determined to stand by his men and see that every one of them was brought back to where they belonged. "What have they done that makes them unworthy?"

"Lucas, and Emrys are too young, they have done nothing of note. Saffir seeks pain then repents for it at the temples of the old gods and the new. He has an inner darkness that must be addressed before he can sit at the table."

"What about Lionel? You cannot object to him. There is no one more responsible, more educated, that he is." Liam said, squaring off with his friend, not thinking of him as the king.

"You have been distracted, old friend. Unfortunately, he has responsibilities outside your household." He tossed a letter down on the table in front of Liam. "You remember his father? Alexander?"

"The man was evil. The most dreaded instructor we ever had." Liam shook his head and picked up the letter. "It is hard to believe that a solid, kind-hearted man ever came from that household."

"Well, believe it or not Lionel has a sister that is now his ward, or will be soon." Arthur pointed at the letter. "Alexander is dying. He has requested to see his son and that Lionel take his sister into his care."

"That is going to be hard. He does not talk about the man at all." Liam rubbed a hand down his face. "Alright. I will send Emrys and Gerard with him. They were going to meet the twins from Gore and bring them to Redbourne. Lionel's home is on the way. They can leave him there and retrieve him on the way back with the twins."

"Will that be enough time for him to make peace with the old monster?" Arthur asked, handing Liam the letter.

"It will have to be. It is all the time he has."

To Be Continued in "Cast from Camelot Book 2: The Blue Knight."

About the Author

Born in Hardisty, Alberta Monica developed an undeniable love of reading at an early age. Homeschooled during her primary years, her mother not only taught the basics to her five children, but she also read to them at least twice a day. From Anne of Green Gables to Tolkien's Lord of the Rings the stories and the people behind them instilled a love of the written word.

As soon as she could hold a pencil Monica began to write her own stories. Her first complete work was 'Monkey Millionaires' in which a pair of monkeys became millionaires by selling ice cream. While it was a huge hit among the kids in the neighborhood it was just the beginning. After discovering the TV show Spartacus, and full immersion into that fandom, Monica was disappointed to find there was very little fiction to satisfy her desire to indulge a love of Roman era romance. The spark was then lit to write the stories she wanted to read herself.

Despite some eye-opening experiences (it's not as glamorous a profession as the movies would have you believe) she would not change her journey in the slightest. When she is not working or writing, Monica is a single parent to a little girl. Nothing makes her happier than when her daughter tells her that she wants to be a writer, "Just like you, Mommy." So, to keep inspiring a very special little girl, and to bring some elements of romantic Rome and the romance of real life to some not-so-little girls, she is pleased to be writing as M. Francis Lamont and brings you "The Champion's Prize" the first of her centurion saga and many more stories to come. She encourages everyone to "Live with Passion. Live with Purpose. And most important of all, Never Lose."

Welcome to the beginning of something wonderful.